Under-Heaven

Under-Heaven

TIM GREATON

Focus House Publishing

Wilton, Maine

Published by Focus House Publishing
ISBN-13: 9798605355953
Cover photography by T.J. Greaton
Cover graphics by Wizards Prism Art & Media

Printed in the U.S.A.

To Joan my beautiful wife and to my three amazing children who were all so patient during my thousands of writing hours – I can barely find words to express my love and thanks.

Acknowledgements

To my mothers, Marilyn Jordan and Ruth Greaton – It is hard to imagine what kind of a man, let alone what kind of a writer, I would have become without your love and guidance over these many years. Please know you have all my love

To Marilyn Nulman and Mark Reader – In every author's life there is usually one writer that teaches and inspires. I was so fortunate to find two of you. Thank you.

And to you, my readers – It's impossible to describe how much I appreciate your continued support. Please know that I strive every day to tell better stories… all for you, dear readers, all for you.

Table of Contents

1

The Angry Man

"I told you, I'll handle your mother!" the gaunt, disheveled man said, smashing his McDonald's shake down on the table. Pink liquid exploded everywhere.

Jesse froze as a thick drop oozed from the table edge onto his sneakers. Swallowing hard, he felt dread clamp around his chest. He knew his father was only seconds away from what his mother called a "hellva bad scene."

Jesse's eyes darted around the room. No one was nearby, though a woman with a baby stroller and another family with two boys a year or two older than him sat on the far side of the restaurant. On one hand, he hoped they were far enough away to avoid what was about to happen, but on the other he prayed he wouldn't be his father's only target. His rememory wasn't very good yet, but it seemed to him that his father got meaner with each passing day. Try as he might, Jesse could never understand where his father's outbursts came from, and whenever he asked his mother she would only say, "Just be glad you're still a little boy."

Seeing his father's cheek muscles tighten his face into the shape of a bare skull, Jesse stared down at the floor and held back the tears. Pressing his lips together, he tried to ignore the hot feeling in his eyes. At the edge of his vision he could see his father's fists clenching and unclenching. Jesse's little body started to quake.

Suddenly, a trickle of pee came out from down there.

Doubly terrified at what might happen if his father found out, he tried to keep his five-year-old body under control. But when that big hand smacked loudly into the pink mess on the table, a tiny bit more pee trickled out.

"That bitch never controlled me, and I'll be damned if she'll start now!" his father exclaimed.

Not daring to move, Jesse kept his eyes glued to his goop-spattered fries. At the top of his vision, he saw his father shake off his hand before wiping it on his already grimy green jacket. Anger was scribbled like red crayon across his face. He glared at the two families across the room.

Taking a chance, Jesse felt his crotch. It was dry. Maybe he hadn't peed that much, at least he hoped not. He yanked his hand back up and waited for his father's unshaven jaw to stop grinding back and forth. Sitting there, Jesse regretted begging his mom to let him go out to eat with his dad. It was weird because when they weren't together, he missed his dad so much it hurt. But lately it seemed that when they were together it was worse than missing him. Maybe he was beginning to understand why his mother wouldn't let his dad live with them anymore.

Jesse winced when his father's angry gaze swung back his way. Too scared to speak, he averted his eyes and wondered, not for the first time, if he might somehow be to blame for the way his dad was acting. Though his mother insisted he had nothing to do with it, how could she be so sure? Jesse tried to remember if he had said or done anything that morning or any morning to get his father so upset. As usual, his memory wasn't up to the task. He couldn't recall doing anything wrong.

Fighting back tears, Jesse wished things could go back to the way they used to be, back when his father had still been his best friend. Yes, his mom loved him, cared for him, and always kept him fed and warm, but it was his dad who always used to wake him up early Saturday mornings so they could watch cartoons and play video games together. And it was his dad who always used to rush into their apartment after work, ready for a wrestling match even before he changed out of his work clothes. The memories almost brought a smile to little Jesse's face. But then something had happened; just like that, their cartoon mornings, video games and wrestling matches had all ended. It was almost as if an invisible hand had reached inside his father's chest and pulled all the fun out of him. He started getting angry a lot and coming home later and later from work. It finally got so bad that Jesse would already be in bed by the time his dad came through the door. That's when the arguing between his parents had started.

Now, sitting at the milkshake-splattered table, Jesse feared his dad had disappeared, somehow replaced by a dirty, angry man who just plain scared him.

His father gestured at the tray in front of him.

"We came here to eat, so eat."

Hesitantly, Jesse picked up a French fry, the one with the largest blob of pink goo. At another time it might have been delicious, but he took only one tiny bite before poking it into his half-eaten cheeseburger. He could feel his dad's eyes boring into him. Fear traced chills up and down his neck. Maybe he should have offered taken out his bag sooner.

"I'm sorry, Jess. I'm not mad at you."

Relieved, Jesse raised his head to find the lines in his father's forehead had smoothed.

"I brought it, Dad!" he blurted out, desperate to avoid a return of his father's angry mood. He reached into his jacket pocket and pulled out a crumpled plastic sandwich bag. "It's my piggybank money, just like you wanted." Jesse studied his father's face as he handed the bag across the table.

Instead of the happy expression Jesse had hoped for, his father's lips thinned as he reached across the table.

"I thought you—"

Jesse was going to add "wanted me to bring my money" but his father waved him silent. Dark eyes stared at him for a moment before examining the little bag of bills.

"You did good, Jess." Gaunt fingers wiped away tears.

Why is my dad crying?

After taking all but one of the bills, his father handed the bag back. Just then, a fast food worker approached.

"Is everything alright?" the older boy asked.

"We had an accident," his dad said in a gruff voice.

"I can see that," the worker said cheerfully. "But don't worry—"

"Just clean the fucking mess up!"

The boy's pudgy face turned red. His arm rose, and for a tiny moment it looked like he was going to stick up his mean finger, but instead he gave a weak smile, nodded and moved away.

Jesse didn't dare say a word.

"Useless little prick," his father said. "Someone ought to fire his ass." His head snapped toward the service counter where two other workers, an older man with glasses and a young woman, were talking quietly.

"D'you hear that? You should fire his pimply ass!"

The woman's head snapped up and her mouth opened as if to say something, but the man with glasses put his hand on her shoulder and whispered something. She gave Jesse's dad one final angry glare then disappeared into the cooking area. The older man didn't look their way again as he sprayed cleaner and began wiping the front counter with a cloth.

"Just a bunch of friggin' losers," Jesse's father said. He was looking at Jesse again. "Don't quit school, Sport, or you'll wind up working here with these retards!"

Though his insult reverberated across the restaurant, the older man in the service window ignored their side of the restaurant and continued swirling his cloth around the stainless-steel counter.

His dad reached across the table and put his hand on Jesse's. Jesse tried to hand the bag back to him.

"No, Jess," his dad said in his friendly voice. "Put that back in your piggybank when you get home—and don't tell your mom. I don't want her to be mad at you."

Jesse nodded. Of course, he wouldn't tell her. She was already mad enough at his father.

"Excuse me," the older boy said, having returned with a washcloth in hand. Jesse's father stood and moved out of the way so he could wash the table. Jesse started to get up, but the boy waved him back down. "No, you're okay. Just move your food for a second."

Jesse slid his tray out of the way and in moments the boy had washed everything clean.

"I'll be back with a mop in a minute." The boy's voice cracked, making the word "minute" sound like it came from a girl.

Jesse fought the urge to giggle.

"I'm going to the bathroom," his dad announced.

"I need to go, too," Jesse said.

"Goddamn it then! You go!"

Jesse froze. He stared at his food.

"Well, do you have to go or not?" his father asked.

Jesse's eyes lifted and settled on several beads of sweat forming at his father's hairline. Dumbly, he shook his head "no."

"You're as bad as your friggin' mother!" His father got up and stomped toward the bathroom. "She can never make up her goddamned mind either."

Jesse wiped at a stray tear as his father disappeared into the bathroom. As soon as the door closed, he quickly snaked his hands under the sides of his legs and felt around. Thankfully, the backside of his pants was dry. His Wolverine underwear must have absorbed most of the "scared pee."

Glancing toward the service counter, Jesse could see the girl had returned to whisper with the older man. They gestured toward him and then toward the bathroom. Jesse had seen his father thrown out of enough places to know what came next. Ignoring the feeling of damp superhero underwear against his private place, Jesse hurried over to stand beside the restroom door.

"Hey," his father said, swaying to a stop as he came out a couple of minutes later. He had a goofy grin on his face, and his eyes rolled back and forth as though he was having a hard time focusing. If it weren't for the way his father held onto the half-open bathroom door, he probably would have fallen.

"So now you needs to go," his father slurred.

Like a cluster of teachers in a schoolyard, all three of the workers were watching them.

"Can we leave right now, Dad?"

"Sure, Jess." His father reached down to tousle his hair and missed. He grinned and tried again, this time managing to run his fingers across the top of Jesse's head. "What-whatever you want, Jess. You know you're my little sport."

Jesse hated his father's drastic mood changes, but this one couldn't have come at a better time. He tugged on his father's hand and kept tugging until his father was tripping over cracks in the sidewalk a block from the restaurant.

"So'd'ya have a good time, Je—"

His father stumbled and yanked Jesse's arm before catching his balance. He laughed then stopped and claw-gripped Jesse by the shoulder.

"I asked you a question!"

Jesse winced.

"Yeah, it was fun."

His father grinned. Drool ran down one corner of his mouth and formed a bubble in his whiskers.

"Me and mom's getting back together, y'know. She's gonna let me come—"

His father stumbled again but this time didn't have Jesse's hand. Arms wind-milling, he staggered off the sidewalk and fell onto his butt. Jesse was afraid he'd get hit by a car, but his father just laughed, got awkwardly to his feet and hopped up onto the curb, which he then proceeded to walk like a tightrope. He took only two steps before falling flat on his face.

Jesse was terrified.

"Come on, Jess," his father said, rolling over and reaching up with a grin. "Help yer ol' man up."

Jesse reached out as asked but he wasn't big enough and fell on top of his father who smelled like cigarettes and body odor. His dad tickled him for several seconds, but Jesse was in no mood to laugh. Somehow, they both got to their feet. "Don't be so sad," his father said. "It won't be long 'fore I move back to-to the apartment."

Jesse nodded. The chilly breeze made his damp underwear cold and uncomfortable.

"No, serious," his dad said, swinging his arms wildly as he started walking along the curbing again. "I'm coming back. Your mom loves me, y'know. We're family, and families live under the same-same house."

Jesse faked a smile.

His father gave up the dangerous balancing act and staggered back into the middle of the sidewalk. Though still unsteady, he managed to stay on his feet.

Jesse and his mom lived in an apartment up over a laundromat, where if Jesse stood on the edge of his bed and peeked over the two-story building across the street, he could make out the very tip of McDonald's yellow arches. It didn't take them long to cover the short distance, but Jesse's father was breathing hard by the time they reached the front door. Back when he lived at home, his father could easily have run that distance.

Jesse knew something was wrong.

"Karen," his father said too-loudly into the intercom. He waited only a second before pounding the button again. "Karen, we're back. Open the fucking door!"

"Okay, okay," Jesse's mother said through the speaker.

The door buzzed, and Jesse's father shoved it open.

"Bye, Dad," Jesse said, rushing past and bolting up the stairs. He was already in his bedroom by the time his parents started fighting through the closed apartment door. His father, like always, wanted to come in and talk. His mother wanted no part of it, so they yelled back and forth for a long time.

Jesse knew he should have changed his pee underwear, but instead he crawled into bed, pulled his blanket over his head and started to cry.

≈ ~ ≈

Under-Heaven

2

Under-Heaven

…sometime in 1945

At first, she didn't tell me I was dead. Instead, she said, "You've moved on."

I had no recollection of anything before that moment. It was as though I had just magically appeared standing before her. A heavyset woman in her fifties, I guessed, she had a cheerful smile and a graying stack of brunette hair tied in a bun at the top of her head. Reminding me of a nurse's outfit, her high-collared white dress was loose and hung below her calves. Her white stockings barely covered the ankles above her white shoes.

My gaze swung to the small, white home beside us: a bay window protruded from a wall to the left of an unadorned white door that opened onto a porch barely large enough to seat two people; a set of five white steps dropped onto an immaculately cut, green lawn. Beautiful flowers of every imaginable color surrounded the porch.

I wondered how I had gotten here and who this woman was, but the questions made me uneasy. I felt as though a part of me didn't want to know.

"Can you talk?" she asked.

My thoughts too jumbled to speak, I nodded.

"Take your time, Nathaniel," she said. "There's a lot to get used to. For now, let me show you around your new home."

Uncertain, I accepted her grip, which was warm and gentle. Though I was almost ten years old, it seemed odd to be left alone with a stranger. Questions littered my mind, but I sensed even the tiniest inquiry would be like a scalding pot. Forcing any dangerous thoughts away, I followed her up the stairs and froze. There, between two white wooden chairs, sat a pure white lobster trap. Fear crawled like a spider along the back of my neck. I shivered and followed her into the house.

"I'm your grandmother," she said as we walked into a tiny living room. Two over-stuffed chairs and a couch sat snuggly against the walls. The cream upholstery matched the carpet. The ceiling was white as were the walls, which were noticeably devoid of pictures. The only end table in the room had a single brass lamp.

"You can call me Grandma Clara if you like," she continued. "You have quite a slew of relatives looking forward to seeing you, Nathaniel, but we'll probably wait a little while for that. Okay?"

"I guess," I said, finding my voice.

A growing queasiness in my stomach wouldn't allow me to question why there was no radio in the living room nor why I didn't recognize my own grandmother.

As unadorned and white as the living room, my new kitchen additionally had no cabinets, no refrigerator, no stove and, of course, no sink. I wouldn't have recognized it at all if it weren't for the small round table and four chairs in the middle of the otherwise empty room.

"Where's the food supposed to go?" I asked.

"You won't be eating here," she said.

I was imagining a cafeteria or local restaurant as she led me across the hall to the last room, which held only a bed and a rocking chair. Though oddly austere, the house had a warm, comfortable feel.

"It's usually quite peaceful here," Grandma Clara said as we returned to the front porch.

I paused.

"Nate, are you all right?" she asked.

I stood at the railing and consciously avoided looking at the lobster trap that inexplicably sent fear coursing straight to my heart.

"Yeah, I guess," I said, but I knew something was wrong, maybe with me but definitely with this place.

I stared out at the circular neighborhood of identical small, white homes. They were all single-story with small porches, bay windows, light gray roofs and brilliant floral displays, not one distinguishable from another—except for one thing: I couldn't see a single other white lobster trap.

Lucky me.

I glanced at my trap, but a sense of uneasiness immediately forced me to look away again. Somehow, I knew my anomalous porch furnishing could lead to dangerous memories.

I let my eyes follow the string of identical homes, which were like the pearls of a huge necklace. The necklace surrounded a circular, white cobblestone street which was completely self-contained with no entry or exit roads. The round median consisted of a thin strip of meticulously maintained grass and a large pond with a stunning, two-story cherub statue at the focal point. Powerful streams of water spouted in four directions. For a long moment, I gazed up at nearest of the four cherubs but soon withered beneath its gentle smile and white eyes.

Something was very wrong.

Sighing, I leaned over the rail and saw blossoms of every conceivable shape and color stretching luxuriantly toward the sun from the base of my porch. But even their rainbow hues and bouquet of scents couldn't break through my malaise. Instead, the fresh country smell caused my uneasy stomach to twitch again.

I quickly stood upright.

Examining my new neighborhood, I could see no fences or walkways, but the neatly mowed grass wasn't matted down anywhere, which was odd since men and women were milling about—mostly in pairs—all across the deep green surface. At least a dozen people knelt in the median and faced the fountain as if in prayer. As I looked out at the scene—immaculate homes, vibrant flowers, people dressed mostly in white, lush green grass—it seemed too perfect. Even the white cobblestones of the circular street were too bright. I could not see a single smudge of dirt or mud on the road's surface. Oddly, there were also no cars.

I turned my attention to the people at the pond's edge and wondered why nearly everyone in this place was dressed completely in white. Of the dozen or so people kneeling at the water, there were only two exceptions: one man had dark shoes and bizarre slacks that were black up to his knees but then white from that point upward; the other really stood out because his clothes were colorful to the point of being garish. His green plaid pants, yellow striped shirt and green hat, made him look as though he had just stepped off a fairway at Staber's—

My breath caught at the thought of my hometown golf course. Any further reflection scurried to the outermost reaches of my mind when I realized my hands were trembling.

Focusing instead on the people kneeling by the water, I wondered if they might be watching fish or turtles. Abruptly, the man with the bright golfing outfit made a fist and jabbed a finger down at the pond.

"You better hope I never see you again!" he spat. Then he got up and stomped up onto a porch four homes down from me. "And that's what I think of this goddamned thing!"

Suddenly a white child-size tricycle flew off his porch and landed with a metallic thump on the grass in front of his house. One of the white rear tires was still spinning as he disappeared behind a slamming door.

I glanced back toward the people at the shoreline. None paid any attention to the angry man and instead kept their gazes focused on the unusually calm spots of water in front of each of them. I shifted my focus to the spray of water cascading from a cherub's polished marble hand. Water splashed and churned as it struck the pond's surface and sent small waves rippling across the pond to lap gently at the shoreline. But those ripples never affected the circular spots of water in front of each kneeling person; those circular areas remained as motionless as glass. Confused, I watched as two of the pond-side people got up and moved away. In both cases, tiny waves immediately erased the motionless spots and began to lap at the shore. I was still trying to unravel that mystery when it came to me!

I snapped around to look at my grandmother.

"I know what's wrong with my house!"

"It seems quite nice to me," she said with a smile.

"Maybe I missed it," I said, striding back inside. I looked again through each of the three rooms. I didn't see any additional rooms or doorways. "There's no bathroom!"

"You won't need that anymore," Grandma Clara offered, having followed behind me.

"You mean I'm supposed to use an outhouse?" I'm sure my face scrunched with disgust at the thought of it. Billy Ganglin's family still used an outhouse. There had been large black spiders crawling on the walls and the smell had been worse than all the dog poops I'd ever cleaned up. Worse was that after I sat my naked butt on the wooden bench, I could have sworn something splashed underneath me. Terrified, I yanked up my pants and had run. After my one visit to the hole from hell, I swore I'd never go into such a place again.

When was that? I wondered, but my mind had already clamped shut. Unable to even remember the boy's name, I struggled to recall the thoughts that had just been so clear in my mind. The effort sent my heart racing. My entire body quaked. Fear washed over me like a chill rain.

I gasped.

"Are you okay?"

I took a deep breath. "Yeah, I guess."

"Nate—I hope it's okay to call you Nate?"

I nodded.

"Nate," she continued, "you don't need to go to the bathroom anymore."

"I'm supposed to hold it?"

"Nate, nobody here goes to the bathroom. We just don't need to anymore."

"Oh." I nodded with feigned understanding. Though I knew her statement was ridiculous, I also knew it would have been improper to point that out. Until I figured something else out, I would sneak out back when I had to go.

I didn't allow myself to stop and consider any of this too deeply. In the back of my mind, I knew it was preposterous for an almost ten-year-old to get his own house, and it was equally crazy for that house to have no radio, no appliances, no sink and no bathroom. Of course, it all made about as much sense as a perfect circular neighborhood populated by people dressed mostly in white—which, come to think of it, included me.

Since when are jeans white?

My stomach roiled with fear. I wanted to understand but at the same time lacked the courage to search inside myself for answers. At that moment, staring at the strange woman who called herself Grandma Clara, I realized that a secret was locked inside my head. I knew it wasn't just something bad; it was quite possibly the most horrible and terrifying secret there had ever been. I imagined a steel-reinforced prison inside my mind, and I further imagined a fang-filled creature locked just behind that prison door. In my hand I held a key, a key that I feared I would someday have to insert into the lock and turn—

I threw the imaginary key and raced out onto the neatly mowed grass of my new neighborhood. As I ran, my feet left no imprints in the perfect grass.

~

Though Grandmother Clara visited every day, she was still a stranger to me, and I found myself missing other people that I knew I should have but couldn't remember. I suppose that emotional confusion might have played a part in the way my subconscious mind began to dole out memories...

The bright red school bus reeked of disinfectant, which made my five-year-old mind wonder if a lot of kids threw up during their first ride to school. My stomach sure felt funny. Terrified, I sat on one of the hard leather seats and craned my neck so I could watch my mother wave until she disappeared in the distance behind us. I tried to hide stray tears from the other kids as the tall buildings of Providence, Rhode Island slid past. Though I had seen many of the same buildings from my bedroom window, they looked so much larger when staring out through the windows of a disinfectant-smelling school bus. Once at school, the day passed in a blur of new rules and odd social moments with more kids than I'd ever seen together in one place. What made things worse was that our only teacher, a young woman with frizzy red pompom hair, spent most of her day coddling one brunette girl who couldn't stop crying. Though I put on a good show, I came very close to crying myself. When, later that day, the same red bus pulled up to the sidewalk in front of my house, I was ecstatic to see not just my mother but also my father standing there. He held four beautiful balloons—which I wound up sleeping with for almost a week, until the air got so low, they were nothing more than drooping pieces of colorful rubber...

Marching out into the backyard of my lonely new home, I could still feel my dream father lifting me up so my mother could smother me with kisses. It was my third day in that strange place, and Grandma Clara had been gone for only a few minutes. I stood on my back lawn and stared at the wall of clouds encircling my new neighborhood. Hesitantly, I brushed my hand along the white mist and walked along its edge. Though damp, the clouds were warm and not as frightening as I had first thought. I walked back and forth along that wall several times and wondered what might be beyond. But, no matter how hard I looked, I couldn't see anything through the fluffy whiteness. Convinced that there must be other children beyond the clouds, I took several steps into the impenetrable border.

Suddenly, I was surrounded by a terrifying gray gloom so thick I couldn't see my own fingers wiggling in front of my face. I stopped, certain that at any moment I would walk right off the edge of a cliff. Peering into the murk and gingerly testing the ground in front of me, I took another step, then another and another. The whole while, I kept telling myself that a new neighborhood filled with children would be just steps away. With my fourth step I saw faint light ahead. Excited to be free of the dense gray mist, I rushed out onto a perfect green yard behind a perfect, small white house.

I crept along the flowerbed that bordered the edge of the nearest house. Peering out into the front yard, I hoped to glimpse even one boy or girl my age but saw only adults milling peacefully within the tidy circle of white houses or kneeling at the edge of a fountain pool identical to the one in my own neighborhood. My eyes flicked from house to house around this new circular road. Confused, I turned and froze as my gaze locked upon the one item that couldn't possibly have been there.

My lobster trap.

3

Falling Hero

Jesse Dropped his Thor hammer. Though it was his favorite toy and he had begged his mother for two days after seeing the movie, not even a superhero weapon was important in comparison to spending time with his dad. Besides, today was an especially important day because they were going to play his mother's favorite game and convince her to join them. Between the loud intercom buzzes, he heard his father's voice. Bolting out into the kitchen, he was just in time to see his mother angrily punch the broken talk button on the intercom.

"Ow!" she exclaimed, scratching her finger on the exposed metal prong. The loud buzzer blared throughout the small apartment for a fourth time. More gently, she depressed button again.

"Wagner," she said, "you do know that just pisses me off, right?"

"Hey, Babe," came his father's static-filled response, "I ain't here to make you mad. 'Just wanted to make sure this busted thing was working."

"Yeah, whatever." Jesse's mother pressed the unlock button and waited until they could hear footsteps coming up the stairs before letting it go.

"I'm going to take a shower, baby," she said. She leaned down to kiss Jesse on the top of the head. "Maybe you and your dad could play a videogame or watch some TV."

Jesse nodded with a secretive smile. Her shower would give his father and him time to set up the Monopoly game. Once it was ready, he knew she'd never be able to resist, especially since she won every time they had ever played—except once when Jesse caught her slipping money into his pile when she didn't think he was looking. He smiled and looked forward to the long game that would give his parents time to talk. What he wanted more than anything was for them to get back together so things could go back to the way they used to be. The footsteps stopped right outside the kitchen door.

"Hi, Babe," came his father's voice.

"You let your dad in," his mother whispered. "I'll be in the shower."

Certain their plan would work, Jesse reached up on his tippy toes to turn the bolt lock. His father shoved the door open and nearly knocked him down. As it was, the edge of the door hit him hard in the forehead.

"Hey, beautiful," his father said, pushing past him.

Unshaven, with messy hair and clothes that looked like they'd been worked and slept in for multiple days, his father was a mess. Snots were frozen to his upper lip and his cold red hands were embedded with dirt. Worst of all, he stank of vomit and body odor. He glanced around the kitchen and took several steps to peer into the living room.

"Babe?"

"She's taking a shower." Jesse said, wishing his father had done the same before coming over. No way would his mother want him around looking and smelling like that.

"That's a hell of a way to treat guests," his father said, but there was no anger in his voice as he reached over and grabbed a paper towel to wipe under his nose. Most of the snots came off.

"So, where's the game, Jess?" he asked.

Jesse's shoulders sagged. Though he didn't understand what caused it, he recognized the glassy look in his father's eyes. That look meant it wouldn't be long before he started talking too loudly and getting mad for no reason. Jesse was certain that a few minutes after his mother got out of the shower they would start fighting. The only question left was would his father leave when asked or would he make her call the police again? Jesse wanted to cry. Why couldn't they just be a normal family?

His father made a loud rasping noise at the back of his throat then spit in the sink. "Go on, Jess. Get the game."

Jesse trudged to the hallway closet and pulled out the worn Monopoly box. The sight of it depressed him even more because he remembered the happy times they used to have playing together. His father would keep telling his mother how badly he was going to beat her, and she would say things like "Bring it on" and "Give it your best shot." Then throughout the whole game his mother would help Jesse count his money and keep track of his properties, while his father would whisper not-so-secret plans about how the men were going to team up and crush her. The game always ended with his father going broke and bargain selling all his properties to his son, then helping him until he, too, lost to the all-time champ. Jesse could envision his mother's triumphant grin and could hear the cheerful father of his past saying, "We'll get you next time, just wait and see." Then he and Jesse would go on a tickle attack and chase his mother all through the house until they had her pinned down, laughing and gasping for mercy on her bed.

But there would be no laughing tonight.

Jesse returned to the kitchen to find his father rummaging through the cupboard.

"Where the fuck is my Best Husband cup?" he asked.

Jesse wasn't sure but thought it might have been the cup his mother had thrown out a few weeks before. That same night, she had been crying for no apparent reason and had thrown out several things, including something from the kitchen cabinet, a dried flower from the family Bible, and a stack of old letters from her bedroom.

"Well, guess I'll just have to use this one," his father announced pulling out a mug with a cartoon of a large-chested naked lady on the side. Not remembering ever seeing it before, Jesse guessed it had come from the top shelf where he could not reach—even after climbing onto the counter.

"When your mom finds my cup, we can put this one back!" His father slammed it down on the counter with a simultaneous whack and sharp clink. Glazed eyes stared at the broken handle.

"Glad it wasn't my cup," he said, grabbing both pieces and shoving them way down into the trashcan. "Your mother didn't like that cup anyway. 'Made her feel bad about her tiny boobs."

Jesse knew talking like that wasn't nice, so he didn't mention that he liked his mom's boobs; they were soft and snuggly whenever he fell asleep in her lap.

Having no choice but to wait for the argument that was inevitably coming, Jesse dropped the game onto the kitchen table. Apparently forgetting the need for a cup, his father turned on the kitchen faucet and scooped several handfuls of water to his lips. The way he slurped might have been funny if Jesse hadn't been staring at the twigs and bits of dried leaves that covered the back of his father's green jacket. There were even small clumps of dirt or animal doo-doo tangled in the back of his father's long, stringy hair. Had he been sleeping in the park? The thought of his dad living out in the cold made Jesse want to cry.

"Everything okay?" his mom called out.

"Everything's fine," his father said, winking at Jesse. "We men are just waiting for our lady to get out here."

The bathroom door slammed shut.

"Go on, set the game up," his father said, spinning a chair around and settling down backwards on its seat. Jesse suddenly realized his father's hands were shaking. Blood trickled down from one of his nostrils.

What was wrong with him?

Jesse didn't dare to say anything, but he couldn't stop staring as the whiskers of his dad's upper lip began to stain red. His father sniffled and wiped the back of his hand under his nose.

"What the hell!" He pushed back from the table and rushed over to the sink. He tried to wipe the blood from his face, but when he glanced back at Jesse the red had spread to his lips and beard.

"I'll go get Mom!"

"No!" his father yelled. Then more calmly, "Everything's okay, Jess. It's just a little nosebleed." He yanked a half-dozen paper towels off the roll and blotted his face.

Jesse was terrified by the bright red stains that bloomed all over the white paper sheets. His father wiped several more times then held the clump of towels under his nose. Jesse could still see red patches in the whiskers around his mouth and chin.

"I have to go," his dad said, his voice muffled by the bloody towels. "Tell your mom I'm sorry, but I couldn't stay for the game. It's a work thing. She'll understand." His father rushed to the door and opened it. "I love you, Jess."

Without another word, his father slipped out the door and stumbled down the stairs. Jesse heard the outside door open and shut. Normally, he would have raced to his mother's room to watch his father get into his truck and drive off, but he knew it would be really bad if his mother found out what really happened. So, instead, Jesse pushed a chair over to the sink, climbed up to shut the faucet off, then pulled out a handful of clean paper towels and began to wipe the stainless-steel basin.

His lips quivered and tears started to fall as the towels turned red.

4

In Fear of Memories

I had been in that strange place for two weeks and almost daily had flashes of memories that churned my emotions like ocean waves breaking against a rocky shore. I was tormented by recollections of children teasing me and throwing things at me, but they were nothing compared to the reoccurring memory of a bearded man whose breath smelled like chewing tobacco and whose powerful visage left me gasping in terror.

How could I ever make sense of these bits and pieces of my life when I was too frightened to hold any one image in my mind long enough to understand? Just thinking about the man with a bulldog thick neck and arms like tree limbs sent chills sweeping up and down my spine. Each time I envisioned him it was as though my imaginary monster was reaching a clawed hand through prison bars for me.

Nerves already frayed to the breaking point, I didn't know how much more I could take. As much as I feared answers, I resigned myself to finding out more. Though Grandma Clara usually wore some version of a nurse's outfit, the one she wore that day was longer than usual with a high frilly collar and lacey cuffs. It made her look both elegant and professional, which seemed proper given what I had to talk to her about.

"Is this Heaven?" I asked.

"No, Nate."

"Then where?"

"There are many names, but I like the term Under-Heaven."

"How did I die?"

"I don't think that's for me to say." Her eyes squinted in sympathy.

"Why?"

"Because you already know."

My monster rocked viciously back and forth. It was like all the terrible people from my past, or what I thought was my past, wrapped into one horrifying body, and it wanted out. The key to its cage was in my hand again. As though it was scalding hot, I dropped it and forced the vision away.

"Why don't I remember?" I asked. Just voicing the question made my chest tighten and my throat constrict.

"You will, little one," she said. "But it has to be at your own pace."

"I hate not knowing, but I'm also terrified of what I might learn."

Grandma Clara drew me into a tight embrace. "I'm so sorry I can't help you with this."

"It's not fair," I said, pushing her away. "I have to get this over with." Even as the words left my lips, I knew it was a lie. I knew I didn't have the courage to face that monster, and I doubted I ever would.

"You have to choose your own timing, Nate. That's part of growing as a soul. I have faith you'll remember when the time is right."

I closed my eyes and was suddenly overcome with the image of my mother. I hadn't realized before then how much she looked like my grandmother only younger. My body clenched at the sight of her tear-filled eyes.

Why were you crying, Mom?

What a horrible past I must have had! I stared at my grandmother.

"Why do you even come here if you don't want to help me?"

"Oh, Nate, I—"

I didn't hear what she said next because I was already racing out of my house, down the stairs and onto the white cobblestone road. I skirted the fountain pool and bolted to the other side of the circle. My mind was filled with a sense of terror as I sprinted between two houses on the furthest side of my circular neighborhood. Like my own backyard, the grass was beautifully manicured and bordered with every manner of lovely blossoms. And, like my own back yard, beyond the grass and flowers rose the ever-present, billowing white clouds.

Sliding to a stop, I fell to my knees and stared at the edge of what I now realized was a trap. Under-Heaven was my own personal prison. Though I desperately wanted to disappear into that wall of white and somehow escape the mean children and the terrifying man with tobacco breath who kept trying to pry their way into my mind, I sensed that to enter that border of whiteness a second time would make everything about my new life horrifyingly clear.

My monster shook with anticipation. It wanted me to know!

Why couldn't this all be a dream? Why couldn't things return to the way they were?

Were?

What was I thinking? I knew nothing about my past. How could I crave the return of a time I couldn't even remember? And how could I be so frightened of my memories but yearn for them at the same time?

Claws raked across steel bars.

I winced. No matter how deeply I searched inside myself, I couldn't find the strength to overcome my fear. I couldn't face my past. Not now, not ever!

I tried to concentrate on the grass, the flowers, but the vision of that prison door remained stuck in my head. Huge claws were now scraping loudly across the steel mesh that covered the prison window. That monster—and that man—would soon be free!

A part of me knew that only by facing my fears could I find peace, but I was no more capable of facing that monster than I was of pretending my new neighborhood was anything other than what it was: a prison. I was stuck here in the sameness of Under-Heaven much the way my own memories were trapped within the jail inside my mind.

The monster is me, I thought, making the crazy connection. But if that's true, why can't I find the courage to face myself?

Even though I didn't have an answer, I knew I was right. I pressed my hands to either side of my head and squeezed, but the terrible thought wouldn't stop.

I am the monster.

I shook my head, clamped my eyes shut and willed myself to see only darkness, but that prison shone like a beacon in my thoughts. The iron door was shaking, and violent thumps left large protruding dents. I yanked my eyes open and screamed, but my monster's piercing howl overwhelmed my own strangled cries.

I am the monster.

I am the monster!

Every mind has its limits, and mine had just been reached. As my conscious mind collapsed, so too did my muscles. I fell limp to the grass and wept. I wept for everything that had been lost and forgotten. I wept for the fear that enveloped me every day. Mostly, though, I wept in frustration at my own cowardice.

Tears came from a very deep well and ran for a long time.

I am the monster...I am the monster...I am the monster...

It seemed like an eternity before that damning phrase slowed and finally stopped its relentless march through my mind. Sometime during that period, I sensed a hand reaching out from the clouds to gently stroke my hair, but when I looked there was nothing but swirling whiteness.

Exhausted and confused, I finally got to my feet and returned to my prim little home.

Grandma Clara was already gone.

5

Mental Doors Can Crack

I had been in Under-Heaven for over a month when my routine was suddenly changed. I woke earlier than usual one morning at the sound of my grandmother coming in through the back door.

"Today we're going to begin your first lesson," she called from the living room.

"Lesson?" I said with a yawn, rolling out of bed.

Rather than explain, she passed my door and went into the kitchen. I followed to find her sitting at the table, removing a deck of cards from one of the many pockets in her nurse's outfit. I settled into the seat beside her and watched as she dealt out seven cards to each of us.

"Do you know how to play Rummy?" she asked.

Once again, I found myself at a loss as to how my memory worked. Though I remembered only snippets of mostly terrifying people from my past, I immediately remembered how to play Rummy. We played several hands, of which I won one, but when we changed games to Fish, I won three out of four. It was her turn to deal but after shuffling the deck she placed it face-down on the table and looked quizzically at me.

"Why is it," she asked, "that it's okay to keep secrets playing Rummy but not when you're playing Fish?"

Suspecting this was part of the day's lesson, I explained that in Rummy the rules allowed you to keep your hand a secret, but in Fish the rules say when someone asks you for a card you have to give it up.

"So not all secrets are bad?" she asked.

"I guess not," I said.

"Can you be more specific?"

"A secret is okay if the rules allow it, I guess."

"What about if a person keeps secrets from himself?" she asked.

So that's what she was trying to get at. My monster immediately began banging on its prison door.

I flinched.

"I'm too scared," I told her. "I can't."

"But in your case, who's making the rules?"

I was starting to lose the logic of her card game analogy. The sheer terror I felt at what might be hiding inside my head rendered all logic null and void. I could barely breathe when I thought about that thick man with the tobacco breath, forget think rationally.

"Nate, who makes the rules about your memories?"

"I guess I do," I said grudgingly.

Grandma Clara dealt out another Rummy hand.

"That's it?" I said. "That's all there is to that lesson?"

She smiled warmly.

"Now I just have to teach you how to let your grandmother win more often."

And she went on to teach me that lesson pretty well.

~

As the days passed, lessons became a regular part of our routine; though not all of them were as much fun as playing cards, I found myself keeping something from each of my grandmother's teachings. It helped that the subjects varied each day. Sometimes we talked about seemingly random events in history; other times the discussion would be about Under-Heaven, and yet other times her past would be our focus, but inevitably all of our lessons swirled back to questions about morality. Surprisingly, as much as we talked about right and wrong, my grandmother never preached; she simply engaged me in conversations that illustrated how every person was responsible for his or her actions.

Oddly, her lessons also made me yearn to take responsibility for my own actions, but how was that possible when I couldn't even remember them? I began to feel as though I had an obligation to remember my past but wanting to remember and being brave enough to actually do it were two entirely different things. It was true that scattered images of ocean waves and boats began to join my brief memories of people, but they came and went so quickly that I had no idea what any of them meant. I only knew that every fleeting snippet caused my stomach to clench and my mind to swirl with fear. It should have come as no surprise that my monster was about to get its first claw through my prison door.

It was the end of a day and my grandmother had been teaching me about John D. Rockefeller, an oil tycoon accused of corporate tyranny in the late-1800s and early-1900s. People said he crushed all the competition then overcharged for his products. However, later in life—after gifting huge sums of money to colleges, hospitals and museums—he became known as the world's most charitable person. Though he had hurt a lot of people in business, he seemed to have helped even more with his charity. She made me promise not to pass judgment about what he had done, but instead asked me to think about what I might have done differently had I been in his place.

As I followed her out into the backyard, I was still thinking about whether it would be okay to hurt one person as long as I helped ten other people. I waved as she strolled toward the misty barrier at the edge of my new world and smiled just before she was swallowed up by the swirling whiteness. Turning back to my house, I was halfway convinced that maybe it would be okay for someone to inflict pain on one person as long as they helped others, but what if the person being hurt was Vicky—

Vicky! I had a sister!

I suppose it was the shock of it that sent me tripping face-first onto my back porch. Though bones don't break in Under-Heaven, mental doors can crack…

I'd been a pretty typical kid, I think. I hadn't liked fourth grade very much and on that last day of school was happy to be free and run home. I ran nonstop all the way to my house, which was tucked up a woodsy dirt road that ran off from Burgess Street. It was a long run, but my feet were flying so fast I imagined I was The Flash and that the neighbors never even saw me pass. Okay, so old Mr. Kipswitch did wave at me from his porch rocker, but everyone knew he had supernaturally sharp eyes. I think I could have outrun my dog Whiskey that day as I soared into my yard. I was anxious to see the energetic hairball who my mother always kept fenced out back until I got home.

Whiskey and I were nearly inseparable and if it weren't for my parents insisting I go to school, we would never have been apart. He was a golden retriever and my best friend. My parents used to say we grew up together, but I knew the truth: I grew up with Whiskey's help. He had always been the wiser of the two of us. I couldn't even count the times he had stepped between me and some trouble I had been about to get into, and it turned out that he'd have his paws full that summer as well. I raced past my father's rusty, red 1928 Ford pickup, leapt over one of my mother's flower patches and careened up the stairs into the house. I stopped short.

Unusual for this time of day, my father was propped at the edge of his favorite rocking chair, his fingers weaving strands of heavy twine into a dilapidated old lobster trap that sat like broken furniture in the middle of the floor. I wondered why he wasn't still out to sea. That morning, like every morning, Whiskey and I had watched from the hill above our house as the Miss Kane sailed out of the harbor. The Miss Kane was my father's boat, named after his third-grade teacher. My mother said it was because he had always had a crush on the woman, but my father insisted it was only because she inspired him to work hard in school.

"Did Miss Kane break down?" I asked.

"No, son, I just had something to take care of. That's all."

My father was dressed in a blue button-up shirt, which seemed odd for him at any time but especially unusual on such a warm day. Normally, around the house, and even out on his boat, he wore T-shirts. He reached over and switched off the knob to our three-foot-tall cabinet radio.

"Ma Perkins" went silent.

"Whiskey's out back," I said, shuffling my feet, hoping to be excused.

My father said nothing at first as his practiced fingers returned to weaving new twine into the vandal-ravaged netting. I knew it could take him up to two hours to mend a single trap, and I also knew that even then it would be one of the saddest-looking lobster pots in use off the coast of Maine. His mishmashes of wood and netting patches, though effective, didn't look especially nice. Most of my father's traps had been salvaged from the dump or purchased from the wives of unsuspecting lobstermen. Stiff competition for the shrinking lobster populations meant most lobstermen would never knowingly allow a single trap to pass onto a competitor, especially not one from out-of-state.

My father worked hard at his new career as a lobsterman, but making a living was never easy, and that combined with what my father called "competition with all the kids coming back from the war" made things especially tough. My mother said President Roosevelt had done everything he could to help poor people, but I couldn't see that he had helped my parents very much. Even so, my mother adored President Roosevelt. When he had died two months earlier, she cried for an entire afternoon. Just a month later, when the war with Hitler ended, she cried again because, "Our dear president died too soon to see Germany surrender."

I desperately wanted to get into the back yard—after all, my dog was waiting—but I knew my father would just call me back. Respect for your elders came first in my family. I tried to calm my hound-wrestling instincts. Whiskey would just have to wait for another minute or two.

My father pulled two pieces of new twine into a knot. Finally, he looked up. "How was the last day of school?"

"Okay, I guess," I shrugged, "but Tommy Edds spit on my seat again."

"Why?"

"Like always, he said I was a flatlander and that I should go back to flatness where I belonged."

By Maine standards, flatlanders were just about anybody that came from outside of the state of Maine, though people from New Hampshire fared better in Mainers' minds than flatlanders from other places. We, unfortunately, had come from Rhode Island where my father had lost his job at a bank over three years earlier. We may as well have been from the East Indies, though. Most Mainers joked about flatlanders and didn't mean anything by it, but fishermen were a different breed. To them, flatlanders were invaders, and my father was the worst invader of all because he was out on their sea pulling their lobsters.

My father's lips thinned, but he did his best to hide his anger. "Kids say some mean things sometimes, Nate. They'll get used to us in another year or two."

I didn't bother to mention the obvious: that we had already been in Coldwell for three years and still weren't welcome. I knew my father was having the same trouble on the docks. Though he and Mom never talked about it in front of my sister or me, someone had been cutting my father's traps loose at sea, and last week a dozen of his traps behind our house had been torn up. One thing was certain: the Maine lobstermen hadn't welcomed my father to their shores any more than their kids had welcomed me to their classrooms.

"It's okay, Dad," I said. "Most of the kids are nice anyway."

The truth was that only two of the kids at school
were nice to me, and they were both girls. One was Gracey Vachon, and though her parents had been in Coldwell for over twenty years, she also got called "flatlander" a lot. It apparently didn't matter that she had been born in Maine. The other girl was Trudy Jackson. Her father was a fisherman, but she had liked me ever since Whiskey and I chased a skunk out of her yard a few months before. It had probably crawled back under her barn later that night, but our friendship held. The other kids either ignored me or picked on me.

"Did you see a sheriff's car on your way home?" my father asked.

"Nope." I said, suddenly alert.

Something was up, probably something to do with the other lobstermen. My father wasn't the type to come home from work early unless it was serious. And to call the police was about as serious as things could get in a small, shoreline town. I'd only seen a sheriff in Coldwell three times since we had moved here, twice because people died of old age, and once when a bear got stuck in the Gradshaw's basement window the previous spring.

"It's nothing, son, but when you see the sheriff pull in the yard, why don't you take Whiskey out for a run? I'd like some privacy when I talk to him, okay?"

"Okay," I said. Though I was curious, being a kid sometimes meant you had to wait for information. Besides, I had a dog to see. My father returned to his trap repair while I rushed into the kitchen and pecked my mother on the cheek. I would have been embarrassed to do that in front of the kids from school, but it was a chore I secretly enjoyed when there was no shame to be found.

"Hi, Mom; Bye, Mom," I said as I bolted out into the backyard.

"Nice to see you, too, son," she called after me. I could hear the laughter in her voice.

Like a reddish-blond cyclone, Whiskey hit me chest high and sent me sprawling on my back. I rolled to catch him in a chokehold, but he was too smart for that. By the time I swung my arm around for my famous dog-wrestling move, he had jumped back out of arms' reach. There we were, two adversaries eyeing each other, each trying to guess the other's next move. It occurred to me that a certain ball of fur had already bested me; after all, I was lying on my side in the grass, and he was standing comfortably on all fours just a few feet away. He'd been planning this, I thought, and I knew my only chance of winning would be to trick him.

"Okay, you win," I said, rolling to my feet and brushing grass from my blue jeans and button-up, plaid school shirt. "You're too smart for me."

Whiskey let out a little yelp and pawed the ground. He swayed his neck back and forth staring at me. His hind legs were slightly crouched. He was ready to pounce.

"No, Whiskey, you win," I said, shaking my head. "I'm not going to fight you anymore."

His head stopped swaying, but his rear legs were still in a crouch. He wasn't buying it. I knew this was going to call for drastic measures, so I turned and took two steps back toward the kitchen door.

"Whulp, whulp?" came the question.

I glanced back just long enough to say, "I told you, it's over. You win."

I was another step and a half toward the door when a familiar flank appeared beside me. With a shameless lack of honor, I dove on his back and snaked my arm around his neck in my famous dog-wrestling move. We fell to the ground in a heap with me on top.

He gave only one final "whulp" before licking my cheek.

Once again, boy had proven victorious over dog.

In retrospect, I think Whiskey was smarter than I gave him credit for that day. I think he was just letting me win, one of his many ways of showing me how much he loved me…as much as I loved him. We were friends for life.

Unfortunately, neither of us knew how short those lives would be.

6

A Colorful Friend

I was still trembling when my grandmother arrived the next morning. Though her brow was wrinkled with concern, I was thankful she said nothing as she hugged me and settled onto the kitchen chair beside me to start our lesson. That day, I was to learn about archangels, the original angels and guardians of Heaven. I listened as well as I was able but found it hard to concentrate. I couldn't get the vision of that ominous prison door out of my head, only now the door had a crack running halfway up from the bottom. I could hear my monster gouging at the steel from the other side. It wanted out, it wanted me.

Not for the first time, I wondered if my fear would subside if I could somehow find a way to leave my Under-Heaven. Grandma Clara had explained that though there was only one Heaven, there were so many levels of Under-Heaven that I would never be able to count them all even if I had a math teacher to help. Most of the people in my Under-Heaven seemed to remain for only a few days, or on rare occasions maybe a month. In contrast, I had been there for three solid months...every day of which I had been accompanied by an overwhelming sense of fear and confinement. I'd often thought it might have been easier had there been other kids to play with. Unfortunately, children were seldom placed in the same Under-Heaven—something about peer pressure, my grandmother had once tried to explain. All I heard, however, was that my prison sentence wasn't going to get any easier.

As always, I grimaced at the thought of having trapped my memories much the way I myself had been trapped.

I am the monster!

"So, the archangels spend a lot of time in the Under-Heavens," Grandma Clara was saying, "making sure the pure souls are not mistreated when the demons come for the unlucky—"

She gasped.

"Are demons really that scary?" I asked.

"No—I mean, yes they are but...." Her voice trailed off as she stared out my large kitchen window.

30

I turned and was stunned to see a red-haired boy, maybe about eight years old, running past my front porch. I couldn't help the smile that spread like a sliced melon across my face. I was just standing to get a better view of him racing through the grass a couple of doors down when my grandmother tapped the table.

"Nate."

I immediately settled back into my seat but couldn't stop my feet from tapping the floor as she attempted to renew our lesson. She tried to explain that archangels were the only angels allowed to interact with new souls across family lines. "…so that's why family angels don't usually mingle on the grass or near the fountain pool."

I chanced a quick look out the window but couldn't see the redheaded boy anywhere.

"And they serve ice cream to the singing goats," she said.

I focused on her again and nodded.

"Ice cream…goats."

"Huh?"

She shoved her chair back and got to her feet. Hoping she wanted to move our lesson outside, I stood and fought the urge to look out the window again.

"That is why children shouldn't be grouped together." She pointed toward the floor at my feet.

My eyes followed her finger to the floor, but when I didn't see anything, she gave me a confused look.

"Nate," she said, "are you going to tell me you didn't notice the color of your sneakers?"

My excited thoughts about the new boy in my neighborhood melted faster than ice in a fire as I glanced down again. Sure enough, my sneakers were black…and black was just as bad as any other color.

You see, in Under-Heaven everyone's clothing changes color in response to how much guilt they harbor. White clothing and white shoes mean you are guilt-free and will likely move on to Heaven-proper. Anything other than white, however, means you have varying degrees of guilt. And with enough color, a soul might well become one of the damned. According to Grandma Clara, if a person's color is dramatic enough, demons can nab you at any time. Usually, though, they prefer darkness and will steal unlucky souls from their beds at night.

Though I'd never actually seen a demon, I often heard screams at night when some of my more colorful neighbors were forcibly relocated. By morning, they and their homes would be gone. Sometimes other homes with other residents might have appeared, but often the vacant spaces just became more beautiful grass—

Grass that the new boy and I can play in.

Even as the thought crossed my mind, I felt color wicking up my ankles. I stole another glance and, sure enough, the cuffs of my white jean pant legs were beginning to turn blue. Having my grandmother staring at them as it happened didn't help, but even that added guilt couldn't quash my intense desire to meet this new boy. His arrival was easily the most exciting thing that had happened since I had arrived in Under-Heaven.

With a sigh of resignation, my grandmother pushed her chair in. I braced myself for…what: a punishment, extra lessons? But my Grandma Clara's puckered brow turned into a gentle smile. She pointed toward my feet, which I suddenly wished were hidden under the table again.

"I'm worried about the color," she said. "But it's hard to deny that smile of yours." She turned toward the window. "Just promise me you'll be careful."

My chest was tight with excitement. Was she saying what I thought she was?

"First, come on over here," Grandma Clara said. She turned to look out my large kitchen window.

I joined her at the counter and followed her gaze toward the far side of beautiful cherub fountain where I could see the redheaded boy running across the grass with his arms spread like the wings of an airplane. Other than myself, I had never seen anyone run in Under-Heaven. The sight made me even more eager to meet him.

"What do you see?" Grandma Clara asked.

Was that a trick question? The boy soared across the grass, swooping first left then right. He was running and playing, having a great time. I should have been right there beside him.

"Look at his shoes and pants, Nate."

Suddenly, I saw what she had been trying to point out. The boy continued to run but rather than picturing myself with him, all I could see were his blue sneakers and pants that were tan almost to his waist. The exhilaration I'd been feeling drained away like water from a rusted bucket. If my understanding of color in Under-Heaven was correct, the redheaded boy might soon be on his way to Hell.

Under-Heaven

When my grandmother had first explained the color system to me, I thought it was the silliest thing I'd ever heard. It seemed obvious that all a person needed to do was take off their colored clothes and change into white ones: problem solved. The demons would be fooled, and life in Under-Heaven could continue. But there were a few problems with my theory. First, there were no changes of clothes in Under-Heaven. A person retained only the clothing they arrived in. Our bedrooms had no closets or bureaus to store garments in, and there weren't any stores at which to purchase new outfits. But even if we had access to other changes of clothes, it wouldn't have mattered because in Under-Heaven your clothes changed colors on their own. For instance, whenever I thought about slipping out of my house early before Grandma Clara arrived to give my lessons, my sneakers would begin to turn black. It was as though my clothing could actually read the level of guilt I felt. The one time I actually had skipped a lesson, by the time my grandmother found me hiding behind a house two doors down, my sneakers had already turned black and the cuffs of my pant legs had turned blue.

Other than those few occasions, I had never personally been concerned with the color code in Under-Heaven. My clothing had always remained pretty much white all the time. And, my few brushes with color had only lasted for a few minutes before my clothes turned white again. The only color that stayed with me since arriving in Under-Heaven was the bright red stain on the left shoulder of my T-shirt. The two times I had ignored the monster in my mind to ask Grandma Clara about it, she had shuffled the question aside, something she was especially adept at doing.

So, there I stood crestfallen to think that a boy even younger than me might have to go to Hell. I didn't know what he could have done that was so bad, but as I watched him race across the grass, I knew I had to at least talk to him.

"Just this once?" I asked my grandmother.

She encircled my waist with her arms and kissed me on the cheek. Normally, I would have pulled gradually away but this time I let her hug me for as long as she wanted. The thought of a boy my age going to Hell was enough to make me appreciate the comfort.

"You go ahead and meet him," she told me. "But you keep an eye on your colors. Promise me."

I dared a brief glance down at my sneakers and was relieved to see they had returned to their typical white tone. So far, I was safe. I nodded.

"Now that we have that settled," she said, "I have some important people to see. I don't know what fool approved of both you boys being in the same Under-Heaven, but I'm going to give them a good talking to—of that you can be sure."

Thankful I wasn't that person; I hugged my grandmother one more time before hurrying outside to introduce myself to my new neighbor.

It took all of two seconds for the redheaded boy and me to become fast friends. That first day, we played right up until dark, right up until a kindly man with glasses, a white beard and a cane called for Ricky from one of the front porches on the opposite side of our circular neighborhood from my house. The man was, of course, dressed entirely in white. Not daring to bring it up when we first met, I had completely forgotten about Ricky's little problem. I glanced down and was pleased to see the tan color in his pants had receded to knee level. Maybe he had nothing to worry about after all.

"That's my Uncle Sedrick," Ricky said as we jogged up to his house. He introduced us.

"It's nice to meet you, Nathaniel."

"You, too," I said, feeling awkward to be talking to an adult other than my grandmother. Since I'd arrived in Under-Heaven, I had stayed pretty much to myself. I waved to both him and Nate then ran back home.

The very next morning, I woke to the sound of knocking at my front door. Confused, I looked out the window at the dim morning sky and estimated my grandmother wouldn't arrive for another hour or two; besides, she never came through the front door.

Hoping that demons didn't knock, I crept out into the hallway.

"Who's there?"

"No one special," came a familiar voice. I opened the front door to see a huge smile smeared across Ricky's freckled face. My eyes traveled down to see the tan color of his pants was still down at his knees. Maybe he was going to be alright.

"Wanna do something?" Ricky asked.

I yawned and nodded. "Sure, but I can't go far because my grandmother will be here in a while."

"She comes every day?" Ricky asked.

I nodded.

Ricky took a couple of steps to the side and settled onto the chair beside my lobster trap. Just catching sight of the sinister contraption sent my monster into fits. Not for the first time, I wished I knew how to get rid of it. My grandmother had already ignored the question—twice.

I sat at the top of my stairs with my feet propped on the second step. The smell of flowers and morning dew should have been pleasant but stoked my ever-present sense of dread instead. I wondered if giving into my monster would have allowed me to understand the fear, but I lacked the courage to go back. No way could I face my own death.

"I heard screams last night," Ricky said. His chair creaked. I imagined he was tilting it back on two legs.

"It happens most nights," I said.

Oddly, Ricky didn't ask where the screaming came from. Maybe his uncle had already explained it to him; or maybe, like me, there were certain things he didn't want to face. Ricky's chair creaked again, and just the thought of looking back in the direction of the trap caused my monster to growl.

"Looks like there aren't as many houses as yesterday," Ricky said.

I nodded. "It changes every day—"

"Bet I can count them before you!" Ricky announced.

Laughing, I leapt down onto the grass and counted as quickly as I could. Ricky raced down beside me. We were both furiously mumbling and pointing as we spun in slow arcs.

One, three…ten…twenty-one—

"Forty-three!" we shouted out at the same time.

"I was first!" I yelled, not really sure but willing to see if he would fall for it.

"No way. I was," Ricky said. "And you were sticking your tongue out like you need it to count or something."

"At least I don't count on my fingers," I jibed back.

"That's only because my shoes are on and I couldn't use my toes."

That sent us both into fits of laughter.

When the silliness passed, we settled onto my stairs, and I explained that I'd never seen less than thirty of the small homes and the most I had ever counted was fifty-two. Without going into details, I added that people came and went fairly often in Under-Heaven and that their little white houses came and went with them.

I heard a door open and close. It must have been my Grandma Clara arriving through the back. I knew I should have hurried inside, but Ricky and I were still talking when she came out and leaned on the railing above us.

"So, who's your new friend?" my grandmother asked.

We got to our feet.

"My name's Ricky," he said. "It's nice to meet you, Ma'am."

"I'm happy to meet you, too, Ricky, but I'm guessing there might be a certain gentleman waiting across the way for you." The expression on her face suggested it wasn't really a guess.

Yes, Ma'am," Ricky said. He glanced at me before his eyes dropped to the grass near his feet.

Horrified, I saw the tan color creep from his knees all the way up to his waist. Thankfully, it stopped there.

"Now, now, Ricky," Grandma Clara said gently, "I don't think any harm has been done here. Missing a lesson or two isn't the worst thing. Even so, why don't we all get today's discussions out of the way?"

Ricky and I looked at each other and back at her. We both nodded.

"Tomorrow, Nate," my grandmother said, "why don't we skip a day so you can take a little free time."

I perked up, but Ricky's depressed posture didn't change.

"Ricky," Grandma Clara offered, "what do you say I smooth things over with a certain angel?"

He looked up, eyes wide, smile returning to his freckled face.

"Would you, Miss Clara?"

"Of course, Ricky. Let's get you back home." Grandma Clara held both our hands so we couldn't romp all the way to Ricky's house.

With angels there apparently wasn't much smoothing over needed. Grandma Clara simply winked at Ricky's Uncle Sedrick who was sitting patiently on the first porch swing I had seen in my neighborhood. I knew from my own experience that souls arrived in Under-Heaven with one special item from their life. For some it was positive, like a favorite hairbrush or a lawn statue; one time I had actually even seen a cheerful elderly woman arrive with an antique car. But some items were not seen as positive by their owners—items like my lobster trap. The way Ricky settled down beside his uncle suggested he was probably one of the lucky ones. I hoped that meant his swing carried good memories. I clamped my mind shut at further thought of my own special item.

"It's kind of you to escort my young rascal home, Clara," Sedrick said pleasantly.

"No problem at all," Grandma Clara said. "Your nephew and I already have an understanding about what happened this morning."

"Oh good," he said. "So, I shouldn't have to go over all that again. Splendid." The man's lopsided smile was infectious. I grinned. Ricky smiled, too, but whether it was in response to his uncle's demeanor or the lecture he'd just avoided, I couldn't have said. As we walked away, Grandma Clara turned back to Sedrick.

"By the way."

"Yes, Clara?"

"I'm willing to give these two young men the day off tomorrow, if that would work for you?"

Again, his face lit up with the infectious smile.

"Of course. Of course. I've a ton of things to attend to in Heaven anyway. Ricky and I will finish up today, and then he'll have a deserved break. Thank you for the suggestion."

The walk back to my house was brief and quiet, but silence was always comfortable with my grandmother. We skirted the tall cherub fountain and its large water-filled basin. There were five or six people kneeling and gazing into the water. I, of course, now knew what they were doing, but fear of what I might learn would never have allowed me to go near that pool. I felt a slight sense of panic just from being so near it. I gripped Grandma Clara's hand tightly, encouraging her to make a wider arc around the gushing marble sculpture and was relieved when she veered away.

"About Ricky," Grandma Clara said as we settled down in my kitchen. I braced myself because I knew how much his colorful clothes bothered her, "I think befriending him is too dangerous."

I shook my head. No matter what she said, my mind was already made up. I liked Ricky and, though I didn't understand why his clothes weren't as white as mine, I knew he was a good person.

"I'm worried, Nate." Grandma Clara pointed at my pants.

As I stared down at my sneakers, which had already been black from my lesson-skipping guilt, I saw my jeans now sported several inches of blue.

"That could be the beginning of a slide to the underworld," she said.

I had never liked the term "underworld" because it sounded too much like Under-Heaven, and it gave me the willies to think I was anywhere near Hell. Though I felt certain my color problem would only be temporary, I nodded.

"I'm sorry about skipping the lesson today," I said, in hopes of derailing any further discussion about Ricky.

"You don't have to be sorry, Nate. You have every right to make friends. It's just that…well, I know you like Ricky; I do, too. But maybe you need to be careful about how much time you spend with him. Maybe it's something for you to at least think about."

Probably the most appealing thing about Under-Heaven was that I was the one in charge. I knew my Grandmother Clara's suggestions were only that. She would never have tried to force me to do anything. Of course, her warnings about the underworld had been ever-present as I suspected her advice about Ricky would now be, but warnings were not the same as orders. Besides, she had such a kind manner that even if she had been able to order me around, I doubt she would have done it.

"There's something else, Nate," she said. "I really do trust the goodness of your soul, but I'm worried about how you might take it if things don't go well for Ricky. As much as neither of us wants to think about it, we have to accept that he might wind up in the underworld."

"It won't happen," I insisted. "He's good."

"I think you're right, Nate," Grandma Clara said, "but that doesn't mean he's safe. Sometimes good people go down there, too. In many Under-Heavens, this one included, souls aren't judged by their actions. Instead, they're judged by their own feelings of guilt."

"You mean Ricky wouldn't actually have to do anything wrong to go to Hell?"

She nodded. "In this Under-Heaven you just have to believe you did something wrong. Here, your own belief makes your color change."

"Why is Ricky like he is, then?"

"Only he and his angels know, Nate," Grandma Clara said. "But he must feel very guilty about something."

"That doesn't mean he's bad," I asserted.

"The demons don't care, Nate. If he's ever colorful enough, they're going to come for him. And I pray you're not too close if and when that happens."

7

A Bloody Past

Ricky and I often hung out on the curbing of the road. Not only did it make for a great place to sit, it was also far enough from the cherub fountain that I didn't get shivers unless I looked directly at the mirror-like spots of water where people stared. Ricky was already at the curb when I finally finished up my Greek mythology lesson and was able to join him. Unlike his usual smile, he greeted me with a serious expression.

"I have something to tell you, Nate."

"I'm game."

"Nate, it's scary."

My mental prison door shook.

"What?"

"It's about the red stain on your shirt, Nate. I've been asking around, and I know why it's there."

I was thankfully sitting down because otherwise I think I would have crumpled to the grass. My stomach felt as if an invisible pair of hands were twisting and squeezing it. I could barely breathe.

Ricky slid closer and put a hand on my arm.

"You okay?"

I nodded. Fear zigzagged through my body. I felt the urge to vomit, which was especially odd since I wasn't even sure souls could vomit. We didn't eat, so what could come back up?

"Tell me," I said, touching the red spot on my shoulder.

"Maybe I shouldn't," Ricky said.

I knew he was right. The monster inside my head was jumping up and down, pounding on the prison door, roaring with delirium that Ricky's information might let it out. At any moment, I feared it might be free to rip and tear at my sanity. I stiffened and swallowed hard. I was petrified to know, but I also knew that sooner or later I would have to face those memories.

I dug inside myself and grasped what few granules of courage I could muster. Now had to be the time. My monster clawed at the bars. I prayed that I could survive with my friend at my side.

"Nate?"

If it weren't for the firm grip Ricky had on my arm, I think I might have tipped backwards into the grass. I tried to speak but couldn't make myself say the words. Invisible hands twisted and tore at my midsection. Gales of fear ripped through my body. I gritted my teeth.

"Nate, do you want to know?"

I forced my frozen neck muscles to move. Almost imperceptibly I nodded.

It was a sign of true friendship, because Ricky did one of the most embarrassing things of all for a young boy. He pushed closer until his hip was beside mine. His arm slid around behind me until he had one hand on each of my shoulders. My friend embraced me tightly before he spoke.

"Nate, a red stain means you were murdered."

Razor sharp talons tore long gashes across the mental prison door. The door exploded outward…

It was during the second week after school let out when the sheriff returned. Whiskey and I had been romping through the myriad trails around the local mica mines when we heard the siren. Fear clutched at my chest. Since my father had recently been involved with the police, I feared he might be at the center of this commotion as well. The mines were on the western side of town, just beyond Staber's Golf Course. Normally, Whiskey and I would have skirted the edge of those meticulously groomed fairways on our way home, but in my rush to find out what had happened, we raced past holes three and ten. I'd like to say we were greeted with waves and smiles as we interrupted a dozen or so golfing men, but only dour and rude expressions were offered our way.

One older man had been getting ready to swing when we burst through a small clump of bushes within a few feet of him. Menacingly, he raised his club but dropped it when Whiskey spun and bared his teeth in my defense. I won't describe the gesture I received, but it was better than a golf club to the temple. We raced on.

The siren fell silent before we reached Main Street, but it was obvious where the sheriff had gone. People flanked both sides of Main Street and every head was craned down the hill toward the docks. Clusters of people were hurrying down to see what was going on.

The Coldwell coast consisted mostly of steep, craggy cliffs that rose fifty feet above often crashing ocean waves. The main village had been built above the only actual beach for several miles in either direction. Whisky and I followed the other people down the steep access road to the beach and commercial marina. As we crested the last small hill before the road made its final precipitous plunge to the docks, a gust of wind filled our noses with the strong smell of salt and seaweed. Below us, Shore Road ran to the left and right, parallel to the ocean, dead ending just a few hundred feet each way. A wild array of wooden docks and sea shanties lined the short street on the ocean side with only a few walkways and short strips of beach for the occasional swimmer brave enough to risk the notorious Coldwell undertow. On the inland side were various fishermen's bars and bait shops with two diners also built against the steep slope. If you walked to the end of the road in either direction, you were greeted with sheer, stone inclines that only a person with ropes and hooks could have climbed.

As I looked down at the main pier, I suspected that more than one car had raced down the paved hill and right out onto the wide, main wharf. Probably in response, two horizontal rows of wooden posts protected the entrance to the pier. Tires were stacked five-high over the top of each pillar. I wondered if a car would bounce off those tires or just hit hard and stop. Foot traffic could pass, but it would have been impossible to drive a vehicle through the blockade. Parked in front of the tire surrounds was a Lincoln County Sheriff's cruiser. Blue lights flashed along its roof. I studied the people clustered on the wharf but couldn't make out the cause of the commotion.

Then the breath caught in my chest. Miss Kane's double masts were poking up like two weathered telephone poles at the end of the dock.

What was he doing back so early? Normally, he came and went like clockwork, out with the sunrise and in just before dusk. The only two exceptions I could think of was the recent time he had called the sheriff and the one time over a year ago when he had his ravioli night. Though my father's near-ancient lobster boat had an inboard motor, it also had three small sails which, though not impressive, allowed it to crawl back to shore in the event of a breakdown. So, when one day the old Evinrude had quit, he was forced to return the Miss Kane under strictly sail power all the way back from Campfrey's Ledge, which was about six miles off the Coldwell coast. Apparently, lobster boat hulls had little similarity to sleek sailing schooners because my dad likened the ordeal to trying to blow a ravioli across a bowl of pudding. He had not made it back to the dock until three in the morning.

Pushing my way down the hill, I was anxious to learn what could possibly have pulled him off schedule this time. Staring at the Miss Kane's masts at the end of the pier worried me all the more because after offloading his catch, my father normally moored her a few hundred feet offshore and brought his skiff up onto the beach to save docking fees. I'd never seen him tie the Miss Kane to the main pier for more than a few minutes. That combined with his early return and the presence of the sheriff suggested trouble—probably serious trouble.

The sheriff's last visited Coldwell so my father could report another lobsterman had shot at him while they were both out at sea. Though the gunshots went wide, and my father had no proof, his report ruffled a lot of local feathers. That, of course, meant more vandalizing of my father's traps. But even worse were the knives someone had left sticking out of my father's buoys at sea and the two drain plugs pulled from the Miss Kane's hull the week before. Fortunately, she had taken on less than a foot of water by the time my father found her early that morning.

As I stared at the chaos on the docks below, Whiskey pranced at my side, no doubt, wondering why we had stopped. It's doubtful he would have understood my fear. What if something truly terrible had happened? Knowing Whiskey was right and that I was being a baby, I began pushing my way down through the throng again.

Fishermen are a rough and rowdy bunch, but they wouldn't normally have hurt a child. That was likely the only reason I was able to shove my way through the clogged pier. Most eyes were watching a small Coastguard patrol boat slide up alongside the wharf a little further down. My eyes, however, went immediately to my father who was sitting on a weathered post beside the sheriff. I could see blood splatters on his face and neck. He had several large red smears across his chest. His left arm was wrapped in a blood-soaked cloth that, judging from his bare upper body, I surmised to have been his T-shirt. The sheriff, clad in a brown uniform and a wide brim hat, alternated between asking questions and scribbling in a small notebook.

I pushed through the last of the mob and raced to my father.

"Dad, what happened?"

"Don't worry about it," he said. "I'll tell you and your mom about it later."

I knew my eyes were wide, and I couldn't take them away from the bloody make-shift tourniquet on his arm. I didn't remember ever seeing so much blood. I'd always had a weak stomach, and it threatened to heave at the sight.

"But you're bleeding."

My father shifted his body in an attempt to hide his wounded arm, but when he saw my eyes still drawn to the blood, he waved his good hand to get my attention. I blinked and focused on his drawn face.

"Nate, listen to me. I'm going to be fine. I'm with the sheriff now, but later I'll be home so we can talk about this, okay."

I nodded.

"I'm sorry to interrupt, Mr. Thompson," the sheriff said, "but I need to ask you a few more questions."

"Nate," my father said in a quavering voice, "go home and tell your mom there's been another incident. I'll be home as soon as I can, or I'll leave a message at the Danvers house." The Danvers were a wealthy elderly couple who lived only a few hundred feet through the woods from us. They were the closest people we knew with a phone. "Do you understand, Nate?"

I nodded again and was immediately dismissed as one of the Coastguard officers waved to the sheriff.

"We'll need you to confirm that is the man who shot you, Mr. Thompson," the sheriff said.

My father nodded weakly. The sheriff helped him to his feet and supported him as they trudged further along the pier to stand beside the Coastguard boat.

As one, the crowd surged after them, carrying me along toward the unfolding scene. Mostly lobstermen, these men smelled of fish, brine and gasoline. I knew my father had asked me to go home, but I wanted to gather a few more details so I could explain everything to my mother. My eyes kept going to my father's arm, which hung as limp as a mooring rope. Blood had completely soaked through the T-shirt and now fell in thick, red drips that splattered onto the pier. How could I leave without being able to tell my mother he was okay?

To say I was terrified would have been an understatement. The crowd comprised the largest group of adults I'd ever imagined, forget seen, and I had personally never been this close to a sheriff. I wished my dog had been at my side, but I knew he would be waiting at the back of the crowd for me to emerge.

As my father and the sheriff approached their boat, the two Coastguard officers lifted a large, sheet-covered object and placed it along the wide rail of their boat. I gasped, realizing the shrouded object was the approximate shape and size of a man. The series of red splotches blooming across the white material said the rest.

I held my breath.

One of the Coastguardsmen motioned to my father and lifted the sheet. My father looked down, nodded and mouthed the words, "That's him."

I was thankful I couldn't see the face from my vantage.

It was bad enough I had seen the sheet. One Coastguardsman lifted a rifle and handed it to the sheriff. The sheriff examined it then handed it back before making a few notes. The conversation between the four men went on for another few minutes.

By this time, I had begun to hear some of the things the crowd was saying. There were several statements about how flatlanders should go back to where they belonged. I also heard my father's name mentioned along with numerous swear words. Either these fishermen didn't realize who I was, or they just didn't care. But of all the snippets of angry conversation, two sentences reverberated in my mind like hammers against a bell: "The flatlander killed Stretch McGraw…The flatlander shot him dead."

Stretch McGraw, I knew, was the man who had fired a gun at my father the first time. I figured he must have tried again. My father stored a rifle below deck and, judging from the deer he brought home every fall, he was a good shot. Though I didn't know anything about the law, the whole thing terrified me. What if my father couldn't prove the other lobsterman had shot at him first? What if the sheriff tried to say it was murder?

"That's his boy," I heard someone say from behind me. Suddenly, the crowd quieted. They still talked among themselves, but it was more of a whisper.

The gathering at the Coastguard boat only went on for another few minutes before a car horn began to blare from the top of the hill.

"Brrrrr, brrrrrr…brrrrr, brrrr."

I glanced up to find the entire street packed. From the top of the hill to the bottom, there wasn't a bare stretch of pavement. There might have been a thousand gawkers in all. I would not have thought we had that many people in the entire county, forget the little town of Coldwell. Slowly, the throng parted and gave way to a black sedan that, judging from the shine on the paint, looked to be fairly new, certainly newer than my father's rust and red 1928 Ford pickup truck. Reluctantly, the crowd parted and let the black car glide down toward the docks until the press of bodies on the dock hid it from my view.

"Mr. Thompson, the medical examiner is here," I heard the sheriff say. "Why don't we see what he can do about that arm of yours?"

"I need to unload my catch," my father answered. His voice was weaker than I'd ever heard it, but there was conviction in his tone.

"Mr. Thompson," the sheriff said, "you're in no condition for that. Besides, you're under arrest."

"Sheriff, you know Stretch fired at me three times in the last month. How can you think it was anything but self-defense?"

"I'm sorry," the sheriff said. "I know what you reported, but none of that matters for the moment. After the doctor treats you, I'll have to take you back to my office. As far as the law is concerned, I have to arrest you."

My father's head sagged.

"I can't afford to lose my catch, Sheriff. Please?"

"Mr. Thompson, even if I could let you unload your boat, which I can't, you're in no condition to carry anything."

My father looked up, but even that seemed to be a challenge for him.

"I can do it, Sheriff. I have to. I only pulled in a crate and a half before Stretch started shooting, but every penny matters. I have a family. If I leave my lobsters here, they'll die or be stolen."

Suddenly, someone gripped me painfully by the ribs from behind and shoved me to the side. I snapped around to look but couldn't tell which one of the scruffy fishermen had done it. At that moment, the doctor was making his way through the jam-packed group of men. He was a tall, slender man with dark-rimmed spectacles and hair that was graying at the edges of his high forehead. His eyes were so intent on my father and Stretch's bloodstained sheet ahead that he never seemed to notice any of us as he pushed through the narrow aisle that had been made for him.

The doctor glanced quickly as one Coastguardsman peeled the sheet away from Stretch McGraw. From my new position, I could now see the unshaven face of the dead man. His cheeks were hollow and weathered, and his thinning hair was streaked with gray. He looked older than my father, but I couldn't say how much. The way he lay there with his eyes closed it was almost like he was just sleeping.

The doctor reached out and held two fingers to Stretch's neck.

"He's definitely gone," he said.

The Coastguardsman nodded.

"We figured, sir."

"Then, I'll get to him in a minute." The doctor sat his bag down and knelt beside my father's wounded arm. "I'm Doctor Gregory," he said to my father. "Would it be all right if I took this off?" He pointed toward the blood-drenched rag on his arm.

"I have to unload my catch first," my father croaked.

It didn't take a doctor to see my father's pale and haggard condition was growing worse by the second. He hardly seemed able to remain standing, never mind being able to haul lobsters off the Miss Kane's deck.

I was prepared to try doing it myself when the doctor stood and whispered something to the sheriff.

The sheriff nodded.

"Who runs the shanty?" he asked loudly. He was referring to the wholesaler who bought the catch from the fishermen that worked this pier.

It took a bit of jostling, but finally a fat man with unkempt, blond hair moved to the forefront of the crowd.

"That's me, Sheriff," he said, "but I didn't see nothing."

"I figured that," the sheriff told him. "What's your name?"

"Kevin Brett, sir. Most of the fellers just call me K.B."

The sheriff pointed toward my father. "Well, K.B., this man's in a bad way, and I need you to check his boat and buy his catch. I assume you can get a couple of those strapping salts there to help you unload it."

Mr. Brett shook his thick head, causing all three of his chins to jiggle.

"I'm sorry, Sheriff, but I've known Stretch damned near my whole life. I'm all done buying anything from that flatlander!" He emphasized the last word like a curse.

The sheriff's face tightened, and his eyes narrowed near to closed. He jabbed a finger at the fish wholesaler.

"I hope you're listening to me, Mr. Brett, because I've got too many issues to handle here today already, and I'd hate like hell to add the arrest of a lobster broker to my list. I expect you to unload the lobsters from Mr. Thompson's boat and to pay him whatever rate is fair today. Is that clear?"

Mr. Brett's eyes grew wide and his thick lower lip quivered when he spoke again.

"You can't make me buy his catch." But, by the soft tone of the big man's voice, he didn't believe his own words.

The sheriff turned to look at the two Coastguardsmen who were standing beside Stretch McGraw's sheet-covered body. The taller of the two men nodded and tipped his white hat to the sheriff.

I didn't know what kind of a code they shared, but when the sheriff spun back to Mr. Brett, he said, "It appears that these two gentlemen might need to inspect every boat that comes and goes from this wharf—because of all the recent violence, you understand." The sheriff stared out into the faces of the fisherman that now crowded the wharf. "I imagine a lot of these men will get sick of being boarded once or twice a day, and they might start doing business with shanties over in Wiscasset or maybe in Brunswick. I don't imagine that would be too good for your business, would it, K.B.?"

Mr. Brett looked to either side at the faces of his customers. Most of the men averted their gaze. Finally, he refocused on the sheriff for just a moment before his eyes fell to the weathered planks of the wharf.

"It might be best, Sheriff," the fat man said, "if I take Ben's whole catch and pay a fair price for it. Just like you said."

Voices grumbled from all over the crowd. I didn't know if they were upset because the wholesaler gave in so easily, or if it was simply because the sheriff had stood up for my father. I suspect it might have been a little of both.

My father must have been holding himself up by force of will alone, because as soon as Mr. Brett agreed to take the lobsters, he sat down heavily onto the boards of the pier. It took the doctor several minutes to gently remove the bloody shirt and to clean the wound in his biceps with the water from a canteen the shorter Coastguardsman supplied.

"The good news," the doctor said, "is that the bullet passed right through—Ben, is it?"

My father nodded but didn't seem to have the energy to speak.

"The bad news," the doctor said, as he began to wind a white bandage around his arm, "is that this arm is going to hurt something fierce for the next month or—"

I was unable to hear any more of the doctor's comments because the grumbling of the fishermen had gotten louder and angrier. I heard the word "flatlanders" from a dozen mouths, and two or three times I heard the phrase, "Downeast Justice." I knew enough about the local fishing culture to know that life in Coldwell would not be getting easier anytime soon.

The sheriff let the grumbling go on for only a few seconds before he interjected, "If I hear you men say the word 'flatlander' one more time, I will personally drag you to the nearest jail. For those of you who don't know—" His voice grew louder. "—I'm from Massachusetts. Yes, a flatlander. Do any of you have an issue with that?"

There was a deathly silence.

After finishing with my father, the doctor pulled the sheet back from Stretch McGraw's corpse. He checked the dead man's glazed eyes, tapped his arm twice and lifted a stiff limb before letting it drop again. Then he opened his shirt to examine the two bullet wounds that my father's rifle had created. It was morbid, I knew, but I couldn't stop myself from watching. Finished, the doctor drew the sheet back over Stretch's face then, with the sheriff's help, helped my father back toward the street.

"Tell your mother what I said," he whispered as they all but carried him past me through the subdued crowd.

I followed close enough behind to see the two men help him into the back seat of the cruiser. Then, the sheriff got into his car, which still had blue lights flashing, and turned on his siren. He inched through the crowd and up the hill. The doctor's black sedan followed. I watched them both disappear over the last rise.

Distance and terrain had silenced the siren by the time I extricated myself from the mob of fishermen and onlookers. When I reached halfway up the paved hill, Whiskey magically appeared beside me. I pulled him to the side of the road as a black hearse slid down the hill to collect the body of Stretch McGraw.

I shuddered as it passed.

By then the terror of the last hour's events had begun to take their toll. I felt as though I'd been knocked down and pressed by a large rolling pin. Whiskey whimpered as I wiped at my tears. I rubbed behind his ears, and together we made our way home.

8

Difficult Promises

Jesse KNEW he was too old to be riding in a grocery cart, but he'd been doing it for as long as he could remember and couldn't imagine a more fun way to shop for food. For the last few months, however, he had accepted that his big boy legs just wouldn't fit through the holes in the baby seat anymore, so he now rode right inside the cart with all the food. He smiled as his mother pushed past the service desk, but not the woman with the bright red lipstick handed him two lollipops like she always did. The truth was that Jesse didn't really like lollipops anymore (the kids at school always teased him when his lips and tongue turned colors) but it was still fun to reach out and grab the candy-topped sticks as they passed by.

"You look very handsome today," the woman said to him as they rolled further into the store.

"So, do you," Jesse called back just like he had the last two times. Once again, the woman and his mother both laughed.

Of course, Jesse knew you weren't supposed to call women "handsome." That was a term reserved for boys. But he still said it because he especially liked to see his mother laugh. She didn't do that nearly as much as she used to.

"How about some Kool-Aid?" his mother asked.

"Grape Soda," Jesse announced.

"Not this week, Babe," his mother said. "We're living on one income now."

Jesse made a face and stuffed his lollipops into his pocket. He had a pretty good collection with all different colors in his top drawer and planned to offer them to his father the next time they got together. Lately, he didn't think his father had been eating enough.

They rolled quickly down the first two aisles, and Jesse was discouraged to see the picture of plain flakes on a big ugly bag of cereal she picked. He also didn't approve of the boring loaf of white bread, but he kept silent because his heart was set on a cream-filled donut. Last week they hadn't had enough money, but Jesse planned to not ask for any extra things so that he could choose a donut for each of them.

They continued shopping and were just turning out of the peanut butter and jelly aisle when a shopping cart burst out of nowhere and cut them off. His mother pulled Jesse to a stop just in time. As it was, he could have reached into the other cart and grabbed some food if it hadn't been empty.

"You're looking seriously good, Sweet Thang!" said the man behind the cart. He was dressed in blue jeans and a white T-shirt that had a few stains and several large holes. His chest hair was a lot thicker than Jesse's dad's.

"Coming from a man who's been married four times, that's quite a compliment, Doyle," Jesse's mom said. "Now could you move your cart?"

"I hear you sent your old man packing. It's about time."

"I don't suppose you see my son sitting right here in front of you?"

"S'okay. I like kids."

"I bet you do, Doyle," Jesse's mother said, "just as long as they don't get in the way of a good night knocking headboards."

"You're tough, Karen, but I figure it's time you hooked up with someone that's not a loser."

Jesse was mad and scared at the same time, but his dad had told him that sometimes you had to do things that scared you. He stood up in the cart and felt several cans roll under his feet.

"Stop talking bad about my dad," Jesse said. "It ain't nice."

"Take it easy, little guy. I was just trying to get your mom to go out on a date with me. Then you and me, we could be friends." His face split into a lopsided grin, revealing two chipped teeth. "Wouldn't it be great if I could come over and we could…color together sometimes?"

"Doyle," Jesse's mom said, "the only thing that makes me angrier than you stalking me around the grocery store with an empty cart, is hearing you talk to my kid. You and I won't ever be going on a date, and you definitely won't ever make friends with my son."

Jesse gave the man his best "so there" stare and sat back down. Unfortunately, he didn't notice the loaf of bread under his butt until half of it was squished. He pulled it out and kept the squished part hidden near his leg.

Doyle shoved his cart to the other side of the aisle where it slammed into the shelves and sent a half dozen cans rolling across the floor.

"You're really screwing up, Karen," the man said, "'cause you ain't likely to find too many good men like me."

Jesse's mom harrumphed and pushed their cart rapidly away and didn't slow until they reached the hamburger coolers. He didn't like hamburger so was happy when she moved a little further down and grabbed one package each of hotdogs and bologna slices.

"So, what did Wagner have that I don't?" Doyle said, suddenly coming up from behind them.

"I swear I'm going to call the store manager," Jesse's mom snapped. She threw the meat into the grocery cart and shoved their cart forward. Jesse rocked backwards and wondered felt the bread press against his leg. He wondered if any of their food was going to survive.

"Seriously, Karen. Just tell me why you're too good for me."

Their cart jerked to a stop again, but this time Jesse was prepared with his fingers firmly holding onto the edge. Stiff with anger, his mother turned to face Doyle but not before she reached down to grab a can of green beans out of the cart.

Was she going to hit him?

"Okay, Doyle, I'll tell you. First, just the sight of you makes my skin crawl. Second, Wagner may have had his faults, but he at least works for a living…something Marcie says you never did. Finally, I wouldn't date a cheater and a woman beater like you if you were the last man living in Boston. And, if you ask me, you're lucky Marcie didn't break more than your teeth when she hit you with that frying pan in your sleep. I would have tied your wiener to the bumper and driven across town."

Jesse's mother had turned back toward their cart before Doyle said, "You're as much of a bitch as Marcie. Maybe Wagner knew what he was doing when he left you to rot."

"Maybe he did," Jesse's mother said as she grabbed the cart and pushed it rapidly away for the second time. Jesse could see the man holding up his bad finger until they turned down the spaghetti sauce aisle.

"The cops told me that bitch is going to be in jail for a long time," they heard Doyle yell out. "I hope she dies in there!"

"Thanks to you," Jesse's mother whispered.

Jesse kept looking back and was relieved to see Doyle abandon his cart and disappear down one of the store aisles. Jesse waited until they were by the apples before he asked his mother a question that had been bothering him for a long time.

"Am I going to grow up to be bad like Dad?"

His mother stopped pushing and came around to hold Jesse in a tight bear hug. She smelled like a cinnamon and flowers. He hugged her back. When she let go, she looked into his eyes and gently brushed his hair.

"Your dad is not a bad person, Jesse. He…has some problems right now. You and I just have to keep hoping things get better for him. Okay?"

Jesse nodded and wiped a tear from one eye. He hated it when his little boy side made him cry. He would have dropped the issue, but his mother still hadn't answered his question.

"Am I going to be like Dad?"

Jesse's mother reached down and pinched the tip of his nose. It stung a little bit, but Jesse had always liked that. He smiled.

"You're already handsome as your dad. And you have his smile, but you're never going to have the same problems your dad has. Do you know why?"

Jesse shook his head, anxious to know.

"Because your dad and I love you so much we're going to help you avoid all kinds of problems. You're going to have the happiest life you can imagine."

Jesse nodded and thought about it until they finished grocery shopping. But once his mother gave the cab driver their address and slid in beside his car seat in the back, he figured it was time to ask: "Do you promise you'll help me through any problems?"

"Of course, Baby," she said, stroking his cheek.

"Even if I have one right now?" he asked. He kept his eyes from tearing up, but he could feel his lips quivering.

"Especially right now, Baby. What's wrong?"

"I miss my dad."

9

Dark Thoughts and a Missing Angel

I slammed the prison door closed and withdrew, aching and exhausted, to a dark place in my mind. It was impossible to know how long I remained in that solitary place, but even there I couldn't escape the visions of my father's wounded arm dripping blood onto the dock or the red stains that bloomed across Stretch McGraw's death shroud. It didn't help that those stains were so much like the stain on my own shirt!

My eyes snapped open to see Grandma Clara sitting beside me like the guardian angel she was. The crow's feet at the corners of her eyes were creased with worry, and her concern seemed to be well-placed because my stomach was knotted with cramps and my body vibrated with fear. I wanted to sit up but felt too weak. A slow scan of the room revealed I was in my own bed, in my own house. My last memory in Under-Heaven, just before my monster dragged me viciously into the past, had been of sitting on the curb and hearing Ricky say, "…you were murdered."

Mercifully, it was over for the moment.

"Ricky?" I croaked.

"It's nighttime," Grandma Clara said. "He went home several hours ago. He carried you here, you know."

"Those skinny arms carried me," I whispered, intending a joke.

Grandma Clara smiled. "You are right about him, you know. He's a good boy. I don't understand why he can't get his color under control, but I could see his goodness in the way he worried for you."

"I passed out?"

"Your soul is in flux, Nate. You didn't just pass out, you nearly disappeared. Ricky said he could see right through you when it first happened."

I reached down and patted my arms and chest. I felt solid and real.

"How can people just disappear?" I asked, my voice getting stronger.

Her face took on a warm expression with a gentle smile. I remembered my mother giving me a similar look when I was a toddler.

It came whenever I asked questions like, "Why is there a sky?" and, "How come broccoli doesn't taste like pancakes?"

Grandma Clara patted my arm.

"Nate, you're not a living person anymore. You're a soul, and souls can travel almost anywhere they choose."

"I can fly?"

"Souls don't fly, but they can move instantly from place to place."

"How come you don't? I see you walk into the clouds when you return to Heaven."

She nodded. "That's true, but I don't have to leave that way. It's hard on new souls to see people instantly appearing and disappearing. Angels visit the Under-Heavens to give guidance and to help with the transition to the next life. We wouldn't be of much use if all the new souls saw us as something other than human."

"But you aren't human. You're angels," I said.

"That's true, but we still have human souls. By being as normal as possible, we're best able to help new souls, especially those who are having a hard time moving beyond their past life. You, of all people, should realize how much harder it would be if you had only a strange magical fairy to depend on instead of your good old grandmother."

I grinned. Tinkerbell had always been one of my favorite characters. My mother had read Peter Pan to me at least three times from cover to cover before I even started school. I grew somber at the thought of never hearing her soft voice again. The smell of her lilac perfume was lost to me forever. The monster in my mind tittered. The prison door had been returned to its hinges, but it was so bent and distorted that I knew it wouldn't stay there long. Only the scantest of supports held my creature in check. The memories would get me again soon.

I shuddered.

"I could use a little fairy dust right about now."

Grandma Clara got up from her chair and settled onto the edge of my bed, her fingers running lovingly through my hair.

"If I had only one single grain of magical sand, I would happily give it to my favorite grandson."

Right then, I knew having my grandmother was much better than Tinkerbell could ever be. I rolled to lean against her.

"What happened to me?" I asked. "I mean, am I going to completely disappear the next time I remember?"

She squeezed my shoulder then got up and took two steps toward the window. When she turned back her expression was pensive; two fingers held her lower lip. "I'm not sure, Nate. A soul in Under-Heaven isn't supposed to be able to do what you did. It's too early in your evolution for this to happen. Usually, by the time someone learns how to travel they're already mature enough to be in Heaven…or the underworld."

"I've been here a long time, Grandma. Maybe my soul is trying to leave?"

"Possibly, Nate." She moved to my bedside and stroked my hand. "I don't know."

"Is there anyone who would know?"

"Maybe." She moved to look out my dark window. When she turned back to me, her lips were pursed and worry lines creased her forehead. "I'll talk with some of your other angels tomorrow. Someone is bound to understand this."

Though I knew by "other angels" she meant other members of my family in Heaven, I had yet to meet anyone other than my grandmother. She never said as much, but I suspected they were afraid to stunt my evolution any further than it already had been. I had been in Under-Heaven for nearly four months when most souls spent only a few days. Now that I thought about it, Ricky was the longest other resident in our Under-Heaven, and he'd only been there for a few weeks.

"If I had disappeared," I asked, "where would I have gone?"

Grandma Clara shook her head.

"I don't know, Nate. Maybe another Under-Heaven, maybe Heaven, maybe…."

She let the last words drift off, but I knew she had been about to say, "the underworld." Was it possible that my memories were so horrible they could actually send me to Hell? From the look on Grandma Clara's face, she believed it. And if the cramps that knotted my mid-section were any indication, my body believed it, too.

My eyes wanted desperately to close, but I feared the memories would return. It was bad enough to know that I had been murdered but being forced to relive the experience didn't seem fair. I didn't want to be shot by an angry fisherman again, assuming that was how I died. As far as I was concerned, the past was the past, and it could stay right where it was. I didn't need to know any more.

My monster snickered again. It was anxious to send me back to the horror in Coldwell, Maine. I was thankful when my grandmother moved back to my bedside and reached out to take my hand.

"You need to sleep, Nate," she said. "I'll stay right here until you wake."

She might have said something further, but already my eyes and ears had closed for the night.

~

Morning in Under-Heaven was a glorious time. Unlike on Earth, the sun seemed to rise in Under-Heaven everywhere at once. During the night, tiny beads of moisture formed on the surface of the misty cloud ring that surrounded my little neighborhood. The sudden morning brilliance instantly turned the tiny beads of water to vapor, and the vapor reflected the early light in hundreds of spectacular colors. For those first few moments, it was like watching a thousand rainbows. I was sitting on my backstairs, drinking in the display when Grandma Clara settled down beside me.

"It's beautiful, isn't it?"

"Is it this pretty in Heaven?" I asked.

She placed her hand on my knee.

"Nate, Heaven is like this all the time. No matter where you look, there is beauty and splendor."

"Don't you miss it during the times you're down here with me?"

The truth is I didn't know if Heaven was up, down or sideways from my Under-Heaven, but it seemed easiest to think of the Earth and Hell as being below, one on top of the other, and of Heaven as being above.

"When I'm here, Nate," she said, "I'm simply trading one kind of splendor for another."

"Another?"

"You, Nate, you're an amazing boy and I truly cherish every minute I'm with you."

If people blushed in Under-Heaven, I would have been well on my way to cherry red.

"I'm worried, Nate."

I didn't take my eyes away from the dazzling rainbows as they began to fade.

"Me, too, Grandma. I'm scared all the time. It's like I have a creature inside me, just waiting for a chance to tear me to pieces."

My grandmother's fingers gripped gently at my knee. Though only a small gesture, it was immensely comforting. During that brief moment of contact, I felt that I wouldn't have to face the terror of my past all alone. Unfortunately, as soon as her hand fell away, my solitary fears returned.

"It's normal, Nate," Grandma said as she stood, "for a soul to need time to adjust to being dead. And it's true that some souls never really give in completely to the idea. But I've never heard of anyone staying in this type of Under-Heaven as long as you have."

I knew what I wanted to say. I'd been formulating the question for the last half-hour. But even though I had committed myself to asking it, my insides curdled at the thought. "I remember my father killing a fisherman, but that's as far as I could make myself go, Grandma."

I swallowed hard.

By then the morning lightshow had dissipated. The only colors in the cloud wall came from the flowers that grew like a decorative molding at its base. I turned to look into my grandmother's face.

"Maybe you should tell me what happened when-when I died. I don't want to know, but maybe I need to. I don't think I can take any more memories."

Grandma Clara's mouth opened, but no words came out. Finally, she shook her head.

"I'm sorry, Nate, but I don't think that's the solution. If your mind were ready, you wouldn't need me to tell you."

"What if I disappear next time? What if I send myself to Hell?"

Grandma Clara grabbed me by one shoulder and leaned down to look directly in my eyes.

"Nathaniel, are you listening to me? Are you really listening?"

More shocked by her intensity than anything, I nodded.

"You are a good boy and will never go to the underworld. You have nothing to fear about that."

"But last night you started to add something, some other place I could accidentally have traveled to."

"What I started to say had nothing to do with the underworld. It's something you and I will talk about someday, but right now you have some memories to work through."

"But what if I did disappear?" I stood and leaned against the post that supported my back-porch roof. "Could you find me? Maybe I'll just disappear forever?"

She wrapped both arms around me and hugged tightly.

"You are the dearest boy." She released me just enough so I could see her face. "Nate, no matter where your beautiful soul goes, I would find you. You could skip through a dozen Under-Heavens, and I would be there instantly at everyone."

I smiled. I knew that being alone in another Under-Heaven would have been just like dying a second time. I didn't want to die again.

Never again!

Grandma Clara stayed with me for only a short time that morning and then explained she needed to discuss my situation with some of the other angels.

"As soon as I have a clear understanding, Nate, I'll be back, and we'll see what we can do to get you on the right path. Okay?"

I nodded and hugged her goodbye, but as she disappeared into the mist behind my house, I wished she had stayed a little longer. Visions of Coldwell, Maine were still lingering at the edges of my mind and anything, even a lesson, would have been a welcome distraction. As I sat there on my back porch, staring at the swirling whiteness, I wondered if avoiding distractions might have been her plan all along.

~

Over the next three days, worry was like an anchor on my mind. Ricky was occupied for most of each day with lessons, and Grandma Clara hadn't yet returned, which left me alone to ponder my memory of that horrible day on the Coldwell docks. Though a tiny part of me wanted to know what had happened next, wanted to make sure that my father had recovered from his wound and hadn't gone to jail for defending himself, the larger part of me was terrified at the very thought of going back there again. Wasn't it enough to know I had died? Why should I be forced to explore every gruesome detail all over again?

By the fourth morning, I was really beginning to wonder what had happened to my Grandma Clara. She had said she would find a way to help me through all of this—but three days! I didn't know how far you had to travel in Heaven to find assistance, but if three days were any indication, it wasn't quite the paradise I had envisioned. Regardless of the reason for her delay, I missed her and wished she would come back soon.

Once again, I spent my day pacing back and forth across my small living room and twice actually paced outside on the lawn. Unfortunately, every time my eyes wandered toward the porch the sinister lobster trap reminded me of my maritime past. My monster gleefully rattled its cage in anticipation of dragging me back to that terrible place. Nerves on edge, I finally grabbed the trap and carried it around to the side of my house where I dropped it in the grass.

Why didn't I do that before, I wondered.

My relief was short-lived, however, because when I returned to the front yard the ramshackle white trap was back where it had started. Desperate to do something, I gathered two huge armloads of flowers and dumped them on top of the symbol from my past. Unfortunately, the second I turned my eyes away the colorful blooms disappeared from the trap and reappeared on their original stems.

My monster roared with laughter.

I was relieved, to say the least, when the time came for Ricky's lessons to be over. When I arrived, his Uncle Sedrick was sitting comfortably on the porch swing. I waved as I approached.

"Hello," he said, tipping his white hat toward me. "It's nice to see you again, young Nathaniel."

He had a white cane leaning against his leg. It was intricately carved with angels, the old-fashioned kind with wings and white robes—the ones known as archangels, my Grandmother had taught me.

"It's a beauty, isn't it?" he said running his hand over the elegant wood.

I nodded.

"Have you met any?" I asked without offering any verbal greeting. My grandmother always said country manners were hard to unlearn. I had spent nearly half my childhood in Maine, and there, people waved to one another, but "hellos" and "goodbyes" weren't as common as they were in other places.

"Come sit beside an old man while you wait for that rascally nephew of mine." Ricky's uncle patted the swing seat with one palm.

I liked this man with his semi-formal manner and happily settled down at his side.

"Now, who is it you want to know if I've met?"

"Archangels."

He grinned broadly.

"Ah, now there is a story to be told. You might think those fellows with the long wings fill the skies of Heaven like fireflies in a country field, but the truth is there aren't many of them left, at least not in comparison to the rest of us who have made Heaven one of the most popular stops this side of Niagara Falls."

"So, you haven't met any?"

Just then Ricky came out onto the porch. I was happy to see his shirt was white and his pants were only tan colored up to his calves.

Ricky didn't seem at all surprised that his uncle had roped me into a conversation. He didn't interrupt.

"I was just getting ready to tell your friend about my experience with the archangels," his Uncle Sedrick said jovially.

"You've met them?" Ricky asked, echoing my own curiosity.

"Ahhh," his uncle said, "young minds do think alike, don't they? Oh, yes, I met one of the original angels, but you don't so much meet them as bask in their presence."

"Bask?" Ricky said.

"They are magnificent to watch, all white and glowing and powerful. There is strength in them that you can sense even from a distance. And when they talk to you, you feel as though you're the only one they have ever focused on. They make you feel like the most important soul in the universe."

"How many times have you talked to one?" Ricky asked.

I was glad my friend was there because I'm not sure I would have dared to ask so many questions, even though I was quite curious to know."

"Just the once," his uncle answered.

"What did he say?" I interjected, surprising myself.

"I believe he said… 'Hello,' a word with which a certain young gentleman has yet to acquaint himself."

In another circumstance, I might have been embarrassed or even upset by the humor-filled lesson, but Uncle Sedrick's laughter took any sting out of the exchange. I laughed along with him. When Ricky and I bounded off the porch to begin our afternoon adventures, his Uncle Sedrick called out, "Another time I might tell you what he really said."

"What, like 'goodbye'?" Ricky quipped.

I chuckled and, in Maine fashion, waved farewell.

10

Ripped from My Cold Young Fingers

Ricky's uncle assured me that Grandma Clara was all right in Heaven, but he couldn't or wouldn't say why she hadn't been to see me in the last three weeks. Other than Ricky and my occasional discussion with Ricky's uncle, I found myself alone in Under-Heaven. Oh, there were quite a few souls around but, as always, but they tended to come and go so quickly that it actually made me feel lonelier to speak with them than to just keep to myself. There is something intensely sad about having a conversation with someone one day and finding him or her completely gone the next. Those alone times grew more and more difficult with each passing day. Up until then, I hadn't realized how much I had come to depend on my grandmother. I missed her terribly and knew that I needed her.

As I sat on the bottom step of my front porch and held my trembling hands together, it occurred to me that this might be Grandma Clara's idea of how best to help me. Maybe she believed that by forcing me to spend more time alone I would have to face my memories. The creature in my mind had grown so violent in the last few weeks that it felt like a vibrating motor running constantly in my head. My stomach was cramped with fear more often than not, and I had grown used to feeling nauseous most of the time.

Possibly the only good thing that could be said about my troubled state was that looking at the lobster trap no longer seemed to matter. Coldwell, Maine was constantly on my mind now, and my body shivered all the time. Even movement didn't seem to help. I got up and paced in front of my porch and, when that didn't work, pulled off my sneakers—which were safely white—and socks so the grass could tickle my toes.

Visions of Stretch McGraw's dead body and my father's bloody arm continued to fill my mind.

How long could this feeling persist?

How long would I let it go on?

I could see at least a dozen people leaning over the fountain pool. The tall elegant cherubs towered above them like guardians. I wished I could go there and feel safe as well. For the briefest moment, I considered joining them. By then, I knew that a soul could stare into the

pool and see his or her family back on Earth. It was not possible to talk to them or to interact with them, but at least you could see how they were—

And remember!

My stomach cramped with pain.

I gasped, staggered back to my stairs, and collapsed onto the bottom step. My monster wanted out, and this time it seemed to be winning. I didn't think I could take the pain much longer. I looked inward. The creature had riddled the prison door with so many dents and scars it looked more like scrap from a salvage yard than a security measure. One hinge had broken free completely, and the gash at the bottom of the door had spread to about halfway up. I imagined a loud crash before another large dent appeared. I knew my imprisoned beast was only seconds from freedom.

Something had to be done!

I doubled over with an especially fierce cramp. I might have screamed out with the agony. I was now face down, my shoulder and cheek pushed uncomfortably into the grass. Under-Heaven was blurred by tears that streamed freely from my nine-year-old eyes. I heard another monstrous crash and an inhuman roar. Looking inward, I was just in time to see the twisted remains of the prison door heave outward.

It held, if only barely. I knew I had to fight back, but how? Where could I find the strength?

I closed my eyes as physical agony railed against me. I had to fight this. I had to find a way to keep the beast entombed. I struggled to repair the door. I imagined the tear in the steel surface healing itself. Slowly, in my mind's eye, the gap in the steel began to close.

It was working!

I redoubled my effort using every ounce of my personal fortitude. Though I could hear the beast clawing from the other side, and though I could feel the pain in my stomach and my sides, the rip in the door continued to heal. Next, I pushed inward on the dents with my mind. First one smoothed, then another.

The beast snarled and roared. It was a frightening mass of anger.

I turned my mind to the broken hinge.

"Arrrrrggh, ssheeeee!" I heard.

Fear gripped my chest. I couldn't breathe, could barely think.

"No," I whispered as the rampaging creature slammed again and again at the door. Metal screeched and tore. The last hinge snapped. Steel exploded outward.

I wanted to run but—

Through my pain, from somewhere a long way off, I heard Ricky's voice.

"I'm here," he said. "I'm here with you, Nate."

But it was too late. The memories had me, and I sensed that an ocean of blood was about to flow…

Since his arrest at the beginning of the summer, something in my father had changed. It was as though a black curtain had fallen over his eyes. He never laughed anymore, and it was seldom that a smile creased his lips. Though my mother and I often tried to cheer him up, it was a rare occasion to see any joviality in him at all. Only my baby sister Vicky had any success getting through his somber visage, and even then, the moments were brief and sporadic. I knew my mother had been pressuring him to leave Maine, but my father wouldn't hear of it. If he had been committed to Coldwell before, it was as though the death of Stretch McGraw had securely moored him to the Downeast shoreline. He was staying and, by extension, so was his family.

Though my father's arm had healed within a few weeks, he still rubbed it absently at different times during the day. When he did, his eyes would glaze over, and I imagined he was reliving that frightful moment when another human being had been placed at the center of his gun sight. Though I couldn't imagine killing another person, seeing what it did to my father convinced me I never wanted to learn.

The entire dynamic of our family had changed. It used to be my father at the center of all communication with my mother mediating the rough spots. But now my mother seemed to handle everything. My father had become a ghost to us, a man who was almost but not quite someone we used to know. I sensed that my dad was still in there somewhere, but I also sensed that it would be a long time before he found his way back to us.

Each morning, he would gather his lunch, his personal tools (which included a large, formidable fish-scaling knife, which appeared after the probation ruling forced him to turn his rifle over to the sheriff) and his most recently repaired traps, which he would stack neatly in the back of his rusty old Ford pickup truck. Then, like a man going to war, he would kiss my mother somberly and drive off toward the docks.

When he arrived at the pier, there would be a deputy sheriff's car parked alongside Mr. Brett's shanty, the same place it would be when my father arrived back at the dock late in the afternoon. I didn't know if the sheriff's department was trying to protect my father from the local fisherman or the other way around, but it had become a fact of life here in Coldwell, just as it was a fact that the locals no longer spoke to my father. It was almost as if he had gone from flatlander to alien, but I knew it was worse than that: my father had gone from flatlander to murderer. To make matters worst of all, he had murdered one of the stalwarts of Coldwell. Stretch McGraw had known and been known by everybody for miles around, and whenever his absence was noted, it was usually followed by the angry sentiment: "And that flatlander Thompson got off scot-free."

It was in August, on a Friday, when I saw my father pack up his gear and head for the docks for the very last time. Whiskey and I watched through my bedroom window until his truck spun up a cloud of dust pulling out of the driveway. That was the signal we waited for each morning. I slid the window open and Whiskey leapt out onto the porch roof with me not far behind.

When we had first moved to Coldwell, my parents had though it odd that the original owners had built our house on the leeward side of the ledge when so many other locations on our lot offered spectacular ocean views. However, after our first nor'easter, one of the Maine winter storms that sweeps in from the frigid northeast Atlantic Ocean, they understood. Our ledge deflects the worst of the bitter winds and snows and keeps the house relatively comfortable, even during the worst of January-February rants.

Whiskey darted several steps across the roof and easily leapt onto the high, adjacent granite plateau. It wasn't nearly as easy a fete for me. I backed to the furthest edge of the porch roof then, like a long jumper, raced half a dozen steps and leapt as high and far as I could. It wouldn't have been the first time I missed and fell down between the house and the sheer stone bluff where my father coincidentally deposited his grass clippings and fall leaves in a huge pile. But that morning I soared easily across the narrow alley and grabbed a sapling to steady myself from falling backwards.

Whiskey and I mounted the small outcropping and stared out at what my father called God's most beautiful puddle. The harbor was filled with dozens, maybe even a hundred fishing boats sailing in a mass exodus toward deeper waters. From there it looked as though the captains were playing a dangerous game of crisscross chicken. One boat would be heading north, another south and yet a third straight east. Unfortunately, the ocean didn't have yellow lines or streetlights, nor did fishermen moor their boats in a fashion that would allow them to sail out in orderly and safe lines. Instead, it was a melee of speed and skill to flee the harbor. Each morning, I marveled that with all the close calls none of the boats ever collided.

We sat on the hilltop for a full thirty minutes before Whiskey yelped. Sure enough, the Miss Kane's two distinctive masts had finally begun to move. Since the incident, my father's boat was always the last to sail for open water, which probably had something to do with the large Coastguard cutter that appeared off the southeastern horizon at the same time each morning. Guarded on shore and at sea, my father was ready to set sail. Even so, I knew it wasn't every man that would have been brave enough to do what he did. The Coastguard couldn't watch him every minute of every day, and the sea was a big place filled with nasty characters, many whom had Downeast justice on their minds.

As if the death of Stretch McGraw hadn't been bad enough, Stretch's oldest son Karl had drowned recently while trying to man his father's boat. The Coastguard found his Beal Boat—named after the famous Maine family that builds them—listing to the side off the shore of Crane's island. The Coastguard and Marine Wardens felt he had probably run aground on the island's shallow reefs and had somehow drowned while trying to free the hull. By the time they found his body in a shallow pool, seagulls had already ravaged it.

Karl had been seventeen.

In the locals' minds, my father had taken his second life.

As my father's boat dwindled to insignificance, I wondered what school would be like. Though the previous year had been pretty bad, it seemed certain this year would be worse. Already I was hearing kids holler out things like, "Murderer's kid," and, "Shotgun Junior" —never mind that my father had killed Stretch with a rifle, not a shotgun. Tommy Edds had once even called me, "Son of Satan."

Oh, yeah, the upcoming school year was going to be lots of fun.

My mother begged daily for my father to take us back to Rhode Island and find himself a new job.

"What could be worse than this?" she would say.

But I was convinced my dad had already left. The person living with us was no longer her husband or even my dad. He had become something different. The decent loving man we knew had been torn away, replaced by a body in strictly survival-mode. I knew my father never intended to kill Stretch McGraw. But though we all wished it had never happened, it had, and now we were trapped in a community that hated us.

After the Miss Kane completely disappeared from view, I headed back down the short trail and made the much easier return leap down onto the porch roof. Whiskey was only a second behind me. Together we slipped back in through my bedroom window and traipsed downstairs for breakfast.

To an outsider, it might have looked as though my mother loved to cook, but I knew the truth: it was her way of showing how much she loved us. Even in the best of times, lobstering barely paid the bills, so like many poor people, my mother made everything from scratch. That didn't stop her from tailoring the things she made to the tastes of her family. Yesterday, Whiskey and I had picked three quarts of raspberries over in the woods by the Huntington cliffs. This morning, I faced a veritable mountain of raspberry pancakes, one of my favorites. From the bright purple tint of the pancakes, it looked as though my mother was giving them all back to me in a single meal. The butter and tangy fruit aroma was irresistible.

I dug in.

Whiskey wasn't forgotten, either. He got leftovers from the night before. I could smell the pork in his bowl.

"As soon as you two are done, I need you to get me some eggs and milk. I also think your father could use a couple rolls of twine."

I groaned.

"Do we have to, Mom? Tommy lives only a block from the bait shop. I don't want to listen to him again."

"I know he's not very nice," she said, brushing a brown lock of hair behind her ear and smiling understandingly, "but words won't hurt you. I need you to do it."

I nodded. Maybe Whiskey and I could find a decent back trail to the bait shop. The last one we tried took us out on the other side of Wilson's Motel, which was now run by a family with a long name ending in "-ski." I could never remember it or even remotely pronounce it. My father said they came from Russia and were hard, honest workers. The man used to talk with my father after church on the few Sundays we attended, but since the killing that had ended. My father understood and said just by talking to us, Mr. "-ski" would make things harder on his family. I knew from experience that outsiders in Coldwell already had it hard enough. Though, I doubted the "-skis" would have minded me riding through their yard, I felt certain there had to be a direct trail to the bait shop.

About the time Whiskey and I finished eating, my baby sister waddled into the kitchen. Her hair was tousled and stood at least four inches higher than the top of her head, and she wore only one of two pink slippers. I had to smile. I knew a lot of kids got jealous when a new baby came into their house, but I had never felt that way. Probably Whiskey played a large part in that: his love and dedication to me was complete; combine that with the unwavering love I had always received from my parents and I never felt shorted when the Vicky was born. And, now, watching my tiny sister, only half-awake and rumpled, was a treat.

My mother leaned down so Vicky could leap into her arms.

"Good morning, Sweetheart." My mother planted a loud kiss on her cheek. "Are you hungry?"

"Cereal," Vicky said.

Her choice came as no surprise. Vicky had been eating warm oatmeal with maple syrup for breakfast almost since the day she'd been born. My mother had tried to feed her toast, eggs, pancakes and every other manner of morning food, but unless tears were wanted, oatmeal it had to be. Fortunately, my mother felt oatmeal was healthy, so there was seldom an argument.

"Okay, Sweetie," my mother said, putting the small pair of legs back on the floor. "Maybe after you eat, we can brush that mop of yours, okay?"

Vicky shrugged. My sister and I weren't really hair people. Fortunately, mine was short so it usually looked okay even when I just woke up. Vicky, I knew, was in for a much tougher life. Her hair was already below her shoulders and still growing. It would be an ongoing battle to keep that mess under control. I couldn't imagine having to comb and brush my hair all the time. Taking baths every other day was bad enough. Of course, I did brush my teeth twice a day, but that wasn't so bad. Besides, it gave Whiskey a chance to drink cold, fresh water from the toilet bowl, something my mother would have been shocked to find out.

As soon as my sister was situated in her highchair, a bowl of food on the tray, I accepted a short shopping list and two, one-dollar bills from my mother. She didn't need to remind me to be careful. I'd run similar errands a dozen times already that summer, so she knew I wouldn't lose the money or drop the groceries. Of course, I never told her how I had left her eggs in the hot sun on a granite ledge a few weeks before so that Whiskey and I could explore a creek down behind Miller's Dairy Farm. The egg carton had been so hot when we got back, I was surprised the eggs hadn't been hard-boiled when my mother took them out.

I opted to take my bike this time. Though I hated the look of the new steel basket my father had bolted on a couple of months ago, it sure came in handy when you had a lot of stuff to carry. Whiskey waited in the driveway only long enough to see which direction I was taking before he dashed off toward the logging road that ran perpendicular to our gravel driveway. I'd only seen two logging trucks on the road all summer, but the big trucks had done a great job of breaking down the small saplings that might otherwise have been a nuisance. The logging road traveled all along the backside of Main Street. If only we could find a trail from there straight to the bait shop. Today, Whiskey and I would look harder.

We were all the way to the huge, dead oak tree wider than my father's truck when I stopped the bike. We had already passed the trail to the -ski's motel, and I felt certain there had to be another trail veering off to the bait shop nearby.

"Find a trail, boy," I said to Whiskey. But instead of darting into the woods they way I intended, he bounded further down the logging road. Suddenly, he stopped about fifty feet up the road and waited, amber eyes staring back at me.

"Ruuff," he said.

"No, you're too far," I told him. "We need to find a trail in here," I pointed into the woods beside me.

He raced back to my side but paused only long enough to paw my pant leg before darting back down the road again. He stopped and turned to look at me.

Maybe he was trying to avoid wood ticks, I thought. We usually had to pick a half dozen off from him each time we wandered off the main trails. He barked several more times and waited.

"No," I called out. "We need to find a trail here."

He reluctantly came back but again pawed my pant leg and turned to face further down the road. This wasn't like him.

"What is it, boy?" I asked.

He yelped and raced back to where he had been.

Something wasn't right.

I pedaled to catch up and slammed on my brakes when it came into view. Just down over the hill, sat the tattered netting and mended frame of one of my father's lobster traps. I grew nauseous because sitting inside his trap was something sticky, something red, something blood.

The trip to the store was forgotten as Whiskey and I raced home. When my father arrived late that afternoon, he found the door closed and locked. My mother had Vicky and me sitting beside her in the living room. Whisky was, of course, plunked down near my feet. My mother's trembling hands were red from wringing themselves together. I had never heard her raise her voice so openly in front of her children, but my father barely had time to unlock the door and step inside when she made her proclamation.

"Ben, we are packing our things and leaving here tomorrow."

"I'm not about to—" he began to say, but my mother cut him off.

"My children will not live another day in this town. Your son found one of your traps down the western logging road, a road everyone in town knows he uses, just about a half mile from here. There was blood and the remains of a dead chicken all over it!" Her voice had risen almost to the point of yelling.

"Karen," my father said. His palms were facing out as though to ward off her verbal blows. "Traps can be fixed. It was probably just kids."

"That's. Not. All!" she said, her words fired like blistering shots. She held up my sister Vicky's bloodied doll. "Nate found this inside the trap."

My father's eyes widened.

"All the more reason to believe it was kids," he said, but there was no conviction left in his voice.

"Ben!"

In that moment, I saw my father's anger sink beneath his concern. He knew what that doll meant, and he knew a threat to Vicky was the last straw. The three oldest people in our house had come to a common understanding: the bloodied doll was an omen that none of us could ignore. My father met my mother halfway across the living room. She hugged onto him fiercely.

"It has to be tomorrow," she whispered though her tears. "It has to be."

My father's eyes were also tearing.

"Okay," he said softly. "The flatlanders leave tomorrow."

I felt such a sense of relief that I almost wet my pants. It was amazing to think that we had been living in that town for over three years, and one single moment could change all of that. For my part, I had never formed any friendships in Maine so had nothing to regret by leaving. Once again, I had my dog to thank. Whiskey was my best and only friend, and that was the way I wanted it.

I went upstairs to brush my teeth and when I returned, Vicky was sitting quietly behind the couch playing with one of her unspoiled dolls. She spoke softly to the little brunette about some imaginary event. I would happily have gone to hug her the same way my father was hugging my mother, but there were some things a self-respecting boy just couldn't do. Instead, I settled back onto the couch to enjoy the sounds of her imaginary conversation. I also watched my father stroking my mother's hair and smiled.

My dad was back.

Whatever ill the locals had intended by stealing and abusing my sister's doll, they had actually done us a favor. Not only had my father returned from the darkness that had enshrouded him for the last few weeks, we were also finally escaping this horrible place. I had not realized how much I wanted to leave until my parents said it, but suddenly I was giddy with the thought of putting as much distance as possible between us and the town that we had called home for the past three years.

In a display of family teamwork, my parents began packing things up while I worked industriously in my room and filled nearly three boxes of my own. Of course, Whiskey sat on the bed and oversaw the project. When I went down for a fourth box, I learned my efforts had been dwarfed by two mountains of packed boxes in the center of the living room. My parents had also packed a third pile high against the back door of the kitchen. Unfortunately, that also meant we had used every box in the house, and even the few that had been stored in the shed.

I offered to help my mother finish cleaning out the cabinets while my father drove to the general store to see what he could find. When he returned, it was with his truck bed nearly filled with folded cartons of every size. We immediately set to work trying to fill as many as possible. By midnight most of the small items had been packed and my parents agreed we should all get some sleep and finish the rest the following day. My attic room had long since been transformed into four walls, a bed and six overflowing boxes. I had even packed up my sheet and blankets, but I left my sleeping bag out on top of the mattress. Whiskey and I would make do with that.

My sister's room downstairs was the only one left untouched. My parents had decided it would be just as easy to pack her things up at the last minute and save her the confusion of a bare room that night. She'd been asleep for hours.

Though none of us knew what would happen the next day, it seemed to be enough to know we were leaving that wretched place. Both my parents were smiling and relaxed when they came into my room and kissed me goodnight. My father also gave Whiskey a good scratch behind the ears. After my mother shut off the light, she closed my door, something she seldom did, but I supposed she and my dad wanted to talk about the move. Knowing we were finally leaving that horrible place, I contentedly and rolled onto my side and listened to her and my dad's muffled footsteps recede down the stairs. None of us could have known that closed door was just another tiny incident in a stream of events that would comprise the nails of a very large and very bloody coffin.

I fell asleep.

~

Whiskey was snarling and tearing at the door with his claws when I came to. I snapped awake! My Whiskey wouldn't act like that for anything short of an emergency. I struggled to pull my legs free of the sleeping bag, adding precious seconds to my response time. I heard three loud crashes come from downstairs.

"I'm awake, boy!" I yelled to Whiskey.

He stepped aside long enough for me to yank the door open but then—a reddish, yellow fury—he bolted past me and down the stairs.

Terrified, I followed his growls as fast as my nine-year-old legs would take me. The living room light was off, but moonlight from two windows and a narrow shaft of light from the kitchen revealed two shadows shifting back and forth beyond the stacks of boxes piled in the middle of the room. Man-grunts came from that direction. Glass shattered. I snapped my gaze toward the kitchen and heard two dull thumps come from beyond the partly open door. As I leapt the last two stairs to the living room floor, the light from the kitchen illuminated the wrestling shadows.

One of them was my father!

The other was a much larger man in dark clothing. My father's forehead and right ear were coated with blood. The other man had some kind of black paste smeared across his face, so it was harder to tell if he, too, was bleeding. Horrified, I raced across the room, intending to jump on the intruder's back.

"Your sister!" my father hollered to me. "Get your sister out of the house!"

There was a sickening snap as the intruder bellowed in pain. My father roared and twisted away from the heavier man. Whiskey was snarling and snapping like a rabid dog in the kitchen. More glass crashed, metal screeched, and thumps reverberated from beyond the half-closed door. I raced toward my sister's room, but a second man swarmed at me from somewhere near the basement door. As he crossed in front of the shaft of kitchen light, I could see his face was also greased in black. Though short, he was stocky and easily three times my weight.

I tried to veer around my mother's rocking chair, but he blocked my path to Vicky's room.

"Do yourself a favor and go back upstairs, kid," he warned.

I darted to the side, but the man moved to block me again.

"Jesus Christ, Green!" he called out. "Finish that murdering bastard and let's get to hell out of here!"

I glanced backwards. If he'd been talking to my father's attacker, his words were wasted. Though bigger than my dad, the first intruder had fallen limp to the floor where my father's shoe was making wet mashing noises as it struck his face again and again.

It sounded like my father had just killed his second man in less than three months. He stopped kicking and looked over at me.

"Get your sister," he gurgled through what must have been a mouthful of blood. There was something feral and not quite human about him as he staggered toward the man blocking me.

"Ted," the man yelled. "Ted, do something!"

The body on the floor didn't respond.

"Holy shit!" the stocky man said and backed toward the wall.

In the grip of a terror like I had never known, I willed my body to move. I gave the man a wide berth as I hurried to my sister's door and twisted the handle.

Much quicker than he looked, the stocky intruder lunged, grabbed my arm and yanked. I might have passed out from the pain as my shoulder dislocated, but fear for my sister kept me on my feet. At some point, I realized the blood-curdling wail filling my ears came from my own mouth.

Suddenly, like a creature from nightmares, whiskey's angry snarls grew louder. A man screamed. Then I heard gasping followed by the thump of a heavy body hitting the floor.

"Grrrrr, ruff!"

His fight apparently won; my Whiskey was coming for me.

The stocky man spun me around, sending fresh shards of pain into my shoulder, and hauled me tightly up against his rounded stomach. He had one arm around my neck and the other gripped tightly around my chest. I couldn't breathe, could barely think as my father stopped about three feet in front of us. The blood smeared across his face seemed to intensify his wild look of rage. The memory of his eyes and that terrible expression would have stayed with me for the rest of my life—had I been destined to live.

I gasped for air.

"Let him go," my father gurgled. His devastated mouth was identifiable only by its location. Blood ran in clots down his chin.

Suddenly, the kitchen door burst all the way open as Whiskey tore into the room. Still ten feet from me, he leapt over the nearest pile of boxes, his teeth and claws directed at the face of the man who held me. I yanked my head out of the way as my dog flew past and tore the throat from my attacker in a single bite.

I nearly passed out from the agony in my shoulder, but somehow staggered forward as the stocky man behind me slid lifelessly to the floor. My father reached for me, but as I grabbed for his swaying body, my shoulder exploded in pain. I tried to hold him upright with my remaining good arm, but my single hand did no more than slip along his bloody forearm. Helpless, I watched as his eyes rolled upward and his body collapsed.

Suddenly, the front door exploded inward. Yet another man dressed in black stood there. I recognized his sheer size, even through the grease. It was Tommy Edds' father, the man who pulled in the largest lobster catches, sometimes four and five crates a day. Everyone knew Casey Edds, the high liner of Coldwell Bay.

He surveyed the demolished room, the bodies of three men lying on the floor, then me and my dog.

I heard a low growl beside me. I didn't have to look down to know my Whiskey was injured. If he had been able to fly across the room, he would already have been tearing into Casey's throat.

Tommy's father walked into the room and knelt down to press a finger to the throat of the first intruder. He shook his head. Then he stepped over to the kitchen door and glanced in.

"Jesus," he said softly.

I guessed it didn't require a pulse check to know Whiskey's first victim was dead.

"Out of the way," Casey Edds said, moving around the stacks of boxes to get to my dog. I could see the muzzle of his gun rising.

Whiskey growled menacingly. I saw him drop into a crouch. Injured or not, he was ready to fight.

I wasn't going to let anyone kill my dog.

"Get the baby out!" I yelled to Whiskey as I shoved him towards her door and dove the other way, behind our overstuffed chair. A shot rang through the air and plaster exploded above my dog's head.

Agony shot from my shoulder to my brain as I landed on the floor and rolled to see Whiskey's amber eyes. They were not the eyes of a dog: they were the eyes of a friend, a best friend. I glanced behind him and thanked God that I had succeeded in getting Vickie's door open, if only a crack. She was crying.

"Do it, Whiskey!" I screamed. "Get Vicky out!"

Those amber eyes said I love you and I won't leave you, but Whiskey's obedience to my wishes won out over his need to defend his friend. Whiskey spun, nosed the door open and raced into my little sister's bedroom.

Tommy Edds' father aimed for another shot at Whiskey.

"No!" I screamed. I struggled to my feet and charged out from behind the chair. I tried to punch his groin, but the butt of the gun slammed into my forehead. Quick like a snake, Casey reached down and grabbed me by the hair before I could fall.

"Please," I managed to say. I wanted to plead for the safety of my mother and sister, but I suddenly realized no sounds were coming from the kitchen. If my mother had a single breath remaining, she would have been protecting her children. Whiskey had bested her attacker but must have been too late to save her. My mother was dead. I knew it as surely as I knew my own life would soon end.

Another shot exploded in my ear.

I heard Whiskey yelp.

"No, Mr. Edds!" I pushed with my legs and drove my head into the massive lobsterman's stomach.

"Oomph!"

Tommy's father yanked me up by the hair and glared at me through a grease-smeared face.

"God damn it, kid! How the fuck did you recognize me?"

I heard Vicky's window crash. My God, he was doing it, Whiskey was saving her!

The sound had barely registered in my ears when—with a twist and a jerk from a forearm that had pulled thousands of lobster traps from the briny ocean—Casey Edds, the high liner of Coldwell Bay, snapped my neck.

My soul fled that accursed house before my thin body even had time to drop to the floor.

11

Second Chances

Jesse Had been grinning so often that his friend Storm teased him about it all throughout their day of school. Jesse never explained why because he didn't want to jinx anything. Storm was still trying to find out when all the kids crowded outside at the end of the day. Jesse smiled, shook his head and made the mouth-zipped motion as Storm slid into the backseat of his father's fancy black car. Of course, any car that was not covered with rust and dents seemed pretty fancy to Jesse. During his own bus ride home that day, he was so excited that he could barely keep still in his seat.

His father was coming over.

But this wasn't just any visit, and it wasn't one of the crazy plans that he and his dad had tried to cook up. No, this time he had a deal with his mother. This was the first visit of what his mother called a "'speriment."

Just thinking about it made Jesse giddy inside. He had been working at it for what seemed like a lifetime and had finally gotten his mother to give his father another chance. As long as things went okay—not even great, just okay—she said his father could move back in. Jesse ignored the older girl sitting in the seat across from him. Just like Storm, she obviously could tell something was up. Well, she could think whatever she wanted about his stupid grin, because Jesse was about to be part of a complete family again!

When the bus finally stopped across the street from the laundromat, Jesse shouldered his book bag, which only had two picture books and some crayon drawings he'd made for his mother and hurried out onto the sidewalk. On any other day, the cold air might have bothered him, but not even freezing temperatures could ruin his mood that day. Jesse watched through the open bus door for the driver to signal it was safe then bolted across the street, into the laundromat.

"Hey, Jess," Gladys, the big woman with large hoop earrings and a tattoo all the way around her neck, said to him as he went inside. She had only been working there for a couple of weeks but seemed nice enough, which was good because she was also his afternoon sitter.

The last woman had quit the laundromat after being scared during a "hold up," Jesse heard someone say. He always liked it when his father held him up in the air, but maybe adults didn't like it as much as kids did.

Normally he would have pulled out a book to read, but his mind was whirring so fast he couldn't focus. Instead, he just sat there and swung his feet back and forth while watching the laundry customers. There were only a few people at the machines, which was typical. The homeless teenage girl was also in her regular spot, sleeping across three chairs at the back of the long room. Jesse had tried to talk to her once, but after she yelled at him, he had avoided her as much as possible.

There was an unfamiliar man about halfway down the long row of machines. He wore jeans and a long brown jacket that almost touched the floor as he sat. He had been reading a magazine when Jesse first arrived, but now he just kept looking over and smiling. Of course, Jesse smiled back but that was more because he was thinking about his dad than because he wanted to make a new friend. Either way, the man kept waving and making faces at him.

Jesse occasionally glanced at the man but mostly watched the big clock on the wall. He knew that as soon as the long hand got to the twelve, his mother would arrive. The big hand was still three numbers away when the friendly man gestured for Jesse to go talk to him. Jesse snickered and shook his head. He wasn't supposed to talk with strangers. The man gestured a few more times, but Jesse kept shaking his head "no." He wasn't about to get in trouble on the day his dad was going to visit.

No way.

Oddly, the man wasn't paying much attention to his laundry, which Jesse saw spinning in one of the nearby dryers. Instead, he kept moving from chair to chair, getting closer to Jesse. When he was only about five seats away, he pulled a handful of lollipops out of his jacket and held them out. Jesse shook his head.

The man gestured for Jesse to come closer.

"You a pervert or something!" the big woman behind the cash register said.

Jesse snapped his head toward Gladys and was relieved she wasn't yelling at him. She sure gave the man with the lollipops an angry look, though.

Visibly shaking, the man rushed to grab his clothes from the dryer. After throwing everything into a plastic bag, he hurried the long way around the laundromat—apparently to avoid Gladys—and rushed out the front door.

"Good riddance," Gladys said, her hoop earrings swinging as she shook her head.

Fortunately, the next few minutes were incident free. Then, as though she had a clock built into her shoes, his mother arrived exactly as Jesse saw the long hand reach the twelve.

"How was he today?" his mother asked the new babysitter.

"You already know," Gladys said. "He's a good boy. An' if you met my two nephews—straight from Satan's pit, they are—you'd know not all kids are good like Jess is."

"I know he's pretty special," Jesse's mom agreed. She leaned down and kissed him on the forehead. "Aren't you, Jesse?"

Jesse nodded. He knew he wasn't an angel, but until things were worked out between his mom and dad, he intended to be on his best behavior.

Because their apartment was in the same building as the laundromat, they only had to walk several feet outside to get to their hallway door. Even so, Jesse let his mother zip up his jacket and pull his hood over his head. He was glad Gladys didn't say anything about the friendly man before they stepped outside. He wasn't really sure what had happened but didn't want anything to ruin the 'speriment.

"I get paid tomorrow, Gladys, and will square up with you then. Okay?"

"It's all good," the big woman said.

Some days, Jesse raced up the stairs ahead of his mother, but he knew that to trip and fall, even if it only caused a small bruise, might darken his mother's mood before his father arrived. So, he carefully followed her up the stairs. Then, while his mother went into the bedroom to change out of her waitress clothes, Jesse pulled his pretend clock out of his closet. Two days before, he had put away all of his toys except this one. He still wasn't very good at telling time, so had begged his mother to set the hands of the toy clock to the exact time his father was supposed to arrive.

"When the short hand is on five and the long hand is on six," he said. "Short five, long six." He said it a few more times to be sure he could remember it then placed the toy clock on his bed. He would get his mother to reset it for the next visit and the one after that. Hopefully, it wouldn't be long before the 'speriment was over, but until then he intended to keep track.

"Short five, long six," he whispered as he went into the kitchen and stared at the big white clock. The short hand wasn't very far from the five, so it seemed to him his dad would show up soon.

Praying his father would be cleaner than last time and wouldn't have another bloody nose, Jesse hurried into the bathroom to wash his hands and comb his hair. He knew his dad wouldn't care how he looked, but anything that made his mother happy was important to do. He felt certain that tonight would go better than the last time because even though he wasn't supposed to, Jesse had warned his father about the 'speriment.

By the time Jesse finished cleaning up, his mother was already in the kitchen. When he saw her take a package of steak out of the refrigerator, he knew things were going to be alright.

Steak was his father's favorite.

Wanting to be as helpful as possible, Jesse got out the napkins and silverware. He had all he could do not to cheer at the sight of three place settings at the table. Soon, things would be back to normal. They were going to be a happy family again.

He knew it.

"Salt and pepper please," Jesse said.

"Look at that smile," his mother said. She placed a pan on the stove. "You're really excited about tonight, aren't you?"

Jesse gave his best grin and nodded. Soon his father would be there, and they would have their first family dinner together in a long while. His mother handed him the fancy glass salt and pepper shakers, not the plastic ones they usually used.

His grin widened.

"You know what, Jesse?" his mother said.

Jesse stared up at her.

"I promised you that I would really try to make this work, and I meant it. Anything this important to you is important to me, too."

"And it's important to Dad, too," Jesse said matter-of-factly. Sometimes, Jesse thought his father wanted to come home even more than Jesse wanted him there.

Careful not to drop the glass shakers, Jesse placed them gently on the table. He heard the butter beginning to sizzle in the frying pan as his mother placed three plates and three glasses on the table for him to position where they belonged.

Everything was working perfectly.

His mother had just dropped three steaks into the frying pan when the intercom buzzed. She stretched over to reach the keypad and said, "Hi, Wagner. Come on up."

The door downstairs opened and slammed shut. Jesse could hear his father coming up the stairs. His breath caught.

Something wasn't right.

His father was walking funny. Jesse was still trying to figure out what was so different when his father knocked on the door.

"Just a minute…, Babe."

Just hearing her say "Babe" made Jesse so excited he almost peed himself. His mom hadn't called his dad that in a very long time, not since the happier before times.

His mother moved the steaks around with the spatula then opened the door.

"You're right on—"

"Hello, Karen."

Backing away from the door, Jesse's mother grabbed a sharp knife off the counter.

"What the hell are you doing here, Doyle? I thought I made myself pretty clear when we talked last time."

Jesse felt tears forming. Everything with his dad was so close to getting fixed, but now the bad man from the grocery store was going to mess the whole 'speriment up. Jesse tried to think of something—anything—he could do to make the bad man leave.

"Hi, Jesse," the man said, interrupting his thoughts.

Doyle had one hand hidden behind his back, which reminded Jesse how Eric Wiley at school had been hurt by one of the older boys who had been hiding a stick behind his back. Jesse moved behind his mother.

"I told you never to talk to my kid again, Doyle." His mom held the knife up. "Now get the hell out of my house and never come back!"

Doyle took a step back. Jesse might have run forward to slam the door shut, but the man's feet were still blocking the way.

"Karen, I just came to apologize," Doyle said. Jesse's mother looked ready to stab him in the arm when he tried to hand her the bouquet of flowers he'd been hiding. "Those things you told me that day at the store—you really made me think. I wanted you to know I borrowed some money and bailed Marcie out of jail. I also told the police I wouldn't testify against her. The public defender said they would probably drop the charges."

"So, because you finally did something decent in your life, you think I'm going to go out with you. That's never going to happen. Now take your flowers and go. I'd tell you to give them to Marcie, but I'd be afraid you'd just use her as a punching bag again."

Jesse kept watching the bad man's feet. The second they were out of the way, he intended to slam the door closed. There was only room for one man in their house, and that man was his father.

"Marcie wouldn't even talk to me," Doyle said, "and I don't blame her."

"Good for her," Jesse's mother said. "Now please go before Wagner gets here."

Doyle nodded, letting the bouquet drop to his side.

"I just came by to thank you. I'm taking a bus to Arkansas tonight. My brother bought a chicken farm a couple of years ago, and he's doing real good, good enough to offer me a job. So, I figured it's time I grew up and started to act like the man I've been pretending to be."

Jesse's mother lowered the knife, but Jesse didn't take his eyes off the scuffed boots in the threshold.

"Look, Doyle," Jesse's mother said. "Everyone deserves a second chance. I hope it all works out for you."

He held out the flowers again. "You sure you won't take them?"

"Yeah, I'm sure." His mother turned to look at Jesse and gave him a reassuring smile. "I can only accept flowers from two men in my life. And the other one is going to be here in a minute, so could you please go."

"You've got a pretty great mom," Doyle said to Jesse. He winked. "You and your dad are lucky guys."

Jesse wondered if everyone was like him: a mix of both bad and good. He knew for sure his dad was like that, but when he thought about his mother, he figured she was pretty much all good. Jesse hoped he could grow up to be all good like her.

"Have a safe trip," his mother said as Doyle turned and descended the stairs.

Not able to help himself, Jesse rushed forward to close the door. It was then they both noticed black smoke rising from the stove.

"Oh no, the steaks," his mother said, but rather than yelling she calmly pulled the pan off the stove and tried to flip the steaks with her knife. Smoke continued to billow up toward the ceiling, and one of the steaks flopped onto the floor. Jesse wasn't sure why, but rather than get mad his mother began to laugh. Jesse giggled, which of course sent her into even deeper peals of laughter.

She had dropped the frying pan into the sink, and they were sitting on the floor, nearly hysterical with laughter when the intercom buzzer sounded again.

"Hi, Sweetie," came his father's voice. "I'm really sorry I'm late, but…I had to stop and get something."

His mother hugged Jesse one more time then bounded to her feet.

"No, you're right on time," she said, pressing the intercom button, her voice still filled with good humor. "Come on up, Babe."

Relieved that the footsteps sounded right this time, Jesse stood next to his mother by the door. They both fell speechless when it swung open to reveal his father, clean shaven with a clean gray jacket and a pure-white button-up shirt. He also wore dress slacks, not work jeans, and though he still had on his work boots, they almost looked shiny.

"These are for you," his dad said.

And, as if he hadn't already outdone himself, he pulled a bouquet of red roses out from behind his back. Jesse glanced up to see his mother's radiant expression. Though Jesse thought Doyle's multicolor flowers had been prettier, he could tell from the way his mother stared at his father, she liked the roses much better.

Suddenly, his father sniffed, and his eyes roamed the kitchen. "What'd you burn?"

Jesse held his breath.

His mother threw her arms around his father and kissed him full on the lips. Somehow, Jesse didn't think it mattered what she had burned.

12

And Then Came the Warrior

I dreamt my arms were snuggled around a tiny dog. Though darker and entirely the wrong breed, I somehow knew it was Whiskey. Reunited with my best friend once again, tears streaked my cheeks. I snuggled into his soft puppy fur and hugged him tight. We had been apart so long, and even though I hadn't consciously remembered him I realized that one of the driving forces behind my monster had been a desire to remember my dog. My soul had missed Whiskey so much.

"How are you, boy?" I whispered.

He licked my face.

"Me, too, boy. Me, too." I rubbed behind his ears.

He groaned the way he always had when we snuggled.

"I won't ever let you go again," I told him, but already his body was beginning to fade.

"No!" I cried out.

"Whulp, whulp," he said in parting....

It was dark when I woke, and for the second time I found Ricky had carried my unconscious body into my home. He was sitting in the rocking chair beside me. His Uncle Sedrick stood on the opposite side of the bed.

"Hey there, young fellow," Sedrick said. "It's good to see you in one piece. You had us worried."

My grief was so profound that I couldn't find the strength to answer. My parents were dead. My dog and my sister may have been killed as well. Everything I had known in life had been violently ripped—

I tried to block out my grief. But as I looked around, I realized I had no family left, not even my grandmother remained in Under-Heaven. Instead, a veritable stranger stood by my side. Even Ricky, though a dear friend, could never replace my family or my dog? My soul ached for Whiskey. I needed him so much.

Suddenly, my comfortable life in the whiteness of Under-Heaven had turned a dingy gray.

Ricky got to his feet and leaned over me. I managed a wan smile at his color. His shirt was completely white, and his pants had only the tiniest hint of color down at the cuffs. He was as white as I'd ever seen him.

"I'm good for you," I said weakly.

He looked down at his own clothes and smiled. But when his eyes returned, his expression was somber.

"I'd rather you were feeling better and I was more colorful," he said.

I wanted to smile again, but I couldn't find a cheerful emotion inside myself. I was an empty shell. Even the sadness had drained away, leaving me hollow and dry inside. I had nothing left. I had nothing to live for—correction…to be dead for.

"You disappeared, Nate," Ricky told me. "Your entire body vanished. It was only for a minute, but I was so scared."

From where I lay, it seemed a damnable shame that I hadn't accidentally sent myself into oblivion. I'd been killed once; why couldn't I just have stayed that way?

"It was the strangest thing I've ever seen," Sedrick said, "and I've been around for a long while. I don't know where your soul bolted off to, young man, but it sure wasn't here. How do you feel?"

"I don't feel anything," I answered honestly. I was a withered husk of a soul. I was a creature without hope, a creature beyond caring.

Sedrick leaned on his cane and patted my arm with a thickly veined hand.

"Now that you're awake, young fellow, I'll be off. I think your grandmother would like to know how things are going here. I expect she'll be along shortly."

"I thought she was busy with…." I didn't know how to finish the sentence. I had no idea why my grandmother had left me alone for so long.

Sedrick squeezed my hand.

"Your family decided you needed some private time to work through your memories. It seems they may have been right. I presume you did remember?"

"I know how I died."

"I'm sorry you had to go through that," Sedrick said. His brow wrinkled in concern. "I'll let your grandmother know."

He stood erect.

"Ricky, will you be okay for a time?"

"Yeah, me and Nate'll be okay."

Sedrick nodded, but before he could walk from the room, I asked, "Can souls die?"

Maybe I at least had that to look forward to.

Sedrick didn't have an answer for me.

~

When I woke the second time, Ricky was still at my side. It was light outside. My throat felt stiff from disuse.

"How long have I been asleep?" I croaked.

"Three days, Nate."

I looked down at his pants and smiled. He was still the picture of whiteness.

"You stay much longer and you're going to sprout wings," I said.

"Wings or no wings, I'm here until you get better."

"Your uncle?"

"Back in Heaven, I guess. There wasn't room for four of us here."

"Four?" I craned my neck.

Relief flooded into me. The hollow that had been my soul was suddenly filled with gratitude. I lifted myself and leaned into my Grandma Clara. For the longest time I rested in her loving embrace. I didn't ever want her to let me go.

Not ever.

"I'll be on the porch," Ricky said politely.

I wanted to tell him "no," that he was fine. I wanted to say he could stay as long as he liked, but I couldn't bear to detach myself from my grandmother's embrace for even that simple task. It was she who finally separated us though she still held onto both my hands.

"The monster?" she asked.

I looked inside myself. The prison cell was still there, but the door and its frame lay in a mangled waste off to the side. I had paid a terrible price, but the creature was finally gone.

"It's not there," I said. "I remember everything."

She hugged me again.

I had so many questions, so many things I needed to know, but at that moment, nothing seemed as important as just being held. I learned that angels can hold you for as long as you need.

~

True to his word, Ricky never left my side until I was ready to go outside with him. His uncle had come and gone a few times, but it seemed agreed that his lessons could wait. I was a sickly boy who had his grandmother and his friend looking after him. I felt guilty for not thinking of Ricky as my best friend, but the memories had changed all that. I had only one best friend, and he walked about on four legs.

Though my monster was gone, the memories it left behind filled me with a deep sadness. I learned from Grandma Clara that, as I feared, my mother had died that night. My grandmother didn't go into details, but I suspected her end had been as horrible as my father's and mine. Only one solitary shaft of light pierced the gloom of that tragic last day on Earth: my baby sister had survived.

Though wounded, Whiskey had somehow managed to drag and prod two-year-old Vicky through the woods and down the hill to the docks. Under the main wharf, he kept her warm against his fur for the rest of the night. Knowing how the fishermen hated our family, my dog remained quiet throughout the early morning until he heard the sheriff's car arrive. As the lawman walked along the weathered pier to see if my father had launched another skiff, Whiskey began to bark, softly at first but then louder until the sheriff ducked his head under the dock. That's when my dog whimpered and licked my sister's face one last time before allowing the gentle lawman to pull her safely from his blood-matted fur.

I cried seemingly endless tears when I learned that was the last thing my Whiskey ever did. After carrying out my final wish that morning, he had died. We had truly been friends to the grave.

~

Nearly two weeks passed before I felt ready to go outside. Ricky joined me for a stroll around the edges of our Under-Heaven. I was walking a few steps behind him, dragging my hand through the moist clouds that ringed our tiny world, when I realized the tan color had again wicked up his pant legs and was now nearly to his waist. I wanted to ask him about it, but I knew, as with my own monster, a person needed to handle some things in their own way, at their own pace.

Ricky and I started to play a game of tag but somewhere along the way we realized that neither of us was in the mood. So, instead we sat in the grass and spent the rest of the day watching souls migrate to and from the fountain pond at the center of our little neighborhood. We knew that nearly everyone in our Under-Heaven arrived with an object from his or her past. Mine, of course, had been the beat-up lobster trap that once held my sister's bloody doll. Ricky's porch swing, on the other hand, had been a positive symbol from his past life. It was there that he and his mother had shared intimate discussions when his father worked late. But of all the items we had ever seen souls carry with them, nothing could have prepared us for the clump of white hair that we suddenly saw slipping smoothly through the grass on its way to the pool.

"Look," Ricky said, pointing someplace ahead of the mini-wig.

Confused at first, I finally saw the thin strand of twine that connected the wig to a balding man who walked a few feet in front of it. For some reason, he was pulling the hairpiece like you might walk a dog.

But why?

Fascinated, we watched the man settle to his knees at the edge of the cherub pool. He ran his free hand over the water's surface and stared downward for quite some time. Then I saw what might have been the most bizarre thing I'd ever witnessed in Under-Heaven. He drew in the twine like a fish on a hook. Then lifted the hairpiece and placed it gently on his head, the twine dangling behind like a slender ponytail. As he adjusted the patch of hair, it was as though a switch had been flipped. Suddenly, his all-white clothing burst into brilliant shades of blue, green, and red. Even the tuft of artificial hair changed from white to a deep black, which was especially odd given that the ring of natural hair around the man's head remained heavily streaked with gray. It was almost as though he had a dead kitten sitting on his head.

Unable to peel our eyes away from the now dangerously colorful man, Ricky and I were thankful he never looked up to catch us gawking. Instead, he continued to stare down into the water for another few minutes before snatching the hairpiece from his head and flinging it away. It might have gone further but caught up short on the twine that was apparently tied to his wrist. The mini-wig flopped down onto the grass just a few feet from him. By then, it was white again as were all of the man's clothes. Even his shoes were bone white by the time he got to his feet and walked by, completely oblivious to us. Without so much as a glance back, he disappeared into one of the new houses not far from Ricky's home.

During life, Ricky or I might have made some comment or snickered about a man with such an unusual pet, but in Under-Heaven none of that seemed proper. Even small events in Under-Heaven, especially those involving color, had such potentially serious consequences that laughing would have been akin to making jokes about a fatal car accident on Earth. No, we kept our thoughts to ourselves as we got to our feet and returned to Ricky's home.

After he said goodbye and I waved, Ricky fondly brushed a hand along the top of his porch swing before going inside. I stood there for a few seconds, wondering why his color had gotten so bad and why it had remained that way throughout the entire day. I didn't know what made Ricky feel so guilty, but I prayed he would get past it. In the meantime, I was committed to being as good a friend to him as he had been to me. Unfortunately, that made me worry all the more.

It had been nearly four weeks since I faced my monster for the last time, and each day I found I missed my family more and more. I knew Vicky was back on Earth and living her life as best she could, but my parents should have been someplace where I could see them.

"Can I go to Heaven to be with them?" I asked Grandma Clara when she arrived one morning.

"I'm sorry, Nate, but it's not that easy. Your parents are not in Heaven yet. They're in two different purgatories."

"Purgatories?"

"You mother was a Christian, like me," Grandma Clara said. "She believed in Purgatory, so that's the kind of Under-Heaven she went to. And your father, though not a full-fledged Christian, also chose form of Under-Heaven similar to Purgatory."

"Will I ever see them again?"

"I think so, Nate. They're good people, and it's likely they will decide to go on to Heaven. Sometimes in the Purgatories it takes a while, but I believe you will all be reunited in Heaven someday."

"I thought God decided who got into Heaven and who didn't."

"Ultimately, it is his decision, but in the Purgatories, souls have to make their own judgment first. Then God makes a final judgment."

"Why didn't I go to Purgatory?"

She smiled warmly, a look I had grown to treasure, and said, "You mean besides the fact that you didn't even know what Purgatory was until I just mentioned it?"

I shrugged.

"I didn't know about this place either."

She nodded.

"You didn't have any preconceptions about Heaven, Nate, so you were sent to a simple Under-Heaven. Here, you are judged by your instinctive feelings of guilt. Here, you don't have to relive every decision you made in life to decide whether you belong in Heaven."

"Thank goodness for that," I said. I'd had enough of relived memories to last several lifetimes.

"When do I go to Heaven?"

"You'll know when the time is right, Nate. Your instincts will tell you. But for now, you have lessons to learn and some growing up to do."

"I thought no one grows in Under-Heaven."

"It's true that your body will always remain the same," she said, "but you do grow mentally and spiritually. Now that your monster is gone, the rest should become much easier. You'll soon have decisions to make about what you're going to do next, but right now God wants you to relax and take some time to realize who you are and what you really want as a soul."

Even looking back at them, Grandma Clara's early answers seemed more like riddles than actual information. I was often forced to ask the same question in dozens of ways before I could make sense of her responses. That was where Ricky came in handy. He had an amazing knack for interpreting my grandmother's elusive answers. Though he had been a year younger than me when he died, in many ways he was a lot wiser. So, when it came to Grandma Clara's answers, Ricky often found meaning where I only found confusion. Of course, there was always the chance that his interpretations were wrong, but I figured a skewed view was better than no view at all.

As much as I relied on Ricky for answers, he relied on me for fun. At times, it seemed like he had never been a kid at all. Even the simplest of games could sometimes be an effort for him. It was as if he had to work to enjoy himself. One day, though, we were both having an incredible time. Two girls had appeared in Under-Heaven. Though older than us, they were the youngest people we had ever seen in our small neighborhood. One seemed to be about seventeen, and the other I would have guessed to be fifteen or so. Ricky and I had spent most of that morning spying on the younger girl. We ducked behind the fountain, behind other people, crawled in the grass and crept silently along the neighbors' houses like foxes on the hunt. We actually got within ten feet of her and were hiding behind the railing of her porch before she finally spotted us.

It was then that I realized she had grown more colorful as we approached. As I stared at her dark red shoes, green skirt and the light cream bottom half of her blouse, I tried to remember how colorful she had been when we started. Only her shoes and socks, I thought. She waved and smiled when she caught sight of us, but her angel relative, a tall man with a cowboy hat, shooed us away.

Next, we tried spying on the older brunette girl, but she was tough. Within minutes, she had nabbed us for lurking three times. This girl wore a long white dress with shoes as white as my sneakers. She smiled the third time she caught us but didn't laugh like she had the first two times. We decided to move onto another game.

I offered to race Ricky back to my house. He had no visitors that day. I, on the other hand, knew my Grandmother would be waiting for me when I got back. Though my soul hadn't inexplicably flittered away again, my grandmother wasn't willing to take any chances. She now spent most of my waking hours at my home.

"On the count of three," Ricky said. "One. Two. Three!"

Ricky bolted for the win, and I immediately tore after him.

I shudder to think what might have happened if Ricky had been alone that day, because he didn't notice the black creature that swooped down from the sky off to our right. As we rounded the cherub fountain, I saw it and immediately realized it was aiming straight for Ricky's back.

Instinctively, I dove and grabbed Ricky by the ankle. He tripped and fell headlong into the soft grass in front of me. Unable to change its course in time, the mass of black wings and claws careened past, mere inches above Ricky's head.

The creature's scream made my ears ache and my skin crawl.

A demon!

I'd heard Grandmother Clara talk about them, but this was the first one I'd ever seen. Horrified, I watched as it soared upward and banked for another attack. About three times taller than either Ricky or me, the creature had coal-black skin with no fur. The two streaks of red along its cheeks looked like open wounds. Bat-like wings churned at the air as its gnarled arms and legs, all tipped with gleaming black claws, dangled beneath it. A long, pointed tail flicked back and forth like the dangerous water moccasin snakes I'd seen in the swamp at the edge of the Coldwell Mica Mine. The creature's black ears curled back in tall narrow arcs, almost like horns. I felt its hateful black eyes rake over me before it swooped for Ricky again.

Suddenly, a blur of white streaked down from the sky and rammed into the creature's back. The force of the blow sent both objects hurtling to the ground with a small explosion of soil and grass. In a flurry of motion, the white object separated itself and landed nimbly between Ricky and the demon.

I immediately recognized the new combatant. Tall, muscular and dressed in a flowing white robe, he was astounding. His long wavy hair was as white as his garb. Two huge, powerful wings sprouted from his shoulder blades and, unlike the demon's misshapen leathery appendages, they were covered with beautiful snowy feathers.

Awestruck, I couldn't pull my eyes away from the archangel.

The demon snarled and hurled itself at the much bigger archangel, but it might as well have been throwing itself at the open air. With grace and speed, the archangel dodged a dozen different strikes. The demon cackled, spat and struck out twice more with its front claws but to no avail. Suddenly, its barbed black tail whipped from behind, but once again the archangel easily dodged the blow.

Suddenly, thudding like a hammer against wood, a heavenly fist struck the demon solidly in the chest. The black creature staggered back and let loose a scream that would have given any living child nightmares; as it was, the chilling sound was to stay with me for several weeks.

Before the demon could fully recover, the archangel struck it in the chest again. This time, the blow echoed like thunder across my Under-Heaven. Hurled backwards, the demon crashed into the ground and rolled several times before it came to a scrabbling halt on its knees in the grass. After a short struggle, it untangled its gangly limbs and got to its feet. Arms lowered in what looked to be a fighting stance, it flexed its long claws and snarled, revealing razor sharp fangs, but didn't otherwise move. The look of hatred on its drawn face was enough to make me wither inside.

Simultaneously awestruck and terrified, I could not have moved if I tried. The contrast between these two creatures, one of light and goodness and the other of darkness and evil, was almost too much to comprehend. If I hadn't already been persuaded, that one incident would have been enough to convince me to avoid Hell at all costs. Nothing could possibly have been worth exposure to a world filled with those creatures.

The archangel stepped toward the demon. Though about the same height as his opponent, which is to say three times as tall as Ricky or me, the archangel's mass made the demon look sickly and pathetic. Apparently realizing it was grossly outmatched, the vile creature trembled even as it stood its ground.

The hatred, however, never left its black eyes.

I wondered if an archangel would kill a demon. The difference of size alone left no doubt in my mind that he could if he so chose. But would he? I couldn't say why, but somehow, I doubted it.

"Away, foul one!" the archangel said, his voice like a powerful wind.

The demon's lips pulled back into a grimace, revealing rows of deadly sharp fangs.

"That one is mine." It pointed at Ricky.

It wasn't until that moment that I realized Ricky's slacks were entirely tan and most of his shirt had turned a dark shade of blue. Only a few inches below his collar remained white. Maybe spying on those girls had been a bad idea. I glanced down. Strangely the game hadn't turned me at all. If anything, my sneakers were whiter than they had been earlier.

"The other boy," the archangel said, "should never have had to endure even the sight of your foul presence."

The demon's shifted his gaze toward me. I hadn't seen such a look of hatred since Tommy Edds' father had killed me. I shivered, although whether it was from the evil gaze or my brief recollection of my own last day on Earth, I couldn't have said.

"You will go without prey this day," the archangel bellowed. "Leave or I will smite you now and strew your remnants throughout the sky."

The archangel's powerful wings unfurled to several times the width of his already impressive size and hid the demon from my view. By the time the glistening white feathers folded back in place, the misshapen creature was gone.

I tried to get to my feet, but my knees were weak.

The towering archangel turned and stepped toward me. Long, white curls cascaded over alabaster cheeks to frame his glorious smile. Waves of kindness and love washed over me. In that moment, I glimpsed Heaven.

As perfect a creature as has ever existed reached down for me then. And when his hand gently gripped my skinny shoulder, my entire body tingled with warmth and strength. Suddenly, my weakness was gone, replaced by an intoxicating sense of wellbeing. At that moment I would have sworn my allegiance to him forever.

"God loves you, Nathaniel," he said to me.

It came almost as a shock to be reminded that there was a God other than the glowing being in front of me. It would have been so easy to believe he was the One and Only.

I was still awash in affirming emotions when the archangel turned his attention to Ricky. My friend's young body was curled into a near-catatonic ball. I could hear his quiet weeping, and my emotional high was immediately replaced with sympathy and worry for my friend. Knowing how the demon had horrified me, it must have been many times more devastating for Ricky to know that creature had been there for him.

The archangel knelt and lifted my friend's frail body. Upon his touch, Ricky's shirt and pants turned white again. Only his sneakers retained their dark coloring.

"As for you, little one," the Godly creature whispered, "I'm going to bring you home and stand guard outside your door."

"For me?" Ricky said. His eyes filled with tears.

A tender hand brushed back Ricky's red hair.

"I pity the twisted creature that thinks he can pass by me this night. By my word, you will be safe." The air resounded with the authority of his oath.

Ricky began sobbing again, but this time with joy. Then suddenly the sobbing stopped. I braced myself, because I knew what was coming next. I held my breath as Ricky said the words.

"And tomorrow?"

"We'll see," the archangel said. "Salvation must come from within, little one, but I have faith that you can find it if you will only look hard enough."

Ricky nodded and hugged tightly against the archangel's powerful chest. Every eye in Under-Heaven watched as a warrior of the light carried one of the doomed back to his home. Forgotten, but not at all resenting it, I realized that something rare and important had just happened. Even the colorful girl Ricky and I had been spying on earlier was watching in rapt attention, her clothing having turned bleach white.

Grandma Clara hugged and kissed me affectionately on the forehead when I made my way back into my own kitchen.

"Why today?" I asked.

Grandma Clara led me to my bed where I slowly crawled under the covers. She tucked the blankets under my chin.

"I think Ricky has been avoiding the demons for so long that they decided to grab him the second his color was right. I imagine they didn't want to take the chance he would lighten again by nightfall."

I had so many questions, but at that moment her hand on my arm was enough. I think I cried before falling into a deep and much-needed sleep.

94

13

Family Ties

For Quite a while, I'd known the fountain pool was a window back to Earth, and since my memories were no longer hidden, I realized that I no longer feared using it. The truth was I longed to see my sister Vicky, the sole survivor of the Thompson Family Massacre. My Whiskey had given his life to ensure her safety, and I wanted to see her living a good life—at least one of us deserved that.

There were a few other souls leaning over the pool when Grandma Clara brought me out for my first viewing lesson one morning. The cherub statue towered above us, much taller than I had imagined, and the soft patter of four streaming columns of water had turned into a splattering roar that made it hard to think, forget hear, someone speak. A faint mist hovered over the pool and formed a series of competing rainbows, each one more beautiful than the last. As I took in the beauty of it, I couldn't believe that just days before I had been terrified of this place.

"Are you ready?" Grandma Clara said loud enough to be heard over the cascading water.

I nodded.

"First you have to smooth the water," she said, "like this." She gently ran her hand along the top of the ripples. Though the rest of the pool undulated with small waves, the water beneath her hand settled and became perfectly still and smooth. I saw her mouth move but couldn't make out the words. I pointed at my ears and shrugged.

She leaned close and said loudly, "Look into the portal and think of Vicky."

I moved closer to the water's edge and stared down at the mirror-like finish she had created. I tried to envision my sister as she had been that last morning at breakfast: hair snarled, eyes still drooping with sleep, face split with a tiny grin. Suddenly, the clear surface of the pool became a murky white with thousands of faint yellow dots that flickered like candles against a backdrop of snow. Though the lights were dim, one in particular stood out. I knew with certainty that it was Vicky.

"You're seeing her life force," my grandmother yelled. "From this far away, all living people look like that."

"What about the red ones?" I asked.

Though they numbered only in the dozens, the red flickers were easy to see among the hundreds of yellow ones.

"Those are people who will die soon," she said. "Fate marks them a few hours or sometimes a day before it happens. The brighter the red, the closer they are to their last minutes."

I studied the two brightest red spots and wondered how near they were to death. Were they elderly, sickly or just on the wrong side of a fishing dispute?

I glanced away. Though not cynical by nature, the emergence of my memories made it hard not to think like that.

"At night the background turns black, and the lights are bright and beautiful," my grandmother said. "It's amazing to know that all those souls are growing and experiencing life right below us."

"Can I see her up close?" I asked. I was anxious to know how Vicky was doing, how big she'd grown. And I also wanted to get my eyes away from the doomed red lights before one went out. I had experienced enough death to last me an eternity. I didn't think I was ready to watch even a single red light disappear from my view.

"What?"

"Can I see her up close?" I hollered to be heard. I was now beginning to understand why souls tended to visit the pool without their angels. It was much too difficult to talk this close to the rushing water.

"Concentrate again, Nate," my grandmother said, leaning close to my ear. "Focus on Vicky's light and think how much you'd like to see her."

Butterflies filled my stomach. How long had it been? Six months? Eight months? It felt like much longer.

I focused, and Vicky appeared in the water. Taller now, her brunette hair was neatly brushed and at least an inch longer than it had been. I smiled. She and I had never been hair people, and I was pleased to see someone was taking good care of her mop. Staring at her radiant smile, I couldn't believe my mind had been willing to block out her memory. No matter how horrible my last day on Earth had been, something good remained: a gem in the form of a little girl was gleaming at someone; I only wished it were me.

"Your Aunt Donna and Uncle Bert took Vicky in," Grandma Clara said. "She's living in Rhode Island with them now."

I was ecstatic that my sister was no longer in that angry Maine village. Though I knew most of the people in Coldwell were decent, the few bad ones had made a lasting impression on me—though lasting impression might have been an understatement considering I died at their hands. At least Vicky was safe among family and in a town where she would be accepted.

Vicky all of a sudden ran forward so I could only see only her backside. Her dress was light green with a cloth belt of the same material. The belt was sewn into the sides of the dress and pulled back where the ends were tied. The dress's half-sleeves were puffy and fringed with the same white lace that adorned its collar. The tiles on the floor were alternating red and black squares that glowed with cleanliness. I could see the chrome legs of several chairs and a table next to a gray wall on the right. From Vicky's low vantage, I watched her approach a woman from behind. I could only see the woman's legs where she stood beside a white cabinet and the lower portion of a refrigerator. My view ended at the bottom of a yellow skirt.

"If you concentrate, Nate," Grandma Clara said, "you can change your view."

I wanted to get a better idea of where Vicky was, so I tried to imagine I was backing up. Sure enough, my sister shrank to the size of a healthy three-year-old. Above her, my Aunt Donna stood beside a red kitchen counter, which was contrasted above and below by white cabinet doors. She had one cabinet open and was saying something to my sister. Vicky shook her three-year-old head vigorously. I didn't have to hear to know what was going on. "Cereal," she would be saying. "Oatmeal with maple syrup."

It's impossible to describe how great it felt to see her, and not just to see her but to see her smiling, so obviously happy and well-adjusted to her new life. I remembered that horrible night and was thankful that Vicky's door had been closed during most of the violence. Given her age, it seemed unlikely that she would remember even the gruesome noises…noises that were the inevitable result of killing innocent people in their home!

I hated how that thought sent chills across my back. Would I ever be able to accept what had happened to me—to us?

As I watched Vicky pull herself up into her highchair, I wondered how long it would be before she forgot us: my mother, my father and me. It made me sad in a way, but I also knew it would be best. The less she knew and remembered, the more likely she would grow up happy and healthy, without all the ugly emotional baggage.

As my aunt positioned a bowl of cereal in front of Vicky, I looked over at my grandmother and could feel a tear rolling down my cheek, but Grandma Clara politely ignored it.

"How do I shut it off?" I asked.

Though I doubt she heard me, she understood and reached down to tap the surface of the water. Suddenly the portal to my aunt's kitchen was gone, replaced with tiny ripples of water chasing each other to the shore. Mentally and emotionally exhausted, I followed my grandmother back toward home. The splattering roar of water had faded to barely a whisper by the time we reached my front stairs.

Somewhere along the way, I realized I had become the sole caretaker of my family's memories. The pain and responsibility would be mine alone to bear.

~

Grandma Clara had been my only family visitor since my arrival in Under-Heaven, but many times she had mentioned I had a lot of other relatives anxious to meet me, so it came as no surprise when guests arrived. It had been about two months by my figuring since the demon had come for Ricky, and I had been in Under-Heaven for maybe eight months in all.

When I heard the knock at the front door, I figured it was Ricky trying to sneak a day off, but instead it was a rugged-looking man with snow-white hair and a clean-shaven face. He wore a white suit that had a rumpled, lived in look. On Earth I might have guessed him to be in his sixties.

"Hello, Nate," he said with a broad smile. "I'm your Uncle Albert, and this," he stepped to the side so that I could see a thin, angular woman in a white ballroom dress and a white bonnet, "is your Aunt Alice."

She nodded.

"Good morning, Nathaniel," she said through pursed lips that seemed anything but friendly. She had a strong accent that I couldn't place.

"It's wonderful to see you in person, Nate," my Uncle Albert said. "I've been watching you ever since you were a baby, and you've made me very proud."

It was a little weird, I thought, to know people had been watching me for so long. But I said, "Thanks."

"And that incident with that demon and your friend," Uncle Albert continued, "was well-handled. It was touch-and-go there for a few moments, but you thought quickly, knocking him over and saving him the way you did. Nicely done."

My Aunt Alice slapped him on the shoulder. It wasn't a light slap either.

"Now, Albert, you know better than that. What are you thinking? This boy could have been delivered right into Satan's arms, and you found the event nicely done!"

Uncle Albert winked at me then said, "Alice, obviously you and I have different ways of seeing things. And that's okay. But couldn't you allow that I might be at least half right?"

"I could if you happened to be half-right, but you're not." She jutted her chin out and ignored my uncle's impish grin. I immediately liked him.

Aunt Alice, with her severe manner, however, was obviously going to take some getting used to. She was tall and thin, almost to the point of being gaunt. Her dark hair was pulled back tightly and tucked beneath a gossamer white bonnet. Long white pyramid earrings dangled to the top of the tall lacey collar that rose up from her white gown. The delicate silk material was pulled so tightly around her narrow waist that it seemed she should have been in pain. From her hips down, the dress swelled out into large hoops that dropped like a bell to the floor. She could easily have stepped out of the ballroom picture in my sister's Cinderella picture book.

"You have been here for a long while, Nathaniel, haven't you?" Her question seemed like an accusation.

"I guess."

"You guess," she said sternly.

Not knowing what kind of response she wanted, I shrugged.

Her eyebrows rose.

"Why are you here then, Nathaniel?"

"I don't know. To learn, I guess."

"Again, you guess?"

"Yeah. Yes. I know I need to learn."

"Which is it? You guess or you know?"

I wondered how fast anger might add color to my clothes. I didn't dare to look down for fear it was already happening.

"I know I need to learn," I said.

"What about that troublemaker friend of yours?"

I didn't like where this was going. This woman had gotten no more than three feet into my house, and already she wanted to choose my friends. Grandma Clara often asked me to be careful around Ricky, but never once had she said anything bad about him. Apparently, kindness toward others was not a prerequisite for getting into Heaven.

"What about Ricky?" I asked defensively.

"The demons are waiting for him," she said, leaning down to stare me in the eye. "And if you keep fraternizing with him, they'll likely come for you as well."

"Now hold on a second, Alice," Uncle Albert intervened. "Our boy here has a healthy white color." His gaze settled momentarily on my sneakers, then rose to meet Aunt Alice's glare.

"For how long?" Aunt Alice snapped. "Clara has barely gotten this young man to realize there is a path. It's no wonder he's yet to follow it?"

Who was she to make these accusations? My Grandma Clara had been teaching me lessons nearly every day since I had arrived. What more did this woman expect of her…or me? I was rapidly growing to dislike my Aunt Alice.

I tried to pinpoint where and when my Uncle Albert and Aunt Alice might have lived. I had studied past cultures with Grandma Clara because, as she explained, "Earth's history is even more important in Heaven. Up there you actually meet people from all periods, and its best to know something about them when you do." She also said that our genealogy could be traced through every continent and every historical period spanning from Stone Age Asia, Roman Era Europe, Medieval England and ultimately modern-day America. And, she said, the further our lineage goes on, the more all-encompassing and interrelated to the rest of the world we become.

I knew that Grandma Clara had died in 1935, three weeks after I was born. From the look of Uncle Albert's suit, not unlike my father's one suit—only white, I guessed he had died in the early 1900s, but Aunt Alice's formal dress suggested they might be from an even earlier period. I couldn't be sure. There was only so much Grandma Clara's history lessons could do.

"Have you made any decisions, yet?" Aunt Alice asked.

I was unsure what she was really asking, so I shook my head. Time hadn't seemed all that important to me in Under-Heaven, but just then

I found myself wishing I could speed it along. Angels seldom stayed in Under-Heaven overnight, and the sooner this woman left my house, the happier I would be.

Uncle Albert came up beside me and put an arm over my shoulder, coincidentally placing himself between Aunt Alice and my sneakers.

"Alice, I'd like a minute alone with my nephew here, if you don't mind."

I took the moment to glance down. I knew it: my sneakers were black as charcoal. Soon, I expected the color would spread to my pants. Who would have believed my own aunt would be my biggest challenge in Under-Heaven?

Aunt Alice gave my uncle a withering glare, then harrumphed and stormed out onto the front porch. Her wide petticoats brushed both sides of the doorway as she left.

"Quite a piece of work, that aunt of yours," Uncle Albert said with a chuckle. "Don't let her frazzle you though. She means well."

"I didn't think someone like her—I thought Heaven was where nice people went."

Uncle Albert gently squeezed the back of my neck.

"Watch yourself there, young one. It'll be more than your shoes turning colors if you keep up that sort of talk. It's not your place to judge."

"I'm sure she must be nice," I said, "being from Heaven, but she has an odd way of showing it."

"Ever hear about the Wizard?" Uncle Albert asked me.

"You mean the Wizard of Oz?"

He squinted at me. That's when I noticed how bushy his white eyebrows were.

"Not that one. I'm referring to the Wizard of Menlo Park."

"I never heard of that one," I answered honestly. "Was it a book?"

"Not a book, Nate, a man. He was a man who everyone called a wizard because of all his great inventions. His real name was Thomas Edison."

"Sure, I learned about him in school. He invented the phone, I think."

Uncle Albert smiled.

"That was Mr. Alexander Graham Bell. No, Mr. Edison created hundreds of inventions, but his version of the light bulb and the phonograph were two of his most famous ones."

"Yeah, that's right."

"Your aunt and I lived only a short walk from the Edison laboratory in West Orange, New Jersey."

"How'd you meet Aunt Alice?" I asked, truly curious about what had attracted him to her.

He smiled.

"It's not what you think, Nate. I was married to your Aunt Bertrice not Aunt Alice. Bertrice and I were married for forty-seven years. Nice years, too."

Well, that explained why Aunt Alice's outfit seemed more old-fashioned than his did. But where was Aunt Bertrice? I almost asked but kept myself from voicing the question.

He must have guessed what I was thinking because he said, "She's in Purgatory, Nate. Your Aunt Bertrice was always frightened of Mr. Edison and his crazy experiments. For a time there, I think she actually convinced herself he was a demon."

I couldn't make the connection in his logic but continued to listen.

"That crazy old genius actually burned his entire laboratory to the ground one time." Uncle Albert chuckled at the memory. "Yep, he had flames reaching two and three hundred feet in the air. The smoke was so thick it coated the insides of houses blocks away. Rest assured your Aunt Bertrice wasn't too happy about cleaning up after that."

I struggled to understand what any of this had to do with my less-than-nice Aunt Alice.

"She's still there," Uncle Albert said. "Your Aunt Bertrice is still reliving those years in West Orange, still trying to find her way through all the angry words and negative judgments she made about Mr. Edison. Don't you see?"

I shook my head. I had no clue what he was talking about.

"Your Aunt Alice is trying to make you understand that it's important to decide. It's not enough just to be here in Under-Heaven. And it's not enough to just learn the lessons that your grandmother presents to you each day. At some point, you're going to have to find a purpose to it all, Nate. At some point, you'll have to decide."

"Decide what, Uncle Albert? I already know I don't want a demon to drag me off to Hell." I remembered the misshapen creature that had nearly captured Ricky that day. "I never want that to happen!"

"That's the problem, Nate. Knowing what you don't want is only half the equation. At some point you have to decide what you do want. I know your Aunt Bertrice doesn't want to go to Hell, but I also know she doesn't want to forgive herself for all the things she said and did in regard to Mr. Edison. The problem is that she hasn't decided the most important thing: whether she wants to be in Heaven. I'm convinced that when she makes that decision, God will judge her to be a wonderful woman who deserves to be at his table."

"So, I need to decide if I want to go to Heaven?"

"Or not," Aunt Alice interjected. At some point during our discussion, she had come back into the room. "I figured this old fool might need a bit of help before he got too worried about hiding those black sneakers of yours."

If a boy could have blushed in Under-Heaven, I'm sure I would have. It was a small mercy that complexions remain neutral there. My brief expression of horror at being caught, however, must have given me away because, for the first time since I had met her, my Aunt Alice laughed.

I had to admit she had a pretty laugh.

14

Earth, Present and Past

Ricky had become much more serious since the demon incident. In all, the archangel had stood sentry on his roof for three days. During that time my friend had remained inside his house. Twice I had seen his uncle arrive to visit, but both times Nathaniel—I had been thrilled to find the archangel and I shared the same name—had not allowed him inside. On the third day, I saw Ricky out on his porch talking with the archangel for a long time. As I watched from the fountain that day, I remembered envying him a little—enough so that my Grandma Clara had to pull me back across the cobblestone road and into my house. "Before you're the next soul that needs saving," she had said. Of course, my sneakers and the cuffs of my pant legs had already turned color.

Now, almost three months since the archangel had left, my friend tended to play a lot less than he used to. But whatever had transpired between him and Nathanial had apparently helped because his color seldom went any further up than his knees. I raced to his house on one of my days off, hoping he might be in the mood to do something. I knew that wasn't going to happen as soon as I saw the worried expression on his face.

"I want to tell you something, Nate," he said, "but I'm afraid it might be bad for you."

"You can tell me anything. We're friends."

"I'm worried that if I tell you…." His eyes dropped and his left cheek twitched like it sometimes did when he was down. He didn't have to complete the thought. I knew he would never have knowingly put me in danger of meeting a demon, especially one intended for me.

"You think just telling me could make my colors change?"

He shrugged. "Dunno."

"Should we ask one of the angels?" I wondered aloud.

He perked up a little. "Maybe."

The truth is he had me curious. I was almost as anxious to learn his mystery as I was to help.

"What should we do then?" I asked.

104

"Nothing yet," he told me.

"Okay," I said.

We sat in the grass for the rest of the day and picked the petals off from hundreds of flowers, but they of course regrew as fast as we could pick them. We made small colorful hills and castles with them. While we played, we whispered about dogs, and frogs and even my pesky little sister. We laughed a lot, and Ricky didn't seem quite so serious when we parted late that afternoon.

Mentioning Vicky made me yearn to see her, so rather than going straight home I settled at the edge of the pool and focused my thoughts on her. I moved quickly through the white background and flickering lights until I could see a full view of her walking beside my aunt. My aunt and uncle used to visit our house several times a year, and I remembered the way Aunt Donna used to spend more time playing with Vicky and me than she did talking with my mother. I had always liked her and was thankful she and my Uncle Bert had accepted Vicky into their home.

I brushed my hand over the water again to smooth a larger area. The scene expanded. Tall buildings rose beyond my view to either side, and there were dozens of cars moving past in both directions. My sister and aunt stopped in front of a store. I could see my aunt saying something but for me there was only the loud rush of the fountain streams striking the pool. My Grandma Clara had explained that to hear back on Earth I would have to settle into the scene rather than just watch. From her description, I got the impression it would be like sitting inside someone's head, and I didn't think I was ready for that.

I watched my sister for quite a while as she and Aunt Donna went in and out of various clothing stores. From the look of things, Vicky was getting a fancy new outfit. I imagined there might be a wedding or a big party coming up. My little sister sure looked happy about it, or at least about shopping for the occasion. I spun the scene around until I could see her from the front. She was garbed in a light polka-dotted yellow dress that, like most of her clothes, had laced fringes. Two red bows held her hair neatly in ponytails that bobbed in rhythm with her energetic walk. I zoomed in until her cheerful face filled my pool window. I absorbed her image into my mind. It became a nightly habit that would stay with me for as long as I remained in Under-Heaven.

Finally, I reached down and touched her perfect face.

"I love you," I said as the ripples washed her likeness away.

~

Time seemed to speed along faster and faster as my days in Under-Heaven continued. My Grandma Clara said it had to do with the maturing of my soul. Our daily lessons now included more detailed histories of various cultures and their theologies, most of which turned out to have similar basic beliefs. It seemed especially odd that religions which had such a difficult time coexisting back on Earth integrated seamlessly in Heaven. Each Under-Heaven was tailored to the beliefs of the new souls who inhabited it, and as the souls moved on, the perfection of Heaven made conflicts of belief trivial and moot. Of course, those souls who had no tolerance for other people or other beliefs were ultimately condemned to an afterlife more suited to their dispositions. Overall, a simple but effective system.

I also began to receive regular visits from other relatives in my Under-Heaven. They arrived sometimes two or three a day but usually didn't stay long. I was thankful that Uncle Albert had assumed the duties of guide and escort to all of my visitors, because, though most of my relatives were genial, some tended to be less friendly. No matter what the difficulties, however, my uncle always navigated them nicely.

Aunt Alice had also become a regular guest, usually visiting two or three times a week. I came to realize that she was as cool in her affections as Grandma Clara was warm. Even though Aunt Alice wasn't the type to say she loved you often, she did have a way of making you feel important, even if only important enough to be worth correcting you about this or that. The truth is, in spite of her uppity manner, I had grown quite fond of her. And I think she had garnered a certain fondness for me—though it wasn't quite so obvious on the days when I tried to hide my color-ridden sneakers. One time, I had even wrapped them in pillowcases before she arrived. I should have known the cases would turn the same dark shade as my sneakers. Though only for a moment, Aunt Alice had smiled about that.

One out of every three or four visits, my Aunt Alice would declare a "discussion day," which was time after lessons for just talking. Of course, this meant I had to forego some playtime with Ricky, so at first, I found those days bothersome, but more and more I looked forward to them. Often, Aunt Alice would tell me about her fascinating life back on Earth.

She had been born to a minor nobleman southern Russia in 1793. Her mother died during her birth. The owner of about two thousand acres along the Volga River, her father lorded over nearly five hundred serfs by the time he arranged to marry his twelve-year-old daughter Alice to the adjoining landowner, a widowed nobleman. It was an especially difficult time in Russian history. The people were largely either serfs, sworn to work for lords who provided them with the most meager of food and housing, or they were peasants, free to roam within certain townships, though often so poor they were actually worse off than the serfs. My Aunt Alice's father and her new husband believed that by combining the strength of their estates, they would be better able to weather the economic storms that regularly swept up and down the country.

In this, they turned out to be correct.

Though she didn't at first, Aunt Alice grew to love the husband fate and her father had forced upon her. She also came to care deeply about the serfs who worked the land for both estates. She loved those workers much the way a mother would love her children, and as early as her thirteenth birthday she would walk among them, offering support and wishing them well in their daily toils. On her fifteenth birthday, my Aunt Alice convinced her husband to set aside three large rooms on the ground level of their large estate home to serve as a hospital and a welfare area. There she made sure well-trained servants were always available with adequate supplies of food, water and medicine.

In time, word spread of her serfs' superior living conditions, which put pressure on other landowners to begin offering better if not equal conditions. Soon, the region became known for its humane and even caring treatment of most residents, a situation that was noted and definitely not appreciated in higher societal circles.

By the age of seventeen, my Aunt Alice had become the natural mother of two and had begun to personally attend every serf birth within the two estates. Over the course of time, she grew to know most of her serfs by name and was greeted throughout the estates with smiles and waves. These were her people. She loved them and was beloved by them.

In 1812, my Aunt Alice turned nineteen years old. It was a year she remembered well because that was when the Russian economy was brutally shaken and nearly destroyed by the invasion of Napoleon's troops. Though Czar Alexander ultimately chased the French warmonger and his army back to Paris, the victory came at a devastating price. Two hundred young, male serfs, nearly a fifth of her estates' combined work force were sent away as foot soldiers in support of

Alexander's counter-war. Only two dozen were destined to return, and even then, it would be two years before she saw them again. Lacking the strongest backs, maintaining both estates became a struggle. Even after her father's death allowed the two estates to consolidate under a single, noble roof, conditions for her and her people continued to worsen.

Alice's husband, along with many nobles of the time, felt that only by radical change could the country recover. Many were in favor of overthrowing the Romanov Czars and letting the people rule themselves by way of a constitution. For years those sentiments brooded.

Alice was thirty-three years old when Czar Alexander died. Her husband, an old man of sixty-two, joined a conspiracy of three thousand other nobleman who attended the coronation of Alexander's younger brother Nicholas in St. Petersburg. They intended to stop the proceedings and declare rule by the Romanov Czars to be over. Nicholas Romanov, however, retained enough military strength to crush them. It was December 14, 1825 when Alice's husband was slaughtered along with most of the other conspirators. History labeled those men and their movement as "The Decemberists."

I had learned all of this over the course of my previous few weeks' discussions with Aunt Alice. And I had begun to infer that somehow my aunt's own demise had been tied to the same Decemberist movement. As I entered the kitchen with her one afternoon, I thought this might have been the day I would find out how she had died. But instead of beginning a new reminiscence, she said, "Today we dance!"

"Dance," I exclaimed. "Boys don't dance!"

"Up in Heaven they do," Aunt Alice said.

Reluctantly, I agreed to try, but not before I glanced out the front window to make sure Ricky wasn't watching. It wouldn't do to have my friend see me dance. He was nowhere to be seen. Secure in my privacy, I returned to the center of the floor. Suddenly, soft music began to play.

"How'd you do that?" I asked.

"There are advantages to being an angel," she said. "First, we'll try a Russian Waltz." She grabbed my hand. "Here, like this."

15

Receding Footsteps

Jesse surveyed his room and thought it would probably pass his mother's scrutiny. He had hidden most of his dirty clothes under the bed and in his pillowcase. The dirty plate and glass he'd used that morning was pushed to the back of his underwear drawer. Yes, overall it was a pretty good job. At the last minute, he remembered the small hole he'd poked in the plaster wall above his bed with the tip of his Frodo Lord of the Rings action figure sword. For some reason the void looked so much bigger in the daylight. Hurriedly, he moved his tall green Teddy bear against the wall to cover the hole.

Yep, pretty good.

It was Saturday morning, and his father was supposed to take care of him for a few hours while his mother worked the midday shift at the restaurant. Though his last couple of visits hadn't gone so well, Jesse knew the 'speriment was still in process. He just wished his father could keep doing what he did that one time when he showed up really clean in nice clothes. Unfortunately, the last two times Jesse and his mom had seen him, he'd been wearing soot-covered work clothes and his stained green jacket.

"Are you ready, Jesse?" his mother called from somewhere in the living room or kitchen.

Glancing one last time to be sure everything looked good, Jesse nodded and opened his door.

"Ready for my 'spection, Mom."

She was wearing her white and pink waitress outfit when she came into the room. Jesse could tell how much she loved him, because even though she pretended to be stern for these weekly 'spections, she always had a tiny smile at the corners of her lips. It was hard to fail when your mom was proud of you no matter how bad you did. Even so, Jesse wanted things to go smoothly so she would be in a good mood when his dad arrived.

"Um, Jess," she said, her hands on her narrow hips, "I seem to remember someone having their toast and juice in here this morning."

Jesse held his breath.

109

"Well?"

"Maybe that was yesterday," Jesse suggested, wishing he could spin excuses as fast as his friend Storm, who had once told their teacher he only pushed Karen Cushman because he had to go to the bathroom really bad and hadn't seen her. Everyone in class, including Karen, knew it was because he had a crush on her. But the story worked, and the teacher never told Storm's father.

"No, maybe it was this morning," his mother said. "And I don't remember you putting those dishes in the sink." Her tiny smile had disappeared. "So, where are they?"

Jesse stared at the floor.

"Come on, Jesse. I have to finish getting ready, and your father will be here any minute."

"Sometimes things fall off the bureau," he muttered.

"So, they're under the bureau?" she said, her voice stern. "I doubt a glass would fit under there."

"Maybe my drawer was open when—"

"Jesse!" She pulled his top drawer open. "Do you want your clothes all full of bugs?"

"I picked up my dirty socks," he said, trying to change the subject. Of course, he didn't add they were inside his pillowcase along with yesterday's T-shirt.

His mother pulled out both the plate and the cup and placed them on the bureau. Then she started pulling out socks and underwear to shake them out.

"I'll be the only mother in preschool who sends her kid to school with crumbs all over his clothes."

Jesse wanted to say that Taylor Spence had mustard stains all over his jacket and pants the day before, but the look on his mother's face suggested the time for excuses had passed. He was still studying her frustrated expression when her eyes widened, and she pulled his piggy bank out of the back corner of his drawer.

"What's this doing in—" She hefted the plastic pig then shook it. "Where'd your money go?"

Jesse's face flushed. He knew if there was ever a time to come up with a good story, this was it. If his mother learned what had really happened to his savings, the 'speriment would come to a crashing halt. They would never be a family again!

Storm would have known what to say—that was it! His friend would provide the solution.

"I loaned some money to Storm to…to buy a video game. It was one with green bugs and…lots of flying…bat things. He-he's going to pay me back."

His mother pried the bottom off the bank and poured a few pennies into her hand then peered inside.

"One dollar and six cents," she said. "That's all you have left!"

Jesse wiped both eyes and stared at the hem of his mother's skirt. He could see a small bruise on her knee that he guessed might have come from trying to hold the laundromat door open while carrying two baskets at a time. He couldn't think of anything more to say.

The door buzzer rang.

"You and I are going to have a long talk about this, Jesse," she said. She closed his drawer and swapped the bank for the plate and glass on his bureau. "But it's going to have to wait. Right now, I have to get to work."

Jesse trudged out into the kitchen and heard his father coming up the stairs. Something didn't sound right, and for the briefest moment he feared the man named Doyle might have returned, but then Jesse realized his father must have been sick again. From the sound of it, he was staggering from side to side more than moving upward.

"What's going on with you, Wagner?" his mother called out as she threw open the door. She fell silent.

Jesse moved into the doorway where he could also see.

"Hey…, B-Babe," his father croaked from where he leaned against the wall halfway down the stairs. Even with the distance between them, Jesse could smell alcohol mixed with strong body odor. From the looks of his snarled, greasy hair his father hadn't taken a shower since they'd last seen him a week or so before.

"So, what am I supposed to do now, Wagner?" his mother snapped. "You show up—like this—and leave me without a babysitter. Why am I even trying!"

Jesse immediately knew that their 'speriment was in serious trouble. Having to do something, he raced down the stairs to help his father the rest of the way up.

"That's my Jess—"

"Eauuuuuuuuuuuu!" Vomit spewed everywhere.

Jesse felt the hot acid splashing against the side of his face, on his neck and down his shirt. He tried to block it, but his father's next explosion projected onto the top of his head. Jesse opened his mouth to scream and got some in his mouth. Suddenly, his little body revolted and gagged. Though he hated that feeling, his stomach clenched and sent his breakfast up through his throat. Unable to stop it, Jesse puked onto his father's pants, his father's shoes and his father's much larger puddle of puke.

"Awww, gross," his father gasped, then slid down to sit on the slime-coated stairs.

Jesse fought the tears. His throat burned and the taste of bile made his stomach feel like puking some more. Confused, he saw his father chuckling as his large vomit-covered hand try to wipe some of the mess from Jesse's cheek.

Almost as though she had flown down the stairs, his mother suddenly appeared and batted his father's filthy hand away.

"Are you okay, Jesse?" she cooed, wiping his face and hair with her pink apron.

Jesse could see her glaring at his father, who had a silly grin pasted across his face. Fearing that might have been the final straw for his father, Jesse opened his mouth to say he wasn't sick anymore, but instead of words another heave of vomit shot up his throat and splashed onto his mother's bright white shoes.

Jesse burst into tears.

No matter how hard he tried, everything kept getting ruined. How come other kids got to have a normal family but—Jesse wanted to scream.

"It's okay, baby," his mother said. "Sometimes people get sick."

"But you and Dad…the 'speriment." Jesse choked and spit out more of the burning vomit.

His father intermittently laughed and gagged as his mother lead Jesse up the stairs and hustled him into the bathroom. Sitting him on the closed toilet seat, she quickly washed the worst of the foul-smelling stomach acids off from his skin, hair and clothes. She took an extra few seconds to kiss his cheeks and wipe the tears from his eyes.

"Will you be okay for a few minutes while I go help your dad?"

Jesse tried to quell the sobs that he knew weren't helping anything. He wiped his eyes and nodded.

"Can Dad stay until he feels better?"

His mom stared at him for a few seconds, brushed fingers through his wet hair and nodded.

It took her quite a bit of time to help his dad up the stairs. Jesse was already feeling better, so he moved out of the way when she led his father into the bathroom, opened the shower curtain and turned the water on.

"I didn't mean to cause all the mess up," his father mumbled as she pushed him, clothes and all, into the streams of water.

"Wagner, you know Jesse loves you more than anything in the world. Would it really be so hard to pull yourself together for him?"

"I've been trying, Babe, but Harry's been havin' a lot of late work for me—"

"And I suppose Harry also makes you drink while you're working?"

"It's not like that," Jesse's father said, "but it's not easy like you think either."

"I'm sure it's not, Wagner. Too bad you didn't have it easy like I do—working every possible minute just to pay the rent and buy a little food, all so my husband can forget to pitch in because he has to party seven nights a week."

"I gave some money last week."

"Twenty-five dollars doesn't even pay the electric bill, Wagner."

"I could give you my whole paycheck again if I lived here."

Jesse held his breath. A few minutes before, he would have sworn the 'speriment was over, but maybe his father was putting things back on track.

"It smells like vomit in here," his mother announced. She looked down at her clothing and shoes then glanced at Jesse who was leaning in the doorway.

"Want to give me a hand, Baby Boy?" she asked. There was something playful about her tone.

"Me?"

"Yes, Little Handsome, you. Come here for a minute. Maybe you could sit here with your dad for a minute while I go change."

Uncertain why but feeling as though she wasn't being entirely honest, Jesse approached slowly. Suddenly, she grabbed him into a big hug and started tickling him like crazy. The next thing he knew she passed him over to his father in the shower. His mother followed him in.

"Got you," his father announced, tickling him in the most sensitive spot, under the arms. Jesse was soon gasping for breath between gales of laughter as the three of them danced and hugged and played underneath the warm water.

When the playfulness died down, Jesse's mother shampooed his hair and announced it was time for him to go get some dry clothes on.

"Your dad and I need to talk," she said.

Immediately recognizing her serious inflection, Jesse got out of the shower. Of course, his mother had known he would try to eavesdrop, so she opened the shower curtain and watched to make sure he closed the bathroom door behind him as he went to his room. By the time he had changed into a pair of too-long brown pants and a T-shirt with a ripped shoulder, he heard his mother go from the bathroom to her room. He couldn't be sure but thought she had been crying. He must have been mistaken, however, because when he opened his door a few minutes later, he saw her return to the bathroom with a change of clothes for his father. She wasn't smiling but didn't seem upset either.

After they were all cleaned and changed, Jesse's mother and father both went down to clean the hallway stairs. Still, Jesse wasn't sure if everything was okay or if the 'speriment was over, so he snuck to the top of the stairs and tried to hear if his mother sounded happy or sad when she spoke to his dad. Unfortunately, all he heard were faint whispers.

What was going on?

As soon as he heard his mother coming back up, Jesse scrambled backwards and innocently grabbed a chair to pull over to the sink. He was just climbing up to get a glass when his mother asked him the best question he'd ever heard.

"Do you think your father should sleep over tonight?"

Jesse's face broke into a huge grin. Before he could even say "yes" his mother scooped him up into her arms and squeezed him tight.

"I like it when you're happy," she said, setting him down on the floor.

"Dad! Dad!"

Jesse raced toward the door to tell his father the good news and almost ran face-first into the pail of warm water his parents had been using to clean the stairs. It reeked of disinfectant and bile.

"Looks like someone has heard the news," his father said with a grin.

"Can we play videogames in the morning?" Jesse asked excitedly. "And make pancakes for Mom?"

"Sure," his father said, as he pushed his way past to dump the dirty water in the toilet.

"How come videogames come before my pancakes?" his mother asked in good humor. "Aren't I more important than those silly games?"

Jesse was trying to figure out how to explain that she usually slept later than he and his dad, when his father came up from behind her and put his arms around her waist. He tried snuggling against her ear, but she pulled free.

"You still smell like vodka."

"But that's going to stop," he said, "just like we talked about."

"And you're on the couch until you can keep that promise," his mother said.

Jesse was screaming for joy inside. It sounded to him like his dad was moving back home.

"I really have to stay on the couch all night?" his father asked.

"Unless you prefer the hallway," his mother warned.

"Can I sleep on the couch, too?" Jesse blurted out.

Both his parents grinned.

"Yes," his mother said, "but only for tonight. You and your father are not going to be roughhousing late on school nights."

"We wouldn't dream of that, would we?" Jesse's father said, dragging him into the living room and pitching him butt-first onto the couch.

Jesse bounced back up and tipped onto his side. He thought his father was going to bounce him again but instead he jumped onto the other end of the couch, laid down and tried to use Jesse as a footstool. Trapped, he started giggling, but not just because he couldn't figure a way to get free of his father's heavy legs; it was also because they were finally a becoming a real family again. Jesse had wanted that for so long he almost couldn't believe it was happening.

"Wagner," his mother said, her voice sounding strict like it did sometimes, "we need to talk to our son about this." Jesse held his breath because in her hands, his mother held up his piggy bank. "Jesse loaned his money to a friend at school so he could buy a videogame."

His father got to his feet abruptly.

"Babe, I—Jesse didn't do that. He gave the money to me because I asked him to."

Jesse could see his mother's hand shaking and her eyes tearing up. He didn't think his dad should have been admitting any of this. Just when it looked like everything was fixed.

"You took our son's money…and asked him to lie to me about it?" She shook the piggy bank, to which the pennies obviously had not yet been returned and covered her eyes with her free hand. "You took money from your five-year-old son…what, so you could drink, or god knows what else?"

"No," Jesse's father said. "I took his money so I could buy gas."

"No!" she said. "I'm tired of you lying to me. You have a job, you make money, and you haven't been paying any of the bills around here. Why should Jesse have to come up with gas for your truck?"

Jesse's father sat down and buried his face in his hands.

"I'm really sorry, Karen. Harry was good enough to give me an advance a few times when I spent money on just what you think I did. But I swear, when Jesse gave me the money, it was one of those weeks that I had to pay Harry back."

"Wagner, you make this so hard."

Suddenly, there was a loud crash as something slammed into one of the living room windows. An explosion of glass shattered inward and a red brick struck the floor and flipped twice before it lay still on the dark green carpet.

"Largess," someone yelled up from the street. "It's time you squared up with me!"

"Get down!" Jesse's father warned Jesse and his mother.

She grabbed Jesse and pulled him out into the kitchen.

"Who is that and what does he want?" she hissed.

"It's not—I promised not to lie to you," Jesse's father said, moving carefully over to the broken window. He kept his head down. "So please don't ask."

"So, what are you going to do about that raunchy shit you sold me?" the same man yelled.

"I'll make it up to you, Shamus," Jesse's dad said loudly. He looked ready to peer out the window, which Jesse didn't think was a good idea. What if the man threw something else?

"I've already asked my supplier," his father said.

"S'good to hear," the man yelled back, "because next time it won't be just your truck."

Jesse's father chanced a look out the window.

"Holy shit!" he yelled. "My truck's on fire. Call 911. My truck is on fire! No, don't call! I'll deal with it. I'll—"

"Yes, my husband's truck is on fire," Jesse's mother screamed into the phone. "They also threw a brick through my living room window. Please hurry. It's the corner of Pembrook and Tremont, in front of Tremont Laundry."

"Damn it, Karen! Damn it!"

"Is he gone?" Jesse's mother asked.

"Yeah, they're gone," his father said. He was standing in front of the window. "Do you know what you just did? I've got to get out of here. I can't stay."

"Wagner," Jesse's mother said, "the police are on their way, and I want you to tell them everything. Just tell them who the hell threw a brick through our window and torched your truck."

Already Jesse could hear dozens of sirens converging on their neighborhood. He wanted to look out the window but neither his mother nor father was in any mood to be trifled with. Jesse wasn't willing to take the chance.

"I've got to get out of here. I can't answer questions when the cops arrive. I can't."

Jesse had no idea what was going on, but it seemed obvious that at any second their family would cease to exist—again. He wanted to say something to fix things, but nothing came to mind.

"Wagner, I don't know what kind of bullshit you've gotten yourself into, but you have to talk to the police and straighten it out."

"It's not that easy, Karen."

"It is if you meant what you said. Jesse comes first, and all this other crap has to end right now. What if that brick had hit one of us? What if we had been inside your truck tonight? What if Jesse had been inside your truck?"

"But he wasn't. I have to go."

"If you leave, Wagner, it's for the last time. Jesse and I can't go through this anymore. And I won't let you get his hopes up again."

The sirens grew louder.

"Please stay, Dad," Jesse said. He started crying because he could tell from his father's frantic look that he wasn't paying any attention. "We can only be a family if you stay!"

Unable or unwilling to listen, his father stormed past Jesse and in three long strides was out the door. Red and blue lights flashed below the broken window, and a biting cold wind whipped through their living room as the sound of his panicked footsteps receded down the hallway stairs.

16

A Friend's Pain

Ricky and I hadn't spent much time together in the previous few days. One of his relatives from the Stone Age had been visiting, and it seemed they were having a few challenges with communication. I always assumed that since there was only one language used in the heavens it would be easy to talk with anyone. However, it turned out that because hominoids or pre-human people never actually had the ability to speak while alive, they tended to be mute in the heavens as well. Grandma Clara explained there are exceptions, but for the most part a Stone Age angel is usually a silent angel.

"It's hard to believe how people lived back then," Ricky told me when he finally found time to hang out. "They were like Tarzan, only for real."

"So, you've figured out how to talk with your grandmother Amber?" Of course, we both understood that I meant great-great-great grand-mother, many times over.

He nodded.

"She tries so hard to make word sounds, but she just can't."

"So, what do you do?" I asked.

"It's like playing charades," Ricky said. "She acts things out, and I try to figure out what she means. Earlier today, she told me how she once killed a saber tooth tiger!"

I was immediately riveted.

"How?"

"She jumped on its back and hit it on the head with a rock."

"You're kidding?"

"Nope. Her kids were playing near a brook, and the tiger was getting too close."

"'Guess you don't mess with a cave woman, huh?"

"Not with my grandmother Amber, you don't." He smiled.

"Is that how she died?" I asked.

He shook his head.

"No. Her mate killed her."

"Ugh! You're kidding, right?"

"No," Ricky said, "he really did kill her. But he didn't mean to. She had a fever and the tribal medicine woman told him to fetch her some

special berries. Unfortunately, he picked the wrong kind."

"That's sad."

"Yeah, but everyone dies, I suppose." Ricky's eyes had a far-off look.

"Should we talk about…you know?" I asked. I didn't want to say I was anxious to learn his secret, but it had been burning like a firebrand in my mind ever since he mentioned it.

"I really want to tell you," Ricky said focusing on me again. "But it's bad."

I glanced at his clothes. His T-shirt was completely white, and his pants were tan only up to his shins, pretty good for him.

"'Want me to ask Grandma Clara if it's safe?"

"Sure," Ricky said.

Thinking we might play for a while longer, I got to my feet but found he had already started back toward his house.

"'You heading home?" I asked.

He stopped and glanced back but seemed to be looking right through me. It was almost as though I had disappeared again. I patted my arms and cheeks. I seemed real to me.

"Are you okay?" I asked

He blinked apparently realizing I was there again. "I think so. Let me know what your grandmother thinks, okay."

"Tomorrow?"

"Sure, I'll see you tomorrow."

The next morning, I waited anxiously for Grandma Clara to arrive. She had barely walked through my back door when I blurted out the question. Her answer was pleasant but predictably cryptic.

"So, Ricky has a terrible secret," she said, repeating my question as she often did, "and you'd like to know if it would be safe for him to share his secret with you. Is that about the gist of it?'"

"Yeah, that's what I want to know."

"I'd say it was very smart of him to worry before telling you."

"And?"

"And it was also proper of you to ask me first."

"But is it safe for him to tell me?"

"That remains to be seen."

"Grandma, for once can't you just say what you mean?"

"Of course." She smiled sweetly but said nothing more. I wasn't sure, but it seemed she had just brought the craft of evasion to a whole new level.

"Please," I told her. "I need to know if it's okay for him to tell me."

Her brow furrowed and her smile faded. She nodded. "Yes, it should be safe. But you'll need to hurry."

"Hurry?"

"Ricky is leaving, Nate."

"Leaving! You mean the demon is back!"

I raced out the door so quickly that I'm not even sure my feet touched down on the porch, which in Under-Heaven was a real possibility.

"Nathaniel!" I screamed. "Nathaniel! The demon is coming! The demon is coming!"

By the time I rounded the cherub fountain, nearly every soul in Under-Heaven was staring at me. I later wondered if most knew the archangel's name or if they thought I had gone crazy and was calling out to myself. I was still screaming about demons when Ricky hurried out his door.

"Demons!" he exclaimed. His eyes darted all across the sky.

"Don't come off the porch! Not until Nathaniel arrives! Your pants are mostly white, Ricky. He'll protect you. I know he will! Somehow Grandma Clara knows you're leaving—"

His panicked look evaporated to be replaced with a smile. "It's okay, Nate," he said. "Don't worry; the demon isn't coming for me. At least, I don't think so."

"But Grandma Clara—"

"Must have heard my uncle say that I'm leaving."

"But how could he know?"

"Because I told him." Ricky paused, then said, "Nate, I've decided to go back."

"Back?"

"After spending this past week with Grandmother Amber, I've decided."

I stood on the bottom step and stared quizzically up at him.

"I don't understand."

"I never had much of a life the first time around," Ricky said. "I missed so many things. Maybe that's why it's harder for me to have fun. When my grandmother told me her saber tooth story, I realized I had never even seen a lion or a tiger. I want to."

"Ricky, I don't think there are any lions or tigers in Heaven."

"I know, Nate. That's why I'm going back to Earth. I'm going back down there…to live again."

Apparently, Ricky had gone bonkers. The demon scare had been too much for him. I struggled to find words to console and reason with him. He must have read my expression, because he gave me a sympathetic smile.

"So, no one's told you about that yet? Maybe I shouldn't either, but I'm not leaving with you thinking I got dragged off to Hell."

My head swam. Suddenly my friend sounded as cryptic as Grandma Clara, and that took some doing.

"Ricky, I don't under—"

"I'm being reincarnated, Nate. I'm going back to Earth to have a new body and a new life."

"How—I mean…is that—can you really?"

He motioned for me to join him on his swing.

"They don't tell us at first," he said. "Probably because they're afraid we'll choose to go back in hopes of seeing people or places from our old lives. But that's not how it works. The chances of getting reincarnated into the same country, forget the same family, are pretty slim, though one of my uncles said it happened to him. But even if it did happen, it wouldn't do any good because we wouldn't remember anything from our previous life. So, even if we got to see our relatives from before, we wouldn't recognize them."

"I didn't know anyone could go back."

"Neither did I until a few weeks ago."

"You think I could?"

Ricky shrugged.

"If they haven't mentioned it to you, they probably don't think you're ready to decide. But I'm pretty sure that's what you're here for— besides saving me, that is."

"I didn't save you. Nathaniel did."

Ricky chuckled. "Who would have guessed I'd have two saviors, both named Nate?"

"I'm not sure you can call an archangel by a nickname," I joked. "He might feed you to the demons."

"Seriously, Nate," Ricky said, "I think God knew what he was doing when he put us together. I needed a friend. You're the one who knocked me out of the way when the demon attacked, and you're the one who has helped me stay safe since then. I think if I'd been sent to another Under-Heaven, I'd probably be shoveling ashes and dodging pitchforks right now."

I grinned. Neither of us thought Hell was really like that, but my grin faded as I remembered the demon. Any world with them had to be bad.

"I think at some point, Nate, you're also going to have to decide if you want to go back to Earth."

My mind spun with the enormity of the concept, one that I would wrestle with for many years to come.

"Why not go to Heaven?" I asked. "You could, couldn't you?" I pulled at his T-shirt, a reminder that it had been white for a long time.

"I don't know, Nate. I'm not even sure God would let me in Heaven. After all the mistakes I've made, it's hard to say." He shrugged. "'Guess I'll never know."

"Mistakes?"

What was my friend talking about? How could an eight-year-old have made that many mistakes?

Ricky glanced to either side of his porch. There was no one nearby. I felt giddy with excitement. It looked as though he would soon share his mysterious secret.

"What did your grandmother say?" he whispered.

I got up and leaned against the rail.

"Danged if I know."

"What do you think she said?"

"I think she said that if I got here before you left, and if you wanted to tell me, and if I wanted to hear, then it would be okay. But I'm not sure." I sat back down in exasperation.

"I don't think she knows the answer," Ricky said.

"She's an angel. Of course, she knows."

Ricky shook his head.

"I don't think they know as much as we think they do, Nate. Sure, they've been around for a long time, but it seems that even God doesn't have all the answers. He lets us decide most everything for ourselves, and if you ask me, I think it's because he doesn't want to ruin anything for us."

"Ruin anything?"

"Imagine a zoo on one side of town and a carnival on the other. If both were only going to be in town for one day, how could someone else decide which one you should go to?"

I thought I understood, but his example sounded incomplete.

"Choosing between Heaven and Hell isn't the same as choosing between a carnival and the zoo."

"What if the choice is between returning to Earth or moving on to Heaven?" Ricky asked.

"Okay," I admitted. That argument was a little easier to make. "But we're talking about whether or not I should hear your story."

"Yeah, I think you need to decide whether you want to hear about the awful thing I did. Then I need to decide if I dare to tell you."

Maybe I was dense, but up until then it hadn't occurred to me that Ricky's secret was about something terrible he had done. I had more imagined it to be something terrible he knew about. Now, the entire subject took on a sinister tone. What horrible crime had my friend committed? I wasn't sure I wanted to know.

"What do you think?" Ricky asked me.

"I think I'm scared."

"That's it then," he told me. "I'll keep it to myself. It's not that important." But his shoulders sagged as he stared out at our Under-Heaven. Obviously, it was a big deal to him. For a moment I thought he was upset with me, but then I realized that he was upset with himself. He must have been deeply ashamed for what he had done, and he thought I wanted no part of his shame.

"Did you tell your family?" I asked.

He shook his head and gave an insincere smile.

"You know angels," he said. "If you talk about the past, you're really just reminding them."

"So, did you remind any of them?"

He brushed a tear away and gritted his teeth. I knew we were touching on the very heart of Ricky's color problem. I waited several long seconds, and when he didn't answer I wondered if maybe this was a wound that could only be healed by friendship. When I thought about it in those terms, there was no question what needed to be done.

"I want to know," I told him.

His cheeks relaxed, and he nodded. Ricky began at the beginning...

Ricky spun his Buck Rogers atom gun around on one finger as he stared at an older boy sleeping in the hospital bed across from him. There were four children's wards in the Chicago Hospital, ten beds per ward, but Ricky and the other boy were alone in their room. Eight other empty beds lined the walls around them. The older boy's head and both arms were wrapped in stark, white bandages. He had been sleeping soundly ever since Ricky had arrived an hour or so earlier. The bandages on Ricky's nose forced him to breathe through his mouth but he'd endured worse. At least his whole face didn't hurt anymore. Ricky aimed his gun at the older boy but didn't actually pull the trigger. He had almost lost his ray gun in the hallway. The Ward Matron warned him she'd take it away if she heard the loud whirring sound one more time.

"Whoosh, whoosh," Ricky whispered, mimicking the sound. He knew he should have been resting, but he'd been too worried to sleep. He would have felt a lot better if his father had stayed with him at the hospital. At least then he wouldn't have had to worry what he could be doing to his mother.

Though never exactly nice, his father was not violent most of the time, but at night—after the drinking started—he was a person to be feared and avoided at all costs. Most of the time, Ricky knew enough to stay clear. Once his father got ranting, Ricky often hid in his bedroom closet or under the bed; or, when his father seemed particularly loud, Ricky would climb the shelves of the bathroom closet, and crawl up though the scuttle hole into the attic. Fortunately, for both Ricky and his mother, his father did most of his drinking at local bars and at friends' houses, which only left them to worry about the time between when he got home and when he passed out. Most nights that was only a few minutes, but on a bad night it could stretch into an hour or more. A lot could happen in an hour.

Ricky touched his nose and winced.

As time went on, Ricky's father fought more and more with his mother until the fights sometimes happened even when his father was sober. About the time Ricky turned six, his mother began to develop regular bruises that she tried to hide—turtleneck collars, long sleeved shirts, and dark glasses. Ricky knew what was happening, though. He often stood by the bathroom door and listened to her soft whimpering. After particularly bad beatings, she would remain cloistered in there for large parts of the day. By the time Ricky was six and a half years old, he had committed to growing up quickly so he could protect his mother. He planned to grow muscles on top of muscles and to take boxing lessons so he could stand up to his father and keep his mother safe. It never occurred to him, no more than it did to her, that his mother should have left his father.

"Through thick and thin," Ricky had once heard her say to a friend, "marriage is sacred, and Tom and I just happen to be in one of the thicker stages right now." Apparently, that's what you called three to four beatings a week: thick.

Though Ricky was terrified of his father, he also knew that as long as he kept out of his sight for those few drunken minutes each night, he would be safe. Ricky chose to think that by not coming to look for him during his booze-induced rampages, his father was demonstrating that he actually did love him. On the few occasions he had stormed into his son's room to find the bed empty, Ricky would often hear his father chuckle and mutter things like, "Smart boy," or "It's a good thing," before he would stomp off to find his marital punching bag.

Ricky rolled onto his back and stared at the bright white tiles on the hospital ceiling. He tried to understand what he might have done differently. Earlier that night, two days after his eighth birthday, Ricky had overheard a particularly nasty fight. His mother's screams were like sirens between loud slaps and punches. Terrified that his father might actually kill her, Ricky slid down off the shelf in his closet and crept out into the living room. There he saw his father standing over his mother holding a pair of scissors like he was about to stab her.

"No!" Ricky screamed.

Without thinking, he raced across the room. He might as well have tried to topple a tree trunk as he tackled his father's thick thigh.

"Leave her alone—"

His father's huge fist struck him square in the nose.

~

He woke in the Emergency Room in time to hear his father tell the nurse he had to find a bathroom. That was his way of leaving his eight-year-old son to fend for himself.

The doctors and nurses were pleasant, and the hospital actually felt a lot safer than his home, but Ricky was worried for his mother. He needed to know she was all right. What had happened after he had been knocked out? Could his father have done something truly horrible? Is that why he had been in such a hurry to leave?

Ricky didn't sleep much that night.

Relief flooded his scrawny body when his mother arrived the next morning and settled into the seat beside his hospital bed. Her face was thickly coated with makeup and she wore a long-sleeved sweater. Ricky also noticed a spot of blood on her left ear and that she winced every time she moved her left arm.

His cheeks grew hot with anger.

His mother reached out to touch his forehead.

"I should get the nurse," she said. "I think you have a fever."

It's not a fever, he thought. I just hate him!

"It's okay, Mom. I feel alright."

"You can't tell anyone what happened," she whispered. "We need to protect our family."

Though he didn't agree with her use of the word protect, Ricky nodded. He wouldn't say anything even though he'd heard rumors that some Chicago policemen liked to give wife beaters a taste of their own medicine. One boy in third grade actually started smiling every time he heard a police siren pass the school. Coincidentally, he also no longer came to school with bruises or casts on his limbs.

The night Ricky arrived at the hospital, a nurse had said to him, "Your father says you fell down the basement stairs. Is that true?"

Ricky, of course, readily agreed. No one at the hospital could have known that their little house at the edge of the projects didn't have a basement.

Ricky spent four days in the children's ward, longer period than he suspected was normal for a broken nose. It turned out that his young male doctor insisted on having the local police inspect Ricky's home for safety issues before allowing him to be released. Ricky saw the doctor talking with a tall policeman who Ricky assumed would be in charge of the inspection. The policeman left the hospital for several hours then returned to pick Ricky up personally.

The policeman was huge. His head almost touched the ceiling of the police car, and his arms were as big around as Ricky's head. Though it seemed odd not to ride home with his own father, he was exciting to see all the buttons and levers inside the police car. The friendly officer let him turn on the flashing lights as they pulled onto the double concrete strips of his parents' driveway. His father was waiting at the door, a phony smile plastered across his face.

"Thank goodness you're back," he said. He glanced at the policeman then down at Ricky. "You'll have to be much more careful in the future, Son, won't you?"

"Why don't you go on inside, Ricky," the policeman said, his tone serious. "I'd like a few minutes alone with your father."

A thick gauze pad still on his nose, Ricky made his way quickly through the living room, past the fireplace, down the hall, and into his own room. As soon as he got his door closed, he went to the window and opened it a crack. Though he couldn't see the front entrance because of a thick lilac bush his mother had planted several years before, he could hear what was going on.

"…ever catch you hitting that boy or your wife again," the officer growled, "I will personally come over here and pound you into goulash. Do you get me, Mr. Hunter?"

Ricky's dad mumbled something.

"I don't care what you boys do to yourselves down at the rubber plant, Mr. Hunter, but when you're home you will be a gentleman."

"Of course, of course," Ricky's father said.

"I mean it!" the policeman said.

There was a violent slapping sound.

Ricky held his breath until the policeman walked back to his car and backed it out into the road. Within moments, he was out of sight. Just then, the front door slammed shut.

"Ricky, get out here!" his father yelled. "Ricky!"

Terrified but knowing the alternative was too dangerous to contemplate, Ricky trudged out into the living room.

"Yes?"

"What did you tell the doctors?" his father asked menacingly.

"Just what you said…that I got hurt when I fell down the cellar stairs."

His father's face contorted with anger.

"That's a lie and you know it!"

"I know, Dad," Ricky said, tears channeling down his cheeks. His body trembled, but he was too frightened to move. "But that's what you told them. The nurse said so. She said you told them I fell down the stairs." Ricky was crying full-fledged by this point.

"If that's all you said, then what the hell was that policeman doing here?"

"I don't know. I swear that's all I said."

"Did they ask a lot of questions after I left?"

"Not many," Ricky answered honestly.

His father scowled, an expression all the more frightening because he seemed to be sober. Ricky let his eyes fall to the floor. He knew not to walk away while under such intense scrutiny. He was thankful when his father grunted and strode into the kitchen.

"I need a goddamn aspirin and a glass of water!"

Ricky melted back into his room.

The following weeks were the most peaceful Ricky could remember. His father came home early from work every day and spent his afternoons and evenings quietly puttering around the house. He fixed things that had been broken for months or even years. For the first time in a long while they were able to flush the toilet without reaching down into the tank to pull on the chain, and the large strips of floral wallpaper in the living room were pasted back up so they no longer hung down like sagging blades of grass. His father even took the time to fix the cracked shelf in Ricky's closet, a memento of Ricky's many nights curled up on top of it.

During those six weeks, Ricky never saw a single can of beer or bottle of liquor anywhere in their house. Apparently, his father had been serious about quitting, which pleased Ricky's mother and him as much as it surprised them. After a couple of weeks, Ricky even dared to believe that their lives could be normal forever.

It's unfortunate that Ricky hadn't heard the term calm before the storm because it might have better prepared him for the events to come. His father stayed late for work one night, an excuse Ricky and his mother had both grown used to in the past but hadn't heard in quite some time. His mother always used to say that "working late" meant hanging out in a barroom filled with other people who also claimed to be working late. As they feared, when Ricky's father arrived home several hours later, he was both drunk and angry.

Ricky had already been in bed, but he crawled into the attic within moments of hearing something slam into the living room wall. Soon, the sounds of skin slapping skin and his mother's screams filled the house. He endured it as long as he could but finally crawled back down through the hole in the bathroom closet. His nose was still tender from the last time he had intervened, but nevertheless he crept toward the living room.

Like Frankenstein from the movies, his father loomed over his mother who was crouching, hand over her face, against the curio cabinet. Her lips were swollen, and blood coated her left cheek. His father held a tall drink in one hand, but the other was closed into a fist ready to strike again.

"No!" Ricky shrieked.

His father's fist crashed fiercely into the side of his mother's head anyway.

As though in a rerun of their previous battle, Ricky dove at his father's leg. Some of his father's drink splashed on Ricky. He recognized the smell of vodka, which tended to make his father even more violent than beer or whiskey.

His father pitched his glass at the nearest wall while simultaneously tearing his son off his leg. The glass shattered only a second before Ricky struck the carved wooden back of their Victorian couch. With a gasp, Ricky rolled onto the cushions and knew he'd be feeling the imprint of the wooden lion in his back for a long while.

He saw his father's fist already raised to strike his mother again. Her hands rose weakly to ward off the next blow. Not knowing what other weapon to use, Ricky darted across the living room and yanked a thin, half-burning log out of the fire. He rushed at his father.

"Leave her alone!" he screamed.

His father spun and backed away from the torch that flamed just inches from his dripping wet face; reeking of the Vodka that had splashed all over him, he father backed up until there was more than an arm's length between him and the torch.

"S'that what the poleek—poleem—cop told yer ta say?"

Ricky glanced down. His mother was slumped down against the curio cabinet, arms settled around her head. Blood dripped from her left ear onto her shoulder. He couldn't tell if she was breathing.

Dad, what did you do?

Holding the smoldering stick in front of him, Ricky eased over to her. Though he didn't remember hitting his still tender nose again, he could feel blood running from one nostril and clotting on his top lip. Grunting because of the pain in his bruised back, he bent down and gripped her hand.

"Please leave, Dad," he said, his weapon still poised between them. "If you don't, I'll call the police."

His mother moaned.

Ricky said a quick prayer of thanks. Still, her eyes hadn't opened and the blood stain on her shoulder seemed to be growing. Ricky stroked her cheek.

"Mom?"

She didn't respond.

"I have to call a doctor, Dad. You really hurt her."

"She'll be fline," his father slurred, staggering toward them, hands outstretched.

"Don't," Ricky warned, getting to his feet. He waved his torch to show he meant it.

"Look, shun. Yer mom fell and I need to help cleeg 'er up. We can take care' of 'er like a family." He nodded at Ricky and inched closer to the torch.

"She needs a doctor, Dad. I'm calling for help."

Ricky's father wobbled and backed up a step. "What kin doctrans do, anyway?" he barked. "They jus' want to get in your personal brisness!"

Many of the kids at school still didn't have a phone, but thankfully Ricky's parents had had one installed a year earlier. Ricky backed toward the large oak box that hung on the wall near the kitchen archway.

His father lunged.

Ricky jabbed the torch at him.

Sparks flew onto the carpet as the torch scraped against his father's hand. His father let out a bellow that sent a shiver of fear sweeping across Ricky's shoulder blades. Why wouldn't his father just let him make the call?

His dad grabbed at the smoking stick again.

Using the torch like a sword, Ricky yanked it back then jabbed it at his father's face. Suddenly, the Vodka from his father's blue, button-up work shirt burst into flame. In less than a second, his entire chest was enveloped in fire.

"Dad!" Ricky yelled. He dropped the torch.

His father screamed horribly and staggered toward the kitchen sink. Flames had already spread to his hair. Ricky fumbled for the phone and was thankful there were no voices on the party line. He spun the crank and held his breath until an operator came on the line.

"What number can I connect you to?" her pleasant voice asked.

His father was wetting himself down under the kitchen faucet. He seemed to have the flames out, but the burnt odor seemed smelled like a barbeque.

"This is Ricky Hunter." The words rushed out of his mouth. "Both my parents have been hurt."

"Ricky!" his father bellowed.

"Let me put you through to the police," the operator said.

"There's no time," Ricky told her. Already his father—a mass of red flesh and melted tufts of soggy hair—was rushing at him.

"We're at 88 Maple Bend Drive!" Ricky screamed before he dropped the receiver. It fell in an arc and slammed against the wall.

"You little bastard!" his father roared. The pain from his burns seemed to have sobered him up some.

Ricky jumped back, his eyes darting in search of his flaming weapon. By that time, black smoke was swirling up from the overstuffed green chair where he had thoughtlessly dropped the torch. The chemical smell of burning foam was even worse than the stench from his father's scorched hair and skin. Ricky lunged and snatched the torch up. He slapped at the smoldering cushion but had to stop to fend off his father who looked ready to attack.

Having no choice, Ricky abandoned the burning chair and backed toward his mother. His torch now smelled more like chemicals than wood. They had to get out of the house. He knelt and tried to shake his mother awake.

She didn't respond.

Fear held his throat like a clamp. Had his father killed her? Using his free hand, Ricky grabbed her wrist and tried to drag her toward the front door.

By this time, the green chair had burst into full flame. It gave out great gouts of oily black smoke. His father paid it absolutely no attention as he staggered toward his son and wife.

"Little bastard!" he bellowed and surged at Ricky.

Horrified, Ricky dropped his mother's arm and stood upright. His father's face was mostly bright red but a black spot under his right eye looked like a flame-charred hot dog. Two melted clumps of hair hugged his scalded red forehead like fungus. His shirt hung in black tatters with bits of undershirt and skin showing through.

"I'll twist your friggin little neck!"

Fearing his father would kill both of them if he could, Ricky didn't dare to leave his mother's side. By then, fire had begun to climb the purple-flowered wallpaper.

"Mom, wake up! Wake up!" Ricky shook her but still she didn't respond.

Ricky's father lunged and tried to grab him.

Dodging backwards, toward the center of the living room, Ricky knew he had to keep his father's attention away from his mother.

"You burned me, you little Nazi prick. You think you can run this family? You think you're the boss now?" His father grabbed for him again.

Ricky ducked around the back of the couch, which sat at an angle in the corner of the room to allow space for the Victrola cabinet behind it. The Victrola hadn't worked in years, but his parents had kept the old music machine because it had been a gift from Grandmother Hunter. Ricky could feel the machine's large iron horn press painfully against his bruised back as he slid across the narrow space between it and the couch. On the opposite wall, flames were crawling up toward the ceiling. Dark smoke billowed out from that section of the living room in great, curdled black and brown knots. It wouldn't be long before the entire room was thick with it.

Mom, wake up. Please wake up!

Ricky didn't dare to call aloud for him mother for fear his father would remember where she was and hurt her again.

"You did this to us!" His father hissed. "You burned me. You want to ruin this family!"

"Dad, please stop," Ricky pleaded.

His father looked more like a demon than a man as he spread his arms and rushed at Ricky. Ricky shoved the heavy couch away from the wall, making himself a few more inches of room to dart either way. He coughed. The smoke burned his eyes and throat.

"It's all because of you!" his father roared and dove at him.

Ricky threw himself sideways and down, just in time. His father's body crashed into the couch, and if it hadn't been for the old Victrola, Ricky would have been crushed behind it. He crawled along the wall on his stomach. There was less smoke there, but it felt like he was breathing straight from a school bus exhaust pipe.

A hand snaked over the couch and raked his back, but he was able to scramble underneath the Victrola legs and out the other side. Somewhere along the way he had lost his torch.

By then the smoke was so thick it was hard to see and near impossible to breathe. Knowing his father might grab him at any moment, but realizing that if he and his mother didn't escape soon they probably never would, Ricky dropped to his knees and gasped for whatever breathable air he could find. His lungs burned like charcoals as he crawled toward his mother. At any second he expected his father's strong hands to grab him from above. He crawled faster.

His mother hadn't moved at all, and she wasn't coughing when he reached her side. He heard the blare of sirens pulling up to their house. His breath came in hot, heavy gasps. He kept his face as close to the floor as possible and reached out to take his mother's hand.

"The police are here," Ricky whispered.

"Get away from her!" his father screamed.

Ricky flipped onto his back just in time to see a dark boot dropping toward his face. He pivoted to the side and felt a searing pain as the hard sole scraped along his ear.

Flashing lights were barely visible through the thick smoke. Ricky could hear men barking orders just outside. The pain in his ear was nothing compared to the burning in his throat and lungs.

"No!" his father screamed, lurching toward the front door. "Stay out! It's my house!"

Someone pounded on the door, but Ricky imagined his father was leaning against it to keep them out. The smoke had grown so dense that Ricky couldn't see his mother who was just inches away. He brushed his palm against her sticky cheek. He couldn't hear her breathing.

Please be alive. Please!

Coughing and gasping for breath, Ricky rolled her so that her nose was closer to the floor, but even at that level, there was scant anything left to breathe. They needed fresh air. The sounds of crackling fire was all around them now. Ricky gasped, his lungs trying to pull something other than death from the inky blackness around them.

"Get away from the door!" someone yelled.

Suddenly, there was a crash. Ricky sucked in through his nose in a desperate struggle to find oxygen, but only cloying smoke filled his lungs.

"We're coming in!" a gravelly, deep voice shouted.

But it was too late, because Ricky's thoughts had already turned as black as the smoke-filled room...

"That's how I did it, Nate," Ricky finished. "That's how I killed my parents."

"How could you have known?" I countered softly. "Besides, you tried everything you could. You were trying to keep your mother safe."

Tears streaked Ricky's cheeks.

"If I had stayed out of it, maybe they'd both still be alive. If I hadn't used that torch, the fire never would have started."

"Ricky, I think you were brave and right in what you tried to do." I wanted to add that his father was a cruel brute, just like the men who had killed my family, and that Ricky had no choice. But I knew he didn't need to hear that. How would I have felt if someone spoke of my father that way? Instead I reached out and placed my hand on his knee.

"I'm sorry that happened to you, Ricky."

"I'm the one who's sorry." He wiped tears from his red eyes.

"No, I'm really sorry," I said. "I'm probably even sorrier than you."

He stared at me. "What're you sorry for?"

"For being friends with such a crybaby." I grinned

His mood broken, he leapt on top of me and caught me in a headlock. I broke free and vaulted over his porch railing to escape. He dove on me like a hawk on a hare. We rolled in the grass until he had tickled me into submission three separate times.

"Under-Heaven champ!" he exclaimed as I struggled to catch my breath between fits of laughter.

What a vision he was—arms high, smile wide—standing there above me. Though a dark secret had been brought into the open on our last day together, it was his triumphant smile that stayed with me. We parted shortly after that, friends forever.

I never saw him again.

17

Decisions and the Damned

My second year in Under-Heaven seemed to pass in a whirlwind, though there were a few things probably worth mentioning, like the day that a teenaged boy arrived. He appeared several houses down from me with two red stains on his shirt. I was afraid I knew what that meant, and my Uncle Albert confirmed my fears.

"You mean he was murdered twice?" I asked.

My Uncle Albert nodded. "It can happen. Sometimes people are reincarnated, and things don't go any better the second time around."

I'd been thinking a lot about reincarnation since Ricky had left, and that was just one more horrifying reason I couldn't do it. The truth was that I longed for life. I longed for another dog and to be warmed by the sunlight and to feel a cool ocean breeze. My mouth still watered at the thought of strawberry shortcake or even a stack of raspberry pancakes with maple syrup. No one ate in the heavens, and I wasn't supposed to miss food, but I did. Feelings like that seemed to grow stronger every day. I had been in Under-Heaven for over a year, and yet I felt a connection to life that I just couldn't shake. Maybe I had been too young when I died; maybe that's why I didn't really feel dead.

But what was the alternative? How could I seriously consider returning to Earth when someone comes along with not one, but two bloodstains on his shirt? How revolting it was to think that I could have my head twisted off in one life and maybe get it shot off in the next. No, I would never take such a crazy risk! No matter how badly I yearned for life, the horror of my last few moments made it impossible to return, but at the same time I couldn't picture myself in Heaven. So, unable to go up or down, there I was, tethered to Under-Heaven as surely as if I had been chained there.

I crossed the immaculate Under-Heaven grass and knocked on the door of the newest house. Standing there, I felt like one of the women who showed up at our house the first day we moved to Coldwell, Maine. I remembered they had given us lobster salad, egg salad, and three pies. Cynically, I wondered if the husbands of those same women had been the ones who killed my family.

"Hello," the new boy said as he opened his door. He looked to be in his late-teens and had longer hair than any boy I'd ever seen. My eyes quickly fell, however, to the two angry red stains, one on his shoulder and another on his stomach, which marred his otherwise sparkling white clothing.

"I was going to come talk to you," he said, "but my great, great something or other told me you preferred to keep to yourself." He shook his head. "So now angels lie. This place just gets weirder and weirder."

"Normally, I don't talk to the—"

I paused because I had been about to say, "the dead," a term I used to describe anyone who had been in Under-Heaven for less than two weeks, which meant basically everyone. Other than Ricky and myself, I had never seen anyone stay for more than a month, and most souls lasted less than a week. Anyway, I didn't think a newcomer would appreciate being called dead.

"I keep to myself a lot," I said.

"You're the one who's been here so long, huh?" he said, his expression neutral.

"Yeah," I said, "guess I am."

He gave me a small, crooked smile.

"How do you like it here?" he asked.

I shrugged.

"I haven't decided. Guess that's why I'm still here."

"'Don't know whether to go up or down, huh?" The crooked smile came out again.

"It depends on which down you mean," I answered. "I'm not inclined to join the barbecued bunch. I know that much."

That earned me a full-fledged grin.

"Let me guess," he said. "You don't know whether to take use of your reincarnation card or to move on to Heaven."

"I guess that's pretty much it."

"You hoping I can help you decide?"

"Not exactly," I answered. I shuffled my white sneakers across his porch.

"I'm going back," he told me. "I want another shot at getting old."

"Can you?" I asked.

"I'm not entirely clear on all the rules up here," he answered, "but my great, great angel thinks it would be okay for me to do it again. I think anyone can go back. I suspect even the angels could if they wanted to."

"Even the angels?"

He nodded. "It's just a guess, but one of the angels hinted at it the last time I was here. Apparently, they would never want to, though. I guess it's only newcomers that want to go back, and mostly it's just the kids."

"Why kids?"

"I'm not sure, but I think it's hard to grow up in the heavens. There isn't enough stimulus, I suspect."

I thought how mostly uneventful my last year had been and knew he was right.

"Do you remember both lives?" I asked. I didn't want to be rude, but that was the main reason I'd decided to talk with him. "I understand if you don't want to talk about it, though."

"No, it's fine. I don't mind. My first life is the one that I remember most right now, which seems strange since I died that first time over fifteen years ago. The second life feels more like a dream. It's almost like I was sitting inside the head of another person. I have my memories, but then I have his, too. They seem completely separate."

"So, you feel like two different people?"

"Not exactly. It feels like the second person was added on. It's almost like I borrowed that second body, but the first one was mine."

I shook my head. "I can't believe you're willing to go back and do it again."

"I know it sounds crazy," he said, "but I love Earth and I love life. Someday, I might be ready for Heaven, but right now I feel like I have things to finish down there."

"Aren't you worried it could happen again?" I pointed at his two stains. Consciously or otherwise, I had just identified my own single-largest fear.

"Obviously, it could happen again." He grabbed his shirt with two fingers and pulled it out so that he could see both red stains. "I'm hoping it won't, though."

"I don't think I could go through that again," I told him somberly. "I've had a long time to think about it, and I just don't think I could."

"That's okay," he said. "Go on to Heaven. You've got the color for it."

I shrugged. "Maybe I will."

"Want to play a quick game of tag?"

I laughed.

"You bet." It had been quite a while since I'd had anyone to play tag with. "My name's, Nate."

"Nate, I'm Jeremy and YOU'RE IT!" He tagged me and raced off the porch and onto the grass.

I never thought to ask him if Jeremy was the name from his first life or his second. I'll never know because by the next morning he was gone.

Though all houses in Under-Heaven look pretty much the same, it turns out that under certain circumstances, a house can be expanded—downward, to be exact. I learned that the day my Uncle Finneus arrived. At first, I thought I had imagined it, but then I heard knocking sounds a second time. It wasn't coming from either my front or back door.

"Grandma?" I said.

We were sitting across from each other in the living room. For a moment, she looked as baffled as I felt, but then she nodded and pursed her lips.

"This should be interesting," she said.

Mystified, both by the knocking that seemed to be coming from my kitchen and by her comment, I got up to investigate. She followed.

"Open your basement door, Nate," she said. "Whoever is down there can't come up unless you allow it."

"But I don't have a basement door."

"You do now," she said.

The pounding had grown louder and more insistent.

Together, my grandmother and I crept more than walked into the kitchen. A wood grain door now adorned what used to be a blank hallway wall.

"Go ahead," Grandma Clara said. "Let's see which member of the family has managed this little feat." She motioned with her chin.

Hesitantly, I turned the knob and eased the door open.

A smartly dressed man with a curled mustache and a formal suit stepped energetically into my kitchen. He was tall and, all the way from his shoes to his top hat, garbed entirely in black. Maybe I had been in Under-Heaven too long, but that much black nearly hurt my eyes. His shoes were polished to a brilliant sheen, and his suit looked so neatly pressed that I imagined he must never dare to sit down. His hat had a flat top like I remembered seeing on a circus poster once. He was what my mother might have referred to as a "dandy." He removed his hat and bowed, revealing immaculately combed and greased-back, dark hair with a perfect part running down the center. His mustache was trim and looked to be curled with wax at the edges.

"You must be, Nathaniel," he said popping his hat back atop his head and extending a hand. I glanced to my grandmother. She nodded. I shook his hand.

"I'm Finneus T. Buckland, previous of Earth-fame, known as the inventor and distributor of Buckland's Amazing Bottled Tonic, the finest medicine known to man—up until that time, of course." He tipped his hat and bowed again with a flourish.

"Still haven't got that foolishness out of your head, have you, Finneus?" Grandma Clara said.

"Well, well," he said. He eyed her up and down. "It certainly is less than pleasant to see you here, Clara."

She gave him one of my favorite warm smiles.

"Pleasant or not, you old cur, get over here and give me a hug."

He did as instructed but made a face toward me as he dramatically extricated himself from her grip.

"I came to meet my nephew, not to frolic with haggard old angels," he said, turning his attention back toward me. "How are you, Young Fellow?"

"Fine," I said. I could sense there was something very different about him, at least very different from anyone else here in my Under-Heaven. "Are you from Hell?" I asked. It was an uncharacteristically bold statement for me, but something I would find happening more and more as my exposure to my uncle grew.

He laughed a deep and cheerful belly laugh.

"We like to think of it as the other Heaven," he said.

Grandma Clara was grinning like a young girl. I wondered at the connection. Did angels fraternize with the damned?

"You know each other?" I asked.

"He's my grandfather," answered Grandma Clara.

"Correction," Uncle Finneus said. "I was your favorite grandfather."

"Since my other grandfather was dead before I was born, you were my only grandfather."

"That, notwithstanding," Uncle Finneus said, raising his chin in mock indignity, "I was still your favorite grandfather, was I not?"

"You haven't changed an ounce," she said to him. "I'm going to go now, but don't you warp my grandson too much, you hear."

"Now, Clara. You know all the warping comes from above. We folk down below keep things in a much better perspective."

For a brief moment, I was terrified. Even if it weren't for the man's dark color and origin, how could she leave me with a complete stranger like that? I opened my mouth to object, but she spoke first.

"You'll be okay with him," she said, "but keep your eyes open, Nate." Grandma Clara winked at Uncle Finneus. "He's a slippery old coot, and a bit more dangerous than most, given that he's so likeable." She flashed a goodbye smile at Uncle Finneus, and then faded away. I was a little shocked. Other than the one time when I had been sick, she had always used the back door.

My surprise at her exit must have shown because Uncle Finneus said, "Don't fret that none, Young Fella. She was likely just showing off a bit for my benefit."

"Can you fade, too?" I asked.

"Doesn't matter much," he said. "Crawl and skulk is what they'll tell you I do best, and they wouldn't be entirely untrue about that, either."

"Why do you say you're my Uncle if you're Grandma Clara's grandfather? Wouldn't that make you my great, great—"

"Save all the greats, Young Man," he interrupted. "I prefer the term Uncle and that's what we'll be sticking with. Grandfathers are old and withered fellows—two things I am not. I'm currently in the youth of my death, and I shall not have you labeling me otherwise. Are we clear on that?"

"Yes, Uncle Finneus," I said with a grin. How could anyone not have liked this man?

It appeared that, through some unknown-to-me challenges, Uncle Finneus had fought his way up to my Under-Heaven. Grandma Clara explained later that, just like the angels, the damned had access to their family members in the under-heavens. But, over the last few hundred years, Hell had grown so violent that none of its residents had actually succeeded in getting past the other souls in a lineage. As a result, it had been centuries since any of the fallen had actually been to an under-heaven. Grandma Clara thought it was a combination of my lengthy stay and Uncle Finneus' cunning that made his unusual visit possible. She made it clear, though, that he was in Under-Heaven by my sufferance alone. I could banish him back to Hell at any time I chose.

That was a bit of knowledge I would one day find quite handy.

Where Grandma Clara had seemed amused by Uncle Finneus' presence, my other relatives ranged somewhere between shocked and scandalized. My Aunt Alice was solidly in the scandalized camp. She wanted no part of him and would have preferred that I had no part of him either. I allowed them to be in the same room only twice, but both times color shot into my shoes and halfway up my pants before I was able to separate them. Uncle Finneus must have realized how important my consent was to his status in Under-Heaven, because with only a simple discussion he readily promised to stay in the basement when any of the angels were upstairs—the only exceptions being unless I called or unless it was Grandma Clara.

I found it especially fun when both Grandma Clara and Uncle Finneus were together. They were like a couple of bantering old friends. They would talk and tell stories together for hours. Most of the time I was there during the conversations, but sometimes they spent time alone. Grandma Clara once said, "If an angel can't be safe with someone like Uncle Finneus, who can?"

That's what made it all the more confusing when, a few months later, Grandma Clara said she would be away for a while and that Aunt Alice would be taking over her teaching duties. A few days later, Uncle Albert assured me that everything was all right, but he admitted that Grandma Clara was feeling troubled about her interactions with Uncle Finneus.

Grandma Clara remained aloof for almost a year. I considered sending Uncle Finneus back to Hell several times during those twelve months, but each time he would charm me into believing that I needed him right where he was. By the time I realized he was manipulating me, I found myself wanting his company as much as I wanted to be with any of the angels. My color remained pure when I thought this, so it seemed my decision was a good one. Still, I missed my Grandma Clara.

At least once and sometimes several times a day, I would visit the fountain and spend time with my sister. It had been nearly three years since our separation. Though I doubted she had any recollection of our parents or me, she was constantly in my thoughts and in my sight for at least a few minutes every day.

One particular morning, I smoothed the water and saw the familiar lights that represented the life forces of thousands of people. As always, my sister's light sparkled like a diamond among marbles. I zoomed in to find her in the middle of an argument with a blond boy who looked to be about five or six years old. He wore brown knickers buttoned at the knee, and his plaid, short-sleeved shirt with buttons fastened about halfway up, revealed a white undershirt in the wide V of his collar. His face was an angry shade of red as he stood on the brick walkway at the bottom of my aunt and uncle's front stairs.

I watched him shake one fist at Vicky, a motion that might have been more threatening if it hadn't been for the Lone Ranger doll he held tightly in that same fist. In his other hand he held a second doll, this one dressed in buckskins. I guessed that doll to be Tonto. The boy looked ready to charge up the stairs at her, but he didn't.

Curious to know what was going on, I let myself settle into Vicky's mind, something that I had only recently become comfortable with. Suddenly, I could see and hear through her eyes and ears. I had become her unseen and unfelt passenger.

Vicky was sitting on the porch, her feet flat on the top step. A dozen paper dolls with colorful outfits stood all around her, supported by their paper stands. She picked up one curly-haired blond doll by two fingers and held it up so the boy could see.

"Shirley Temple doesn't play with boys," Vicky said. "She's a doll, and dolls are only for girls!"

Though settling into someone's mind doesn't allow you to read their thoughts, you are able to sense their feelings. Right then, Vicky's mood was one of disgust. She seemed to have very strong opinions about this young man and his desire to play dolls with her.

"My parents let me play with them," the boy said. "They gave me these for Christmas." He held up both of his dolls.

"No, Carl. I'll play tag or hopscotch with you. But not dolls!"

I sensed her satisfaction as she made the last statement and wondered when she had formed such strong sentiments about the issue. Vicky carefully stood Shirley Temple back on her stand.

"I don't want to play with you anymore!" Carl said, and with that he pressed both of his western dolls into one hand and pointed fiercely at Vicky with the other. Then he marched to the sidewalk and into the neighboring yard.

"I don't like sissy boys anyway!" Vicky yelled as she watched him stomp up the stone steps of the house next door.

Carl never looked back as he went inside and slammed the door.

I was stunned. I had never seen Vicky so angry before. What made it worse was that I felt she was wrong. I used to play with plastic soldiers, which were just like dolls. And I remember desperately wanting a Flash Gordon doll, which my parents had never been able to afford. Whiskey and I had even used Vicky's dolls on a few occasions to have outdoor adventures. Though I knew kids tended to get over things easily, it pained me to think my sister could have ruined a friendship over something so trivial. I didn't know it at the time, but that event was an early sign of Vicky's attraction to aggressive men, a preference that would one day have terrible consequences.

I stayed with her for a while longer as she played alone with her paper dolls, but her mood seemed somber and unhappy. Saddened by the visit, I backed away until only the light of her life force was visible. I paused for a moment...but then tapped the water and even that view disappeared.

~

To reincarnate or not to reincarnate, that was the question I faced every day in my Under-Heaven. I had been there for nearly five years by the time my sister turned seven back on Earth. In her features I could see a resemblance to my mother, which often brought back related memories of my dog Whiskey running through the woods, and my father sailing the Miss Kane out through the morning harbor. I didn't know if I would ever be able to put myself through that kind of loss again, but a part of me longed to try.

As I looked down at my sister's sleeping form one night, I realized how much she had grown while I hadn't changed in appearance at all. It's true that I had gained a lot of knowledge during my five years in Under-Heaven, but my body remained that of a nine-year-old boy. Soon, Vicky would be physically larger than I was, and she would be moving on to experience her teen and ultimately her adult years.

I envied her that.

As I stared at her nighttime hair, mussed and tangled against her pillowcase, I sensed that one-day I would go back to Earth and experience all of the things I had missed. There is no way I could have known, however, the terrible price I would pay for that decision.

18

Realizations

Jesse stood with the fingers of his yellow, SpongeBob SquarePants gloves entwined in the cyclone fence. The fence surrounded his kindergarten's schoolyard. Out on the sidewalk, his father blew faint clouds of breath into his bare hands and rubbed them vigorously. He was dressed in the same stained, green jacket and black corduroys with a hole in one knee that Jesse had seen him in the last few times he'd stopped by the schoolyard. What had happened to the rest of his clothes, Jesse didn't know.

Glancing behind him, Jesse could see his best friend Heath playing with Storm and some of the other boys on the yellow, plastic slide in the center of the playground. Jesse wanted to run back and join them, but he knew his father would be mad. Besides, talking to his dad was important, too. He turned back to the fence.

"Your mom and me will get back together again," his father said. "You just wait and see."

Jesse nodded, but he no longer believed his father. Since the night the 'speriment had ended, his mother hadn't let his father come over or spend any time with Jesse. She said it was "too dangerous." Jesse had even heard her threaten to call the police if his father tried to see Jesse at the laundromat after school.

No, everything was different now, Jesse thought sadly.

"I'm going to talk to her again," his father said. "Okay, Jess?"

Jesse remained silent as he stared at his father's hands. Dark scabs covered the knuckles on one hand, and both hands were splotched with grime. The ends of his fingernails were black. If Jesse had ever let his hands get that dirty, he knew his mother would have soaked him in the tub for hours, lecturing and scrubbing the entire time. It was a good thing she couldn't see his father now.

"Are you listening to me, Jess?"

Jesse raised his head and looked into his father's eyes. There was still love in those eyes, but Jesse sensed there was panic, too. His father seemed scared that they would never be a family again. Jesse had the same fear. He wished that his mother didn't feel as strongly as she did.

Though his father had let someone throw a brick through their window and had also let his truck get burned up, at least he never hit his family. Some of the kids in school got hit a lot by their parents.

"Maybe we could go see a movie on Saturday, Jess. What do you think of that?"

His father sniffled, and Jesse could see a small spot of blood forming below his nose. A dirty hand wiped at it and smeared it into the dark stubble of his upper lip. He must have noticed the similar smudge on his hand, because he hid it behind his back. He casually brushed the other hand under his nostril, but the red stain had already frozen into his whiskers.

Jesse overhead his mother once say his father's nose bled so much because of "nose candy," and Jesse knew that was one of the original reasons she made him move out. Several times Jesse had tried to put candy up his own nose, but his nose wasn't very good at tasting. After a while he always had to take it out and eat it the old-fashioned way. Jesse gave up on nose candy after a few tries. Maybe his father should have done the same.

"I'm going to go now, Jess," his father said, "but I'll be back to see you soon, okay?"

"Okay, Dad."

Jesse watched as his father crossed the street and walked rapidly down the sidewalk. He kept watching until his dingy, green jacket was no longer visible. Sadly, Jesse turned to look at Heath. His friend was at the top of the slide and shoving the other boys down as they climbed up the plastic chute. Joining them no longer seemed fun because Jesse realized that since his father no longer had his green, Toyota truck he might not have any place to sleep.

Like the blood that had run from his father's nose, tears began to seep from Jesse's young eyes. He would talk to his mom again. He would beg. He would plead. She probably wouldn't give in, but he had to try. With the temperatures freezing cold outside, Jesse was terrified for his father. He turned away from the King of the Mountain game and faced toward the street. He didn't want the other kindergarten kids to see him cry.

After all, he was a big boy now.

≈ ~ ≈

"Why don't you come down and see what I've done to the place, Nate?" Uncle Finneus said to me. In the four years we had lived together, it had never occurred to me to even look down into his basement. One reason, I suppose, is that I imagined it would look like a substation of Hell, someplace I never wanted to visit. But the more likely reason was that, no matter what time of day or night it was, whenever I needed my uncle and would knock on his basement door, he would step right out as though he had been coming up at that very moment anyway. We were just finishing up a game of chess late in the evening when he made the offer.

Now, don't ask me where my uncle got the chessboard or any of the other items he dragged into my home on a regular basis. I had spent my first year in Under-Heaven without so much as a baseball, and I had never thought of or wanted one either. It was true that my angels occasionally brought items to facilitate lessons, like the cards that Grandma Clara had used during my very first lesson, but Uncle Finneus was of a completely different mindset. He always seemed to need something and would say, "I'll be right back." Within seconds he would return with all manner of toys, appliances and tools. But I never let him leave anything upstairs. I couldn't imagine the horrified look I would get from my Aunt Alice if she ever saw, for instance, a stamp collection. Coincidentally, Uncle Finneus had a pretty impressive one he'd shown me a few weeks before.

You might have thought that my uncle was trying to turn me toward the underworld, but actually the opposite seemed to be true. Though Uncle Finneus wouldn't have known how to keep me on the pure path, he always made sure someone did. The moment he saw color creep up any further than the cuff of my pant legs, he would call for Uncle Albert or Grandma Clara, who was now making daily visits to my Under-Heaven again, apparently having resolved any issues she had about cavorting with her underworld relative. Uncle Finneus had once said to my Uncle Albert that he was "...happy to be away from that unpleasantness down below, and by helping my boy up here I'm helping myself, as well." The last part I found particularly believable, if Uncle Finneus was nothing else, he was definitely the king of self-interest.

"So, what do you say, Young Fellow?" Uncle Finneus asked again. "Are you ready to see what I've done with my meager space?"

I smiled and nodded. "Sure, why not."

"By the way, that's game one hundred and thirty-seven in my favor," he said as he placed the last crystal knight in his ornate, folding wooden chess case. "You have yet to win your first."

He was so smug in his win that I had to smile. Though likeable, he was as poor of a winner as he was a sore loser; we used to play checkers a lot until I started to win a few games. I hadn't seen a checkers game in months.

With his chess set tucked snuggly under his arm, Uncle Finneus strode down into his home. I followed. The basement stairs were brightly lit and covered with a plush, red carpet. An unusual spicy scent in the air grew stronger as we descended what seemed like the equivalent of five flights of stairs. Finally, the narrow stairway opened out into an immense, cavernous space.

If an archangel had grabbed my finger and spit in my face, I wouldn't have been any more surprised than I was at the sight of my Uncle's underground home, if anything that enormous could be called a home. Somehow larger than my entire Under-Heaven neighborhood, his space could only be described as palatial. The area immediately around us looked like a king's ballroom. Crystal chandeliers hung from the forty-foot high ceilings. Elegant wood tables and chairs with ornately carved arms and legs were placed strategically throughout the seemingly endless, carpeted floor. There were stuffed couches and chairs with lavish pillows and overelaborate cloth coverings. Paintings twice my height hung from the walls and impressive statues were interspersed amid the exquisite furniture.

We continued down the last dozen stairs to the carpeted floor. Several hundred feet from us, the furniture and carpet ended, turning instead into open space and grass. Judging from the half-dozen white flags I saw, it looked to be a golf course. Distantly, off to my left, I could also see a bowling alley and a large merry-go-round.

"Modest but comfortable," Uncle Finneus said.

I looked up and expected to see a mocking grin on his face, but there was none. He had been serious.

"You could at least have added a pool and a Ferris wheel," I quipped.

He nodded in earnest. "Both fine ideas, young Nathaniel. I will take them into consideration. Come, let me show you around."

If anything, my initial impression of the size and splendor fell far short of the reality of the world my uncle had by some means built directly beneath my feet. It was as though I was walking through one of the grand castles of the Russian Czars my Aunt Alice had described, though I suspected this was on an even larger scale. For an instant, I thought Aunt Alice would appreciate what I was seeing, but I immediately dismissed the thought. I couldn't imagine there was anything about Uncle Finneus that she would find of interest. Other than having similar formal manners, they were as different as two souls could be.

We ended the tour at the far side of my uncle's lavish domain in an area covered with more toys than I had ever seen or imagined. There were toy cars, trucks and airplanes. Molded armies were lined up on half a dozen tables. Two electric trains circled each other on a large platform that was made with space in the middle for two people to stand and control them. One wall was lined with bats, and balls and baseball gloves. There were at least a dozen basketballs. I didn't dare ask where one could use those balls, because I assumed, I would be led directly to a basketball court. What my uncle had created down here defied explanation or belief.

"You can come down here and enjoy these toys anytime you like," my uncle announced proudly. He handed me a Flash Gordon doll, just like the one I had seen in the comic ads and had wanted for so long. I accepted the doll and nodded, but my smile was insincere. Something seemed wrong about all of this, something that I couldn't put my finger on but was, nonetheless, there. I looked over the toys for as long as seemed polite but then pled fatigue and the need for sleep. Together we made the long walk back to the stairway. My uncle led the way up.

"I hope you'll visit me down here often," he said.

Though we were to spend many more years together in my Under-Heaven, it was a visit that I never did repeat. I'm sure my uncle must have found the Flash Gordon doll where I left it on the bottommost stair.

19

Troubled souls

Though Ricky had been gone from Under-Heaven for nearly seven years, I still remembered his grandmother from the Stone Age. So, it was with great surprise that I greeted her at my own door one day. My Uncle Albert, of course, accompanied her. I couldn't imagine what Ricky's grandmother Amber was doing with him.

"I believe you've met," my uncle said.

"Hi," I said, though I knew from Ricky's previous experience that she wouldn't understand me. "I extended my hand to shake hers and hoped she would comprehend the gesture.

She ignored my hand and moved closer to hug me. I returned the hug and was struck by how different it felt. My grandmother Clara embraced me on a regular basis, and I had been hugged by hundreds of aunts, uncles, grandmothers and grandfathers. But to be in the arms

of Amber was like cuddling with a lioness. I felt an overwhelming affection coming from her, but more than that I felt totally safe. Her emotions seemed instinctive and pure, and in that regard, she reminded me of Whiskey. I savored the feeling.

"I know you have met," Uncle Albert said, "but I don't believe you knew at the time that Amber is also your grandmother," he paused, "…removed by tens of thousands of years, of course."

"How?" I asked. "Nobody told Ricky and me that we were related."

"You should know, Nate, from all of your lessons with Clara, that if you trace a family back far enough, everyone is related. It all goes back to that first couple." He didn't say Adam and Eve. One of the first things you learn in the heavens is that the discussion of religion is no longer relevant. It quickly becomes apparent that all Earthly religions are based on the same truths, and that mankind's botched interpretations created most of the religious strife throughout history. For Uncle Albert to give names to the first couple would have been to dishonor the names that other sects might have used. And as far as God was concerned, all labels were true.

"But we are related?"

Uncle Albert shrugged. "Yes, but so distantly the point is moot. You're just as related to nearly everyone else back on Earth."

Just then, I heard Uncle Finneus knock from inside his basement door.

"Come on in," I said, but the wide-eyed look of shock on Uncle Albert's face made me immediately regret it. I didn't know what the matter might be, because my two uncles had always gotten along quite well. Uncle Albert had even beaten Uncle Finneus at a game of chess a few months back.

For better or for worse, Uncle Finneus stepped out into the room.

Amber snarled, pushed me backward and inserted herself between Uncle Finneus and me. Her knees were bent into a crouch and her fingers were extended like claws. Though I couldn't see her eyes, the growl from deep in her throat told me everything I needed to know.

"Uncle Finneus," I said loudly, "now is not a good time. Please go back downstairs!"

I need not have bothered, however, because my voice was directed at the back of his black jacket. He was descending the first stair by the time I finished my sentence.

"Civilized people would know enough to keep savage beasts caged," I heard him quip just before his door slammed shut.

And so, it became normal that during the visits of yet another of my relatives, Uncle Finneus would make himself scarce. It seemed that less than a quarter of my family could tolerate him, which baffled me because, all his faults aside, I genuinely like the man.

Aunt Amber turned out to be one of the more interesting of my relatives and I, like my friend Ricky, found myself gravitating more and more toward returning to life because of her. There was something in Aunt Amber's primitive psyche that seemed completely rooted in those things physical. When around her, I wanted nothing more than to wrestle, to run and to jump. With her, physical communication extended to physical activity. We would romp and play outside for hours whenever she visited. It wasn't long before she became one of my favorite and regular visitors. I suppose that shouldn't have been surprising given that she was my only Aunt who knew how to give a decent headlock.

~

Vicky had grown into a beautiful young girl. By the time she was ten, every boy in fifth grade would turn just to watch her walk by. For her part, she tended to ignore most of them, only tossing her hair and giggling for the benefit of the most troublesome boys. It seemed that the more often a boy was sent to the principal's office, the happier she was to talk with him. I didn't understand her attraction to darker characters, but it became increasingly obvious that with bad boys is where her affections lay.

Whether it was in mimicry of the boys she socialized with, I didn't know, but one day I viewed Vicky in what would soon become a common scene at my aunt's house. She had just returned home from school and wore a beautiful white skirt with an embroidered poodle on the left side, its embroidered leash extending over toward her right hip. Her pale, yellow blouse was partly hidden by a turquoise sweater draped across her shoulders like a cape. A small chain with pink stones held the sweater in place. I'd once heard Vicky refer to the white suede shoes she wore as "White Bucks." Her white anklet socks extended only an inch above the shoes. The outfit was adorable, but the angry set of her face detracted from it.

She hurried across the glossy, black- and red-checkered kitchen floor to stand behind my Aunt Donna. I could only see the back of my slender aunt's blue dress because she was leaning into the refrigerator. In a moment, she came out with two green, glass dishes and sat them on the counter. She wore a frilly, white apron over her dress. As she closed the refrigerator door, I realized that sometime since I'd last seen the room, the refrigerator had gone from white to pink. A pink stove, too, had replaced the previous white one.

Vicky said something to my aunt.

I saw my aunt shake her head and mouth the words, "I'm sorry, but no."

Vicky stomped her White Bucks angrily and began yelling. I settled into her to find out what was going on.

"I'm going roller-skating, Aunt Donna," my sister said, "whether you like it or not!" She started to leave the room.

"Please come back," Aunt Donna said in a carefully modulated voice.

My sister spun to glare at her.

"What's gotten into you, Vicky? Lately, you've been picking a lot of fights. Is something the matter?"

"You don't care about me. You and Uncle Bert just think I'm in the way!"

"We love you, Vicky." My Aunt Donna's eyes were crinkled in concern. "What happened to your family was horrible, and your uncle and I are so very sorry for that. I miss your mother and the others, too, but it hurts our feelings when you say we don't love you."

"Well, you don't." Vicky turned and left the room.

"Vicky, come back. Vicky!"

But my sister kept walking and slammed the door to her room. She was still crying when I backed out and returned to my Under-Heaven. It pained me to know that there was nothing I could do.

≈ ~ ≈

It had been almost two weeks since Jesse had last seen his father. Every day, he had watched snow and ice build up outside the ledge of his third-story bedroom window. Now, standing on his tippy toes to see over the snow, he watched people come and go along the slush-filled streets below and imagined his father was shivering somewhere nearby. Jesse had pleaded several times with his mother, but she insisted that it was too dangerous for his father to live with them. Jesse knew it had more to do with the burned truck than the nose-candy, but both seemed to be part of the issue. Lately, he came to realize that the problems were never likely to be fixed.

It was almost his bedtime when Jesse heard the security buzzer. Moving close to his door, he held his breath and listened. He couldn't understand the intercom's static but did hear his mother's response.

"I told you, Wagner, you can't stay here. Call the police. I'm sure they'll give you a place to sleep."

Jesse was crestfallen. Would it have been so hard for her to say yes? What harm would it do to let his father in, at least until it grew warm enough to be outside again? How could his mother be so cruel? Suddenly, Jesse had an idea. In his five-year-old mind, a plan had formed. It wasn't perfect or fully thought out, but Jesse didn't want to think of his dad sleeping in the snow anymore.

"Mom!" he said, racing out into the kitchen. "Mom, I want to say hi to Dad!"

He was thankful she was in jeans and a T-shirt. She would never have said "yes" if she had not been dressed. Her finger was near but not on the intercom button. Jesse could hear his father trying to say something, but the speaker crackled too much for him to make it out.

"Hold on a second, Wagner," his mother said. "Jesse wants to say hello, but then you need to get off my front stairs. Okay?"

"Hi, Hero," his father's voice crackled. "Are you being good?" Jesse thought he heard cold tremors in his father's voice.

"Dad, can you come up and tuck me in?" He knew he was putting his mother on the spot.

"I'm not sure your mom wants me to, Jess." Either his father's voice was growing clearer or Jesse was getting better at understanding the static. He turned his best sad eyes up toward his mother. He blinked twice but couldn't quite make tears come. It was working though. He could see her struggling with the decision.

"It's late, Jesse."

"He's my dad…." Jesse let his voice drift off but never took his eyes from hers.

"Jesse, we shouldn't."

Jesse knew he almost had her. He didn't dare to say anything more for fear he might break the spell.

"You promise to go right to sleep after?"

Jesse nodded solemnly, but inside he was cheering wildly. The first part of his plan was working. His mother pressed the intercom button.

"You can come up, Wagner, but only for a minute. You have to leave again right after that, okay? No hassles?"

"Okay."

"You're a stinker," she said reaching down and stroking Jesse's hair.

Jesse willed his lips to stay closed and his face to remain neutral. He was afraid that any wrong expression might ruin everything. He knew if they could just talk, his father would know what to do next.

"Why don't you get into your jammies," she said to him.

"Can I wait for Dad first?" he pleaded. He didn't want to take a chance that unsupervised they would get into a fight with each other.

His mother tousled his hair again. "Okay, but Dad's only staying for a minute, you understand. No video games, no snacks. He's just tucking you in and leaving."

"I know," Jesse said in his most innocent voice. This was one night he intended to follow his mother's instructions perfectly.

His father knocked, and Jesse intentionally put himself between his mother and the door. He figured he had to block her view of his father's dirty hands. His mother pulled the chain lock, and Jesse turned the bar in the center of the knob from sideways to straight up and down. His father had taught him to pretend the bar in the lock was like a big stick. Sideways, you could not get through, but up and down you could walk right in. It was one of the best things his father had ever taught him.

Jesse opened the door. His father's hair was snarled, and his face was red from the cold. Jesse guessed he didn't even have a hat anymore. Now that he knew where to look, Jesse could see a faint smudge of red below his father's nose. Hopefully his mother wouldn't notice.

His father's eyes didn't drop to Jesse's level. Instead, they stared straight at his mother's face.

"Hi, Babe."

"I'm not your babe anymore," she snapped, backing away from him. "You look like hell."

Before his father had time to say anything further, Jesse grabbed both his hands and tugged him into the apartment. His father's fingers were cold and felt scaly, and if anything, they were dirtier than before.

"Dad's going to help me brush my teeth," Jesse said. Without waiting for an answer, he pulled his father through the kitchen and down the hall.

"Right to bed after that," she called after them.

His father's hands were so cold they were almost painful to touch. It was like dragging a big ice cube around, Jesse thought, as he led his dad into the bathroom. Gently, he closed the door.

"Dad," he whispered, "I want us to make a plan so you can sleep here with me every night."

"Jess," his father said. "Your mother already said 'no.' I tried."

Jesse turned on the sink water and waited for the water to turn lukewarm. Whenever his hands got cold at the playground, hot water made them hurt, so he figured the same would be true for his father.

"You have to wash up good," Jesse said. He pointed to his father's grimy hands. "If you leave them like that she'll make you leave."

His father smiled weakly. Jesse suspected he hadn't slept much lately. Maybe he didn't dare to fall asleep when it was so cold. He also noticed that his father was still wearing the same clothes he'd seen him in for the last few weeks. It looked as though things weren't going well for him at all, which made Jesse even more committed to helping. As his dad cleaned his hands, a chore that required a scrub brush from under the sink, Jesse retrieved the comb and hairbrush from the windowsill and a washcloth from the closet.

"Face and everything," he insisted. Oddly, his father did as he was told. Somewhere along the way the child had become the parent. Jesse had a mouthful of toothpaste when his mother called to them.

"Everything okay in there? It's been a while."

Jesse spit into the sink in preparation to answer, but his father got to it first.

"No problem, Babe," he said. "I was just cleaning up a little, while Jess did his teeth."

"Good thing," Jesse heard his mother mutter through the door.

Jesse studied his father's face in the mirror. He looked cleaner, but the skin on his face was red and peeling in places. Jesse hoped it wasn't a frost bite. He didn't really know what frosts looked like, but he knew they lived out in the cold. Storm said a frost bit his brother the previous winter, and the doctor had to cut off one of his toes because it turned black.

Jesse tried not to think of his father's peeling skin as he whispered, "I know how you can sneak back in, Dad...."

≈ ~ ≈

I often found myself dreaming about my life back on Earth. One night, the dream was a familiar one: Whiskey and I were hiking along the hills that sloped down into the old mica mines behind Staber's Golf Course. The hillside was steep and treeless. I grasped small bushes and shrubs to balance myself as we made our way down the gravel slope. Whiskey, sure-footed as ever, pranced happily along below me. Though I feared I might slide and roll at any moment, he seemed to have no concerns at all.

By the time we reached the quartz and granite plateau that most of the kids in Coldwell would jump from in the summer, I was ready for a rest. Though the August air was surprisingly cool, even for Maine, I was hot from our hike. Together, Whiskey and I stared down at a perfectly round pool below. I had heard the shaft that formed the small pond was over a hundred feet deep and that at the bottom there was an excavating machine that had been caught in a sudden flood. Some of the kids at school also said there were at least two stolen cars down there. I didn't know if any of that was true, but I'd once seen several Coldwell teenagers leap from my dangerously high perch and dive as deep as their breath would allow in hopes of seeing the tip of the excavating machine. When they resurfaced with huge gasps, I learned that none had succeeded. According to them, no one ever had.

Whiskey laid his head on my lap. With summer vacation coming to a close, we were trying to enjoy as much time together as possible. That's why we stayed later than usual.

I should have known better.

When we began the return climb, the temperature had dropped from cool to cold, and the shadows had grown long and dark, making it difficult to see proper handholds and footholds. My poor decision to stay late had turned a challenging but relatively safe climb into a perilous chore. We had ascended about three quarters of the way when I slipped on a granite shelf and started to slide backwards. I grabbed for the nearest shrub.

It came out, roots and all.

I scrabbled at the mostly bare slope but there was nothing to hold onto.

"Whiskey!" I screamed. I rolled onto my butt and tried to dig my heels into the crumbling slope. It was like scrabbling in breakfast cereal. The edge of the narrow plateau rushed up at me. There was nothing I could do. I couldn't stop myself!

At any second I knew I would hit the narrow ledge and pitch headfirst over the cliff and into the cold water. I'd once heard that falling from a second-floor window into water would hurt almost as much as landing on concrete. The mica mine cliff was higher than a second-floor window!

It's true I had seen those teenagers leap from the same cliff and live, but they had been older and had jumped feet-first. Who knew how I would land? It would be a spectacular belly flop for all I knew. I grasped for another bush, but the leaves ripped off in my fingers.

"Whiskey!"

Terrified I might be the first person to see the bottom of the flooded mine shaft, I kicked and scrabbled wildly. It was no use. Soon, a dead boy would sink past the excavator and maybe land on a stolen car.

Suddenly, a blur rushed down my left side and plunged beneath my feet. My sneakers struck soft, furry flesh—flesh that miraculously had come to a stop!

Whiskey had done it. He had saved me…

When I woke from that dream for the umpteenth time, I remembered every detail of that harrowing day, including how my dog had come only inches from the edge of the cliff side when he brought us both safely to a stop. Whiskey hadn't given a single thought to his own safety that day, or any day. When it came to protecting me and my family, he never hesitated. Not even at the very end.

I desperately missed my dog, my best friend. I missed my parents, too, but at least they still existed. Though they were still working through their Purgatories, someday I knew we would be reunited. But when Whiskey gave his life to defend my family, he had given up everything.

My Whiskey was gone forever.

20

Dominoes Begin to Fall

For the third night in a row, Jesse woke to the muffled buzzing of his Aladdin alarm clock. He gave his stuffed, blue dog a hug, then rolled out of bed and crept over to the closet door he had left open earlier. He reached down under the mass of clothes, some clean, some dirty, and groped until he could feel the blue Genie's arm. He pushed it down. The buzzer stopped. Jesse held his breath and listened for any sound that might indicate his mother had heard it.

Nothing.

Good. He was safe. He grabbed his Star Wars sword, which was really just a flashlight, and crept out into the living room. Jesse climbed up onto couch and pushed the window curtain back so that he could look down at the dimly lit street below. A light snow was falling. The plan, which had been mostly his, was that at midnight his dad would wait across the street until Jesse blinked his flashlight twice before going into the kitchen to push the button that would unlock the security door. Jesse would have preferred they sleep together in his room, but his dad had said it would be better if he stayed in the basement where at least he could stay out of the cold and weather without making his mother mad.

For the third night in a row, however, Jesse saw no one on the sidewalk. His dad never showed up on any of the planned nights. Jesse felt as though he had somehow failed. Maybe he had misunderstood the time, or maybe he'd missed something his father had said. Whatever the reason, their plan wasn't working.

Had his father found a different place to sleep?

Jesse doubted it as he stared at the snow and ice piles that lined the sidewalks. In his gut he knew his father was in trouble. An image of his dad frozen inside a block of ice came to his young mind, but he pushed it away.

Just as he'd done the last two nights, Jesse committed himself to staying awake. After all, sleep didn't seem that important when your dad might be freezing to death outside. Jesse perched up on the back of the couch with his feet on the arm and forced his eyes to stay open.

He knew if he fell asleep and his mother caught him in the living room, his chances of ever helping his father would be ruined. Ages later, when exhaustion finally forced him back to his own bed, he thought, Dad will be here tomorrow. I know he will.

He hugged his stuffed dog and fell into a troubled sleep.

≈ ~ ≈

It's surprising how fast the years can go by, and if it weren't for my nightly visits with Vicky, I might not have even been aware of the time that passed. It seemed as though overnight she jumped from a pretty, elementary school girl to a full-fledged, beautiful woman. It was apparent that the boys around her thought so, too, because I could scarcely view her during waking hours when there wasn't one guy or another fawning over her.

One night, I zoomed in to find her with a boy who wore a faded, blue jean jacket with the collar turned up. I immediately didn't like him or the fact that he looked several years older than her. They were sitting in the front seat of a small, sleek car that I later learned was a Ford Fairlane. The boy, probably nineteen or twenty years old all but forced himself on her, and worse: my sister seemed to be enjoying it! Disgusted with their steamy kisses, I backed away but at the last minute caught sight of something shiny in his back pocket. I spun my view and my breath caught. It was the handle grip of a gun. What would he need with a gun?

As I withdrew and returned to Under-Heaven, my head was filled with concern.

~

If I had been surprised by the appearance of the young man with two red stains on his shirt, imagine how I felt when an elderly man appeared in my Under-Heaven with seven individual, red stains on his white suit jacket. He was the epitome of all my fears and proof they were well founded. If I went back to Earth, I might be murdered again. Of course, moving on to Heaven was always an option, but as Uncle Finneus often said, "I still had too much dirt under my fingernails to give up on Earth just yet."

As I stared at the man and his stains, I was fascinated and revolted at the same time. If I didn't want to spend eternity in Under-Heaven, I would someday need to make a decision, but how could I risk everything by going back down there again? Maybe a talk with this man would help. Having grown out of my childhood shyness, I approached the elderly, multi-murder victim who was sitting on the stairs of his house. His pure white shoes and clothing contrasted boldly with the red blotches that covered his jacket like sauce from a spaghetti food fight.

He nodded at the stain on my right shoulder.

"Guess I got you beat, huh?" he said.

I smiled weakly and swallowed. His red stains swam like danger signs before my eyes. Visions of the violent lobstermen who murdered my family threatened to overtake my courage. I steeled myself because I knew I had to find out as much as I could before this man moved on to Heaven. He was thin, almost gaunt. I suspected he had been sickly at the time of his murder.

"Scary stuff, huh?" he said, pointing a thumb at his jacket. His nonchalant smile suggested the stains on his coat were of no more interest to him than what he'd had for breakfast.

"How'd it happen?" I asked, feeling shyer than I had in years.

"Which one?" he said casually.

I found his tranquil manner baffling. How could someone have been murdered seven times and not think it was a big deal? I'd only been through it once, and the experience had left me in such a turmoil that I had become a legend of indecision in Under-Heaven.

After a long delay, I said, "What about the last time?"

He shrugged and shook his head. "I not sure yet."

I wasn't surprised by his lack of memory. The boy with the two stains said the last life took a while to recall. What I couldn't fathom was this man's calm demeanor.

"You don't seem upset? After seven times, I would've thought...."
My voice trailed off.

He shifted his position and gave a quiet laugh.

"Not as much flesh on these old bones as there used to be," he said. "I think I'll bring a cushion from the couch out here next time."

Filled with apprehension, I tried to shake the feeling that I was speaking with a ghost, which was ironic given that I was as much of a ghost as he was. Nevertheless, I had all I could do keep from spinning around and running for the safety of my own home.

The old fellow reached a gaunt hand out to me. I shivered and backed just out of his reach. I didn't want to chance attaching myself to the bad luck or any curse that might have followed this seven-time victim. Maybe one of the Salem witches had cast an evil spell his way before she burned. To a living person my theory might have sounded spectacular, but from where I stood it seemed perfectly plausible: if there could be demons and archangels, why not witches? And, considering how many times this man had been murdered, he might actually have been alive during those witch trials.

"I don't remember my last life very well just yet," he said, gently returning his hand to his own side. "It takes a while for new memories to settle into your original soul."

"I've heard that before," I said, "but aren't they your memories?"

He nodded. "Sure, but it always takes a while for them to be internalized."

"Why don't they internalize during the years of your life?"

"It's an interesting thought," he agreed, "but it doesn't work that way. While on Earth we have no memory of our past lives. It's only up here that we have a chance to think about it."

Something about what he said sounded essential to me. Maybe this was the very information I needed to make my final decision to move on to Heaven. I asked another question.

"So, when you get reincarnated, you're not you anymore?"

The old man dropped his head. From this angle, his wispy, thin hair barely covered his scalp. If there had been flies in Under-Heaven, I could easily have seen one trying to hide anywhere on his head. He looked back up.

"Your first life is mostly who you are as a soul," he said. "All the other lives feel like strangers at first, but over time those strangers become friends. I've absorbed my first three lives pretty well. I assume in another few decades I will absorb the others, too."

"But right now, you don't remember your last life?"

"Oh, I remember it, but not as well as I will."

"How can you not remember how you died?" My morbid curiosity fueled the terror in my own head. Suddenly the man's red stains became prominent again. I desperately wanted to bolt away but forced myself to stay…and learn

"The first death is always the hardest." He gave a reassuring smile. "I was an old man, as you see me now, when it happened the first time. It's not easy to let go of that first life. Thinking of that arrow in my stomach still makes me uncomfortable."

"You were killed by Native Americans?" When I was alive everyone called them Indians, but the term had changed over the years, and my grandmother had taught me that a group of people deserved the respect of being called whatever they wished.

"Yes, a wonderful nation of people. It's unfortunate that they were so ill-treated by the Europeans who took over."

"You like them, even after they murdered you?"

"Of course. Besides, I deserved it."

"What did you do?"

"I stole corn seeds."

"You were killed over seeds?"

"Back then, seeds could have meant the difference between life and death. The Indian tribes used to move around from region to region, and many of them would plant crops in a field so that they would have something to eat when they came back to a particular area. By stealing their seeds, I could have forced a famine on their families."

I nodded. It did sound serious when he put it that way.

"I'm pretty sure I was shot this last time," he said.

I was almost afraid to ask, but I did.

"By who?"

If he had said by a lobsterman, I'm certain I would have fainted; instead he said, "I'm not sure yet, but I think it was my brother or sister."

"So how long before you think you'll leave for Heaven?" I asked.

"Who says I'm going to Heaven?"

I let my eyes roam up and down his white suite and sparkling white shoes again. Maybe there was something about Heaven and Hell I didn't yet understand. Lord knew the angels didn't specialize in straightforward answers—and my Uncle Finneus: let's just say he wasn't exactly facile with the truth.

"You look too white to go to Hell," I said.

"You're probably right about that," he said with a chuckle, "but I wasn't thinking of going to Hell. I'm going back to Earth."

"But you've been murdered a lot already," I blurted out.

The chuckle subsided, but the old man still retained his smile.

"True enough," he said, "but I like it down there." He nodded his head. It seemed as if he was already plotting his next life. He squirmed and rubbed at his lower back. After a few seconds of silence said, "If you'll excuse me, I think I'll go rest on that comfortable couch in my living room. It was pleasant speaking with you, though."

I thanked him as he eased up onto his frail legs and went inside. My head swirled with confusion. How could anyone endure as much trauma as he had, and yet still be willing to go back for more? Though my quandary remained, I think a tiny seed of understanding began to grow that day. Deep in thought, I returned home.

"Was talking to him a good idea?" Grandma Clara asked.

"I'm not sure," I answered honestly, settling onto my couch.

Seven stains swam like barracudas through my mind.

≈ ~ ≈

It was on the fifth night when Jesse's father finally showed up. The moon was out, and Jesse could see him standing on the sidewalk three stories below. Something was wrong, though. There were two other people with him: one much larger, probably another man; the other smaller and standing with a slouch; possibly a woman. Jesse felt his heart sink because he knew he couldn't let two strangers into their building.

Hoping his father hadn't seen him, Jesse ducked behind the curtain. His little palm rubbed back and forth across the grip of his Light-saber flashlight. He didn't want to let his father down, but he also knew how his dad's friends could be. Twice in the past, parties with people like that had nearly gotten their entire family thrown out of their apartment. Though he didn't want his father sleeping in the cold, Jesse couldn't allow his loud and sometimes violent friends inside with him.

He just couldn't.

Jesse pulled the curtain back a tiny bit and peeked outside again. All three people were looking up toward the window. Maybe they didn't all want to come inside. Maybe his father's two friends were only keeping his dad company until the door was opened.

He had no way to know.

Jesse wondered if he should wait to see if his father's two friends disappeared, but as soon as he thought of it, he knew the answer: the others could easily hide someplace where he couldn't see them. His father might even have more friends waiting near the door. Jesse didn't want to imagine what kinds of problems it would cause if he let a whole bunch of nose-candy people inside.

That would be bad.

He took one last brief glance out at his dad and his two friends and then—though it broke his heart—five-year-old Jesse let the curtain fall into place for the last time and trudged back to his room. His young mind held no conscious memory of past lives or of heavens stacked upon heavens. Instead it was filled with love for his father and a deep sense of guilt for abandoning him on a frigid, wintery night. Miserable, he crawled into bed and snuggled into the neck of his stuffed dog. Streetlights reflected off the frost that had crawled up the outside of his bedroom window like a disease.

≈ ~ ≈

I wouldn't have missed Vicky's high school graduation for all the pleasantness in Under-Heaven. Each time I had settled into her mind over the last few weeks, she seemed to be filled with excitement and nervousness for the occasion. I had also witnessed half a dozen fights between her and my aunt and uncle. It seemed that the main point of contention between them was Kevin, her latest boyfriend. He was a high school dropout in his early twenties who never seemed to work but always had a surplus of cash. His hair was long, nearly shoulder length, and he wore a black leather jacket even on the warmest days. He and my sister had been dating for the about six months. My sister, of course, liked him because of his rough demeanor. And my aunt and uncle disliked him for exactly the same reason—that combined with their concern over his invisible stream of money. My Uncle Bert had several times used the term "connected" to describe his suspicions.

From the fragments of events I had witnessed during the previous two weeks, I pieced together that my sister would only go to her graduation if Kevin went. My aunt and uncle were deathly against it, but finally offered a compromise: Kevin would be given a ticket to attend the outdoors high school graduation ceremony but could not sit anywhere near the family. Vicky agreed.

Though my aunt's and uncle's position might have seemed extreme, it took on a more moderate tone when you learned that Kevin had twice kept Vicky out all night and had once threatened to beat my uncle's skull in with a baseball bat if Uncle Bert ever called the cops on Kevin again. Neither my sister nor my aunt and uncle were fully happy with the final compromise, but all three accepted it.

Unfortunately, Kevin had no such inclination. My aunt and uncle had no way to know how sorry they would be for not allowing him to join them in the audience.

I was so anxious to see my sister's proud event that I sat at the edge of the fountain pool for two hours before my family arrived at the school. Grandma Clara, of course, had joined me, as had Amber who happened to be visiting that day. I knew many of our other relatives would be watching from Heaven as well.

I tried to get Uncle Finneus to watch, too, but he insisted that the sun was bad for his skin. I had seen him out of doors only twice in the fifteen years he had been living with me in Under-Heaven, and neither time was longer than a few seconds, barely long enough for his shiny black shoes to touch the grass before he hurried back inside. My Grandma Clara claimed ignorance about his aversion to the out-of-doors, but I had silently developed my own theory: I suspected that my Uncle was worried about demons. Though I knew the wretched creatures of Hell were able to go into the little white houses that largely comprised my Under-Heaven, I also knew that the archangels wouldn't have looked kindly upon a demon that barged into the house of a person with my mostly pure white color. In short, I thought that as long as Uncle Finneus was inside my house, he was safe.

Grandma Clara, Amber and I stared down into the pool as the ceremony began. We watched several teachers and school administrators get up to speak. A dozen awards were issued to various students. Then a large man in a blue suit and red tie read the students names, one at a time from a lengthy list. As each was called, the students rose and crossed the stage to shake hands with a tall blond woman in a skirt and formal jacket. Then a shorter brunette woman in a dark pant suit handed each one a rolled diploma tied with a maroon ribbon. Given that Vicky sat toward the back of the throng, and the students were being called from the front first, we had a long wait in store.

I would have settled into my sister's mind to hear what was being said, but that would have been rude to the angels beside me. In retrospect, I'm sorry that I hadn't at least taken the time to scan the crowd and the school grounds for Vicky's boyfriend. Though it wouldn't have changed anything, it might have alleviated some of our shock and surprise when he did show up.

After a long-time watching Vicky's peers accept their graduation certificates, I finally saw my sister rise and make her way to the two women at the front of the stage. Vicky was luminous as she strode across the stage, her long, brunette hair falling in soft curls from beneath her maroon cap. Though her gown was loose and identical to all the others being worn, she had a way of carrying herself that made it look more like a gown than a shapeless robe. I was breathless as she held out her hand to accept her ribbon-wrapped diploma.

Suddenly, we saw the heads of nearly every person, including Vicky, swing to the right of stage. I shifted our view just in time to see Kevin's motorcycle swerve across the grass and kick dirt up onto the people sitting in the bleachers. For a moment, it looked like he was about to skid out of control, but at the last possible moment he yanked on the handlebars and expertly brought the shiny machine to a momentary halt beside several members of the audience on the lowest seat. Like some elementary school bully, he reached out and snatched a floral hat from the head of an elderly woman before moving on. The way she jumped back and gripped at her gray locks made me suspect he had ripped several hatpins out of her hair at the same time.

By then, most of the graduating students had jumped to their feet and were jostling each other to get a better view. Caps tumbled and rolled from the stage like a maroon avalanche. The motorcycle once again kicked up clods of soil as Kevin swirled to the base of the stage, right below my sister.

He held his hand up for Vicky.

A dozen men and women, most in suits but several in faculty graduation robes, raced from various locations to converge on Kevin's motorcycle. One balding man actually got hold of a handlebar, but Kevin's fist swung so hard we could see blood explode from the man's nose as he fell to the grass. The other pursuers paused, looking from one to the other. One woman in robes dropped her eyeglasses and fell to her knees to retrieve them. For a moment, I thought the closest three men were going to attack Kevin, but a woman on the stage threw up her hands and shouted something.

Kevin waved for my sister to join him, and I was saddened to see a grin stretched across her face. She flung her cap, dropped her diploma. Then—robe still over her clothes—she slid down from the stage and hopped onto the back of his motorcycle. More chunks of turf and dirt spewed all over the would-be pursuers as the motorcycle tore away with my sister on the back.

I didn't need to look to know how Grandma Clara and Amber felt about the scene. Somber, we all turned away and went into my house.

"That Kevin's quite a fellow," my Uncle Finneus said as we came through the door. I made a special point to remain between him and Amber as we all settled into the living room. "I think she's in for some interesting times with that young whelp," he finished.

"How did you see?" I asked, suddenly realizing the obvious incongruity.

My uncle smiled.

"Let's just say there are more ways to view things below than just that silly fountain."

Amber snarled.

My uncle flinched but remained seated.

By holding them sternly in place, you could force a cat and a mouse side-by-side but let go for only a second and a grand chase would ensue. In this case, it was obvious who the cat would be if my enforced cease-fire ever gave way.

"You're not supposed to use crystal balls, you old bat," my Grandma Clara said to him. "It's against the pact."

Uncle Finneus shrugged.

"I've never been much for silly rules," he said. "If no one is supposed to look at the goings on down there, why do you people have that ridiculous fountain? And I'm sure you've got an even more elaborate system in use up above."

"We're not the ones who constantly meddle with the affairs of the living," my grandmother Clara said. "The more you fallen see of the world, however, the more you interfere."

"I resent that," Uncle Finneus exclaimed. "I haven't meddled in more than a decade."

"Ah ha, but you admit that you have meddled."

"Not much," Uncle Finneus said. He let his lower lip protrude dramatically. "Of course, I did have to deal with that Casey Edds character. Now, mind you, it's not that I regret having my fine nephew here in Under-Heaven, but what that fellow did to our family was just not kind."

I was surprised that the mention of my family's nemesis didn't send me into a bout of fear or anger. Of course, I would always retain distaste for the man, but the emotional wound had largely healed over.

"We saw you," Grandma Clara said. "It wasn't your place to punish him."

"If not I, then who?" my uncle said with a defiant pout. "That child-killer deserved no better and probably should have gotten worse."

I suddenly felt guilty at my desire to know what vengeance my uncle had exacted. It's funny, but in Under-Heaven you grow an acute sense of conscience, not just about the things you actually do and say, but also about the things you think. Even as I found myself wishing that my uncle's retribution had been sufficient, I knew that my sneakers were growing darker. Color had begun to seep up my pant cuffs by the time my uncle spoke again.

"I would have killed him," Uncle Finneus said, "but he had a pretty strong following down below, which might have made things too easy for him, so I just lopped off an arm and a foot instead."

Grandma Clara stood. "Sometimes, Finneus, you are just not fit to be around." There was no humor in her voice at that moment; she meant what she said.

Amber had also gotten to her feet. She took the momentary break in manners to express her own opinion. Faster than any living body could have moved, she lunged past me and had my uncle in a painful-looking arm lock before I even realized what had happed.

"I'm not afraid of that wretched beast," my uncle gasped as I pulled him from her powerful grip. He wasted no time getting to his stairway, however. With one foot on his stairs, he said, "Let God, not a Neanderthal, judge me on the propriety of my actions," he said as he disappeared into the cavernous home he had built below. Never mind that Amber was actually many thousands of years removed from the Neanderthals. Also, it didn't seem necessary to state the obvious: GOD had already made a decision about my uncle's propriety, and the scales had apparently not weighed well in his favor.

21

False Hope and Danger

Jesse's father was waiting at the schoolyard fence when all the children filed outside for ten o'clock recess. Jesse spotted him and wished he could somehow avoid going over there. He would be mad because Jesse had made him sleep in the cold the night before. Why couldn't his father have been alone like they had planned?

Knowing he had no choice, Jesse skirted around the monkey bars, made his way up the ladder of the slide and took a quick trip down. Finally, he went through the swings and circled around the merry-go-round. It was important that the teachers didn't see him talking to anyone, or they would have shooed his father away and made Jesse go inside. By the time Jesse reached their meeting spot, his father had moved behind the same tree he always used for cover. Jesse could see him, but almost no one else could.

His dad looked better this time. He was wearing a clean pair of brown corduroys, a fresh black T-shirt and a clean, gray jacket that he hadn't bothered to zip. Jesse was amazed because his father's face was also shaven, and his hands were clean. If he had cleaned up like this more often, maybe things between his parents would have been different.

Jesse closed off the thought. He had tried to fix things, but everything got messed up anyway. He hated it, but that was the way things had turned out.

Staring at his sparkly clean dad, he wondered what had changed.

"I stood outside your window last night, just like we planned," his father said.

"I was asleep," Jesse lied. "I stayed awake four nights, and you didn't come. I thought you found another sleeping place."

"It's okay, Jess," his father said cheerfully. "I just wanted to stop by and let you know that I'm going away for a little bit. I've got a big job planned, and I won't be seeing you for a couple of weeks."

"You're leaving?"

His father nodded.

"Yeah, but just for a little while. Today I'm driving towards someplace warm. In a couple of days, I'll be running around with no shirt on and sipping cold beer at the beach." He wiped a thin hand across the

bottom of his nose. There was no sign of blood on either his upper lip or his hand. Maybe things were getting better. Jesse still held a private fantasy that his father would quit taking nose-candy, and that his mother would forgive his dad and let him move back home.

Once again, Jesse stopped those kinds of thoughts.

"I'll be back soon, Jess. Until then, you take care of your mom, okay?"

"Okay, Dad."

Jesse watched his father cross the street and get into the back seat of a shiny, black car. The car pulled out and drove past the schoolyard. Jesse waved but couldn't tell if his dad waved back because the windows were black. As the car disappeared around the next corner, Jesse had the feeling that something was wrong. He couldn't remember a time when things ever went well for his father. Something felt bad about all this.

≈ ~ ≈

After Kevin's violent graduation performance, Vicky, of course, immediately moved in with him. Though my aunt and uncle hated it, she had turned eighteen and could do as she chose. Fortunately, finding her in China would have been as easy as locating her in Rhode Island, so her new apartment a few blocks from my Aunt Donna and Uncle Bert's house didn't present any challenge to me. Her and Kevin's apartment was in a building located at the edge of one of Providence's roughest neighborhoods. If my sister had gone out the front door and turned right, within a few blocks she would have had to fight for her purse or worse. That was the same direction, I knew, that Kevin often went to meet the men in suits who swapped canvas bags with him. If my sister took a left out their front door, however, in a few blocks she would find herself in a high-end shopping district.

With Kevin's money, Vicky always turned left.

When my view opened one morning, Vicky was lounging on a yellow, vinyl couch with Kevin at her side. She wore a tight, leopard-skin dress that revealed an awful lot of her cleavage. A string of what I imagined were real pearls shone brightly against the pale skin of her neck. On her wrists she wore so many bracelets I marveled that the weight wasn't bothersome. Kevin wore his typical jeans and a dark T-shirt. His leather jacket was draped over a white screen that they used to show home movies. On a small wooden table to his left sat a chrome and green projector case. There was a large wooden cabinet across the room; a sliding door on top was open, revealing a combination radio and record player, a far cry from the old crank Victrola's more common in my time. A record was spinning.

I settled into my sister's mind.

"Want a beer?" she asked Kevin.

"Sure," he said loudly to be heard over the background music. He let go of her waist.

"Are we going out tonight?" she asked as she padded barefoot through the multi-colored beads into a kitchen decorated with yellow swirl & tinfoil wallpaper. The yellow countertop clashed terribly with a green stove and refrigerator.

"We're going to Benny's for a while," he said. "Then I'll drop you back here. I've got some things to take care of."

I didn't know who Benny was, but my sister often pranced around in skimpy outfits so Kevin could show her off to his nefarious friends. Though I didn't like it, I couldn't exactly voice my displeasure from Under-Heaven.

"That'll be fun," Vicky said as she pushed back through the beads and handed him an unopened can.

He popped the top and laughed as foam dripped onto the green, shag carpet. My sister slithered on top of him before he could take a swig. I had seen them together enough to know that at any moment he would carry her to the bedroom with the lake mural on one wall and a mirror on the ceiling. It was time for me to leave.

~

A wide variety of personalities formed my intricate web of relationships in Under-Heaven. Where Grandma Clara was a common sense and loving personality, my Aunt Alice was aloof but supportive; and where my Uncle Albert was generally quiet and congenial, my many-times-removed grandmother Amber was physically comforting and instinctively loving. Even my Uncle Finneus was a fun if debate-worthy character whom I had grown to love. There were also dozens of other angel relatives who came and went, each one adding to the multiplicity that had become my life in Under-Heaven.

As for the dead, I had become a legend among them. Though souls flickered in and out of my Under-Heaven like fireflies on a warm Maine night, they still somehow managed to blend facts and exaggerations into out-of-proportion stories that passed from soul to soul in a never-ending chain. It got to the point where I could hardly walk outside my own home without attracting attention. The dead looked at me like a prophet or immortal in their midst. On the few occasions when I did choose to speak with one or another, the deference I received always came as a surprise.

"Like a god," my Uncle Finneus would say. "They treat you like a god!"

I could hear envy in his voice, but I had no appreciation for any special status my inaction afforded me. I knew sheer cowardice was the only reason I still resided in Under-Heaven. Though I wanted to go back to Earth, I feared that without the benefit of my previous memories and hard-learned caution, I could fall prey to any madman with a gun, a knife or a strong lobsterman's grip. No, ultimately, it was my fear of death by violence that kept me rooted in place. Any importance the other souls associated to my indecision was at best, ill-placed; or at worst, pathetic.

~

My sister had been living with Kevin for only a few months when he began taking her along during his midnight errands. Not only had he given her a small gun to keep between her breasts, he had also taken her several times to a local target-range to practice. I suspect that the way she closed her eyes before firing didn't help but, regardless of the reason, it seemed that unless any future target was at least the size of a house, her gun wouldn't be of much use.

For obvious reasons, I was concerned. I started viewing later and later in the day so that I could tag along during their illicit errands. Though I might have been powerless, it was better to know she got home each night than to stay awake worrying about it.

One night, they had just picked up an envelope from a restaurant owner in a seedy area. Several minutes earlier, I had noticed a stranger hiding in the shadows of an alley nearby, but Kevin and my sister were surprised when the man dressed in a suit stepped out onto the sidewalk from between two buildings.

I settled into my sister so I could hear.

"Vinny's lookin' for you, Kevin," the man said, his voice deep and rolling.

Kevin shrugged.

"So, I'll see him on Tuesday, like always."

"I'm thinkin' he wants to see you tonight."

"Get in the Mustang, Babe," Kevin said to my sister.

Though she willingly joined him on these evening jobs, I knew she was terrified of the people Kevin did business with. She readily slid into the passenger seat of Kevin's new, blue sports car and slammed the door shut. She kept the window open so we could hear, though.

Always the cocky one, Kevin approached the much bigger man and gently gripped the lapel of his suit jacket.

"Who are you anyway?" he asked.

"I'm Joey, Vinny's nephew," the big man said, his eyes narrowing.

"Tell your Uncle Vinny," Kevin said, stabbing a finger into the top button of Joey's white, dress shirt, "that I'll see him on Tuesday, like always. I don't take orders from no thugs like you or him."

"But you'll take our money, huh?"

"Mr. Benarrio is the one who takes your uncle's money. I'm just the guy who carries it for him."

Joey nodded. "That right?"

"Yeah, that's right."

"Then how come Mr. Benarrio says there's two G's missing from last month's payments, Kevin? That's what my Uncle Vinny wants to know. Where'd the money go?"

"That's crap!" Kevin took a step back. "Your people short the big man, and you think I'm going to take the fall? Not likely."

Joey smiled. "Keep talkin' tough guy. Vinny's lookin' forward to hearing how come Mr. B's accountant counted the bag before you got there last night, and the money was right on. Magically, it turned out three bills short by the time it got back to Mr. B, though? You don't know nothing about that, do you?"

Kevin backed up another step.

"Well…something—your guys must have made a mistake!"

"You don't want to talk to my uncle, Kevin, that's okay. But I believe Mr. Benarrio is planning a little seminar for you." The big man turned and started down the dark sidewalk. He stopped, just his wide face visible under dim streetlight. "Goin' to be quite a seminar, Kevin. I'm sure it is."

Kevin seemed to have trouble with the handle before he opened the car door and got in. He fumbled for the keys.

"Everything all right, K?" my sister asked.

"Huh…oh, yeah. I just got some things to straighten out. I-I need some time to think. We're just going to take a ride for a while."

"Okay," Vicky said. She pulled the small gun out of her bra and slid it into the glove compartment.

They drove through the city until Kevin connected with Route 146 heading toward Worcester, Massachusetts. They had been driving for about forty-five minutes when he pulled the Mustang into a rest stop on the right side of the highway. There were no other cars as he pulled down the lengthy parking area that looked like nothing so much as an extra-wide road. At the end, there was a chain with a sign draped across two steel posts. The weathered blue lettering read: "Dam Access."

"What's going on, K?" Vicky asked as he got out and moved to the front of the car where the headlights illuminated his backside.

He pulled a gun from the back of his waist and aimed it at the padlock which held the chain together. Two explosive flashes echoed through the dark night. He kicked at the lock, and then aimed for a third gunshot. After the third crack of gunfire, the lock fell, and the two sides of chain dropped to the ground.

Kevin slid back into the car.

"Just a little private rest stop for us," he said. He pulled the 1963 Mustang down the narrow gravel road. Small bushes and tall weeds made eerie dragging and thumping sounds under the floorboards as they rolled slowly until a steel barrier effectively ended the road. Kevin shut the car off.

I could hear the rush of a lot of water in the distance.

"I'm scared," my sister confessed.

Kevin laughed, but there was a quavering note in his voice.

"We're okay out here," he said. He leaned over to kiss her. I saw his hand reach for her breast.

I backed up and out until I could see the Mustang's dark blue paint reflecting the moonlight. The sleek, new car was parked in a tiny turnaround just a hundred feet from a reservoir and dam. I backed further away until I could see a couple of miles of forested area to the north and east. The dam was on the southern side. A trickle of headlights went back and forth along Route 146, which was a half-mile to the west. I backed further and further into the air until the physical landmarks and manmade lights disappeared to be replaced by the life-lights of the thousands of people who were in Vicky's general vicinity.

It was then that my breath caught, and I felt myself go faint. My sister and Kevin's life-lights had turned bright shades of red!

"Grandma Clara! Grandma Clara!" I yelled as I rushed into my kitchen. Uncle Finneus appeared beside me. Of course, my grandmother had long ago returned to Heaven for the night.

"Out," I said, to my Uncle Finneus. "Out of here right now!"

I was glad when he shrugged and disappeared. The last thing I needed was for his black sensibilities to affect my grandmother's willingness to help.

"Grandma Clara!"

Suddenly she appeared. Her face was tight with concern.

"What is it, Nate?"

"It's Vicky. Her light turned red. She's going to die!"

Grandma Clara's hand shot to her mouth.

"Oh no," she breathed. "That poor child!"

"What do you mean that poor child? We have to do something. We have to stop this!"

Though her body trembled with concern, she said, "I'm sorry, Nate. There is nothing we can do. I can't interfere down there. No one can."

"That's crazy. God created the Earth, everything. Why can't he help my sister?"

"Nate, the Earth, the heavens, even Hell, they're all part of a system. That system can only exist with rules, rules that we can't break."

"This makes no sense. You know what's going to happen!"

Uncle Finneus knocked from the other side of his basement door.

"Not now!" I screamed.

"We have to help, Grandma. I can't just let her die."

"Nathaniel," she said with a measured tone, "there is nothing we can do. I'm sorry."

Uncle Finneus beat at the door.

"I said not now!"

"It's time for me to go, Nate," Grandmother Clara said. "I can't be party to this."

"To what?" I asked, turning to face her. But she had already disappeared.

"For God's sake, Nate, open the damned door!"

I did as demanded, and Uncle Finneus stormed up into the kitchen. He had his hat in hand and his hair was wildly askew. His eyes danced angrily back and forth. I watched as he took a series of breaths to recover himself. He ran his fingers through his hair, and then somewhat calmly placed his top hat back on his head. Within his anger, I thought I recognized a sliver of what had allowed him to fight his way up to me. The fire was still in his eyes as he spoke.

"Do I strike you as a particularly frivolous man?"

I could hear the sarcasm in his voice and didn't think this was the moment to mention that I didn't know what the word frivolous meant. I shook my head.

"Then why, pray tell, Young Nathaniel, would you choose to ignore my knocking when it was evidently URGENT?"

"Uncle Finneus, maybe this isn't the best time for you to drag your point out too long. My sister is about to die, and I need to call Aunt Alice and the others for help. What do you want?"

"Your grandmother was lying."

"Grandma Clara?" I asked.

"None other."

"She can't lie," I said. "She's an angel."

"Can't she now? Then why didn't she admit that she could intervene on Earth if she chose?"

I saw the red glow of my sister's life-light in my mind's eye. Immediately, anger bubbled up at the thought that my grandmother was choosing not to help.

"Are you sure?"

"Positive, Young Fellow."

"Why didn't she tell me that?"

Uncle Finneus shrugged and shook his head.

"Now, I'll agree she's not supposed to meddle. That much is true."

"Is that one of God's rules?" I asked.

"His and Satan's. It's part of the pact that ended the war when Satan was cast down but not destroyed. Neither he nor God are supposed to meddle with Earth affairs."

"But the angels have the power?"

"Yes."

"What would happen to Grandma Clara if did meddle?"

"I'm not entirely sure, but I know it wouldn't be anything too serious. She wouldn't be cast down or anything dramatic like that."

"How do you know?"

"Angels interfere all the time. They're constantly frustrating the efforts of the damn—" My Uncle's expression went slack as he caught himself.

"Of the damned bad people that live on Earth," he finished, but I knew what he'd been about to say.

"So, you can go to Earth, too," I stated. It wasn't a question.

"So, can she," he said petulantly. "Why do you think I was trying to get your attention before she left?"

"Then do it!"

"That's preposterous, Nathaniel. We have rules, too."

"Yes, but you break rules on a regular basis. It's one of your trademarks." I had grown to know my uncle quite well.

"I won't do it," he said. "Do you have any idea what I went through to get up here in the first place? Now me, I'm a pretty levelheaded and nice fella to be around, but there are some downright vicious characters in our bloodline, Nate. And I had to make it past every single one of them to get to you the first time. I'm lucky I wasn't skewered with a spear and turned over a flame for a hundred years."

From someone else about someplace else, I might have taken my uncle's comment to be a metaphor, but after everything I'd seen it wouldn't have surprised me if flame-broiled members of the damned were common. I also wouldn't have been surprised to find my uncle had broiled a few souls himself.

"It has to be you, Uncle Finneus. You have to go and save Vicky!"

"Nathaniel, what you're asking is not—"

"I don't care about the excuses, Uncle Finneus. I don't read the lights as well as the angels yet, but I don't think she has much time. You have to go—now!"

Uncle Finneus went to the living room window. He stared out toward the moonlit backyard.

"I'm sorry, Young Scalawag, but I won't do it."

I don't think any statement in my young life had ever made me as angry as his simple refusal. I didn't have to glance down to know that my sneakers and pants had turned full color. I also wouldn't have been surprised to find my shirt had begun to turn as well.

"I'll banish you." I told him. "I swear to God I will. I'll never let you back here. And if I have to, I'll trade houses with someone so that the demons will come for you right in your basement. I swear, Uncle, you'll do this thing for me, for Vicky, or you'll never see the light of my Under-Heaven ever again!"

His eyes grew cold and black. There was a quiet fury beneath his gray demeanor, which for some reason reminded me of a shark. I could feel his hatred blaze up toward me, but then his eyes swung up and down my torso and his gaze softened.

"Easy, Lad," he said. "Calm yourself. I'll do it. If you get much darker, you'll be joining me down there."

"I don't care," I said. "As a matter of fact, if you don't go help her, I'll damn myself so that I can."

Uncle Finneus smiled.

"That's my boy," he said, patting me on the shoulder. "Sacrifice is always good for the complexion."

I glanced down and, sure enough, my clothing was whitening before my eyes.

"You have to go, Uncle. I can't give you the choice."

He took his hat off and fingered the brim, as he was prone to do when he was nervous.

"I'll go, Young Nathaniel. But, if by some chance I manage to claw my way past those vermin again, you have to promise to let me stay here as long as you're here with no more threats—also, no more banishings to the basement. Those goody-two-shoes angels can either take me or take a hike."

I squirmed at the thought of Aunt Alice being forced to be in the same room with Uncle Finneus. I knew that she would never do it and that I didn't want to lose seeing her completely. But the most important thing was to help Vicky immediately. I offered a quick counterproposal and was fully prepared to go along with his first version if he turned it down.

"I won't banish you," I said, "but you have to agree to work around the angels. Turn invisible or volunteer to go downstairs on your own. Agreed?"

From the way his face broke into a wide grin, I knew there would come a day I'd regret that deal.

"Young Nathaniel, we have a meeting of the minds." He placed his hat back atop his head. "Now if you'll excuse me, I have an errand to run." He tipped his hat to me, shimmered for a moment and then was gone.

I left the door open in my panicked haste and raced to the fountain. Holding my breath, I fell to my knees and smoothed the water with a trembling hand. Though I was relieved to see Vicky's life-light, it was still solidly red. Zooming in on the scene, I prayed that Uncle Finneus would have time.

She was still in the car with Kevin. I felt guilty but pressed through the foggy windows and watched from a close vantage as he groped her various body parts. She was still dressed, but his hands had adeptly found ways inside her tight clothing. At one point, he tore several buttons off her blouse to get more easily at her black and pink bra. For reasons I doubted I'd ever understand, she seemed to enjoy his mauling. She giggled as her own hands reached to unbuckle his belt.

I blocked out my disgust and tried to concentrate on where the danger might come from. This wasn't the first time they had groped each other, and it had never created a problem before. I studied his expression and couldn't see anything to indicate he had murder or suicide on his mind. I backed out of the Mustang until I was about twenty feet above the car. The moonlight was dim, but I could see the weed-covered road.

Just then, I noticed a car pulling down along the wide, paved rest area. When the vehicle reached the broken chain, its headlights switched off, but it continued moving slowly down the narrow pathway. I knew immediately this was the source of Vicky's danger. My muscles tensed as I watched the unfolding scene below me.

22

Desperation

It had been about a week since Jesse's dad had last shown up at the schoolyard. Jesse hoped his father was someplace warm, someplace where he could be comfortable sleeping outside if he had to. His kindergarten class had been finger-painting for most of the morning, and he was secretly pleased that his fingers still had some orange and brown stains as he followed the others out onto the playground. Jesse had forgotten his SpongeBob SquarePants gloves at home. A snowball pelted him in the chest as his foot hit left the last step. There was so little snow left that Heath must have scooped up every last bit just to make the one ball.

Jesse's desperately searched for a weapon of his own. Finally spotting a small snowy area under the merry-go-round, he raced over and scooped up a handful and squeezed it into a cold ball with his bare hands.

It didn't take long to find Heath ducked down behind the slide. Jesse jumped up and pretended to pitch his ball. As Heath ducked, Jesse let the snowball fly for real and caught his best friend solidly in the shoulder.

"Hey, that hurt," Heath blurted.

"Don't start the game if you can't take the pain," Jesse chanted.

"That's a good one, kid," someone said.

Jesse turned to see a huge man with a beard standing near where he had last seen his father. This man, however, wasn't hiding behind the tree; he instead stood near the fence, right out in the open, where anyone, including the teachers, could have seen him.

"You're Jesse, right?" he said.

Jesse didn't answer. He glanced over to Heath expecting to see a snowball flying his way, but his friend had also stopped to watch the stranger.

"I'm a friend of your dad's," the big man continued. "He asked me to stop by and see you."

Jesse glanced up and down the street. Sure enough, there was a black car, which looked a lot like the one his father had gotten into a week or so before.

"Where's my dad?"

The big man stroked his beard and shrugged.

"The thing I'm supposed to tell you," he said, "it's kind of personal. You should come over here so no one else will hear."

Jesse glanced over to see Heath shaking his head not to do it. Jesse scanned the busy playground. Ms. Brentwood was standing next to the slides which were always crowded with kids. She had her back to Jesse and the stranger.

"I can hear you from here," Jesse said.

The man shrugged.

"Sorry then." He turned as if to leave.

"What did my dad want?" Jesse asked, taking a step toward the fence.

"Sorry, kid," the stranger said, pausing on the sidewalk, "but I can't have your dad's private information spread all over the school. He needs your help, but if you don't want to talk to me, I'll just go."

Jesse studied the big man for a minute. His clothes were clean and neat, and though he wore several gold chains around his neck, he didn't look like the dirty people his father often hung around with. He seemed safe enough.

"Okay," Jesse said. He skirted the merry-go-round and approached the fence.

"Jesse," Heath called out.

Jesse knew he should have stayed with his friend, but he had to know what his dad needed. Besides, though the stranger was tall and wide like a TV wrestler, he was also safely on the other side of the fence. Even so, Jesse shivered because the man's black beard and mustache kind of reminded him of a bear. Jesse stopped about ten feet from the fence.

"Is my dad okay?"

The big man shook his head. "I'm sorry, kid, but he's not doing too good."

Jesse felt a knot forming at the center of his stomach. Hadn't his father made it to a warm place?

"What did he want you to tell me?"

The big man seemed to think for a moment. Then he smiled and fumbled around in his pockets before pulling out a crumbled piece of paper.

"Actually, he gave me this note for you."

Jesse could only remember one other time when his father had given him a note. It was on his fourth birthday. Of course, Jesse couldn't read, so his father had drawn a picture of a boy and a toy store. He said that for his birthday, Jesse would get to choose anything he wanted at the toy store. Jesse remembered wanting an expensive video game with four controllers, but he wound up settling for a Superman board game. It was a great present, though, because his father and he had played that game at least five times in a row, and each time Jesse had won.

Jesse wondered what might be on this new note.

"Here," the man said. He pushed the note through the fence with two fingers.

Jesse looked back and made sure Heath was still watching. His friend hadn't moved and was still shaking his head "no." Though Jesse knew his friend was right, he also knew that he couldn't just ignore a message from his father.

Bravely, he walked over to retrieve the crumpled paper.

Suddenly, impossibly, a huge section of the fence came loose, and the big man snatched at him. Jesse dodged backwards, but his boots slipped on the icy grass. He fell. The man threw the broken fence off to the side and seized him with huge, bear-like arms. Helplessly, Jesse kicked and struggled to no avail.

Finally, he bit into the man's wrist as hard as he could.

The fist that struck his temple was nearly as large as his head, but it felt like something more the size of a truck. Jesse's neck snapped sideways. His eyesight blurred and he tasted blood as the man yanked him up by the hair. Pain erupted from his scalp. Jesse fought to struggled to remain conscious as he caught sight of his friend Heath running toward Ms. Brentwood.

A second fist crashed into his head.

Then the world went black.

≈ ~ ≈

Praying that Finneus would be quick, I watched the newly arrived car stop on the narrow, gravel road about two hundred feet from

Kevin's car. I was tempted to rush back into the Mustang and try to warn Vicky, but I knew it would be useless. The living could not hear the dead.

My chest tightened as car door opened and three men got out. Helpless, I lowered my view until it felt as though I was only ten feet above them. In their mid-twenties, maybe early thirties, two of the men wore dark dress suits with matching hats. Probably a few years older, the third man was dressed in casual slacks and a button up shirt. Unlike the other two, he wore no tie, no jacket and no hat. From the way he motioned to the others, I surmised that he was in charge. My mind chilled at the sight of the rifles the suited men were carrying. The leader removed a pistol from his belt.

Terror wracked me. Finneus had only moments to do something before my sister would be killed.

Hurry! Please Hurry!

I wanted to swoop down and scatter these men to the dark forest, but I knew my presence was only an illusion of the fountain pool. I had no more status on Earth than the ghosts that populated The Shadow Knows radio show. My sister was in danger and I could do nothing but watch and pray.

I closed my eyes and asked God for help. It may seem ironic, but I prayed for him to help one of the damned to reach my sister in time to save her. And to stack sacrilege on top of sacrilege, I realized that I was asking God to assist in breaking the "no interference" rule he created. Nevertheless, I prayed. I didn't care about the implications; I only cared about saving Vicky!

I zoomed into the car to see my sister writhing with what looked like pain. Kevin was on top of her, pounding his pelvis against hers. I knew what sex looked like—not only having briefly stumbled across similar scenes between her and Kevin over the last few months, but also having interrupted my parents on a Saturday afternoon when they thought Whiskey and I were still out on the woods trails—however, watching the criminal maul her made me angry, and to make matters worse he was the one who had placed her in mortal danger.

Knowing Vicky's time was up, I zoomed up through the roof to see all three men walking toward Kevin's Mustang, gun muzzles pointed straight at it.

"It has to be now, Uncle," I whispered. "Please get here."

They were only a hundred feet from the car now. I scanned the area for signs of other people. Nothing. I rose a hundred feet above them to get a wider vantage.

Still nothing—

No, wait!

Just slowing to turn off Route 146 into the rest area was a tractor-trailer. It had to be Uncle Finneus! Anxiously, I watched as it crept up the paved parking area.

"Hurry!" I uttered, wishing that my uncle could hear me. I gauged the time and distance. My heart rose to a lump in my throat. The men were closing in on Kevin's car, less than fifty feet—close enough to shoot the windows out, close enough to kill my sister!

I looked to the truck, back to the men. Uncle Finneus would be too late. I had to do something, but what?

I soared down and into my sister.

Suddenly, the car exploded with sound. I could hear Kevin's grunts and her tiny but continual screams. It was impossible to see anything because her eyes were closed.

"Vicky!" I screamed into her mind. "Vicky, you're in danger!"

Her tiny screams turned to breathy whispers. "I love you, Kevin. I love—"

My warning completely unheard, I bolted out of her mind but remained inside the car. Vicky was below me, her eyes closed in apparent bliss. I imagined that just outside the windows, fingers were closing on triggers and that at any moment glass and steel would explode inward. I needed to something, but I had no power there! I was nothing more than a helpless, invisible sightseer. And now I would be forced to watch the murder of my last family member. Whiskey had died so that Vicky could live, but apparently cruel fate had decided that none of us should be left alive.

Powerless, I soared high above the car. Uncle Finneus' truck had stopped back near the broken chain, probably finding the gravel extension too narrow for such a wide vehicle to navigate. I strained my view but could see no sign of a driver running or walking towards the impending tragedy.

I knew my uncle had failed. My sister was doomed.

Only a few feet from the car, the three men fanned out until three separate gun muzzles were pointed toward the Mustang's fogged up windows from different angles. I despaired because there would be no place for Vicky to hide.

"Vicky!" I screamed. "Vicky, you have to run!"

Though my screams were inaudible on Earth, I knew they would ring out loudly in my Under-Heaven, even louder than the roar of the water cascading into the fountain pool. Drawn by my celebrity status and the ruckus, I imagined the dead were already surrounding the fountain. I didn't care. Let them gawk. At that moment, my only concern was for my sister, and with every fraction of a second, her chances were slipping away.

"Uncle Finneus, HURRY!"

Suddenly, the sky above me moved. No, not the sky, a mass of blackness, and that blackness soon resolved itself into a swarm of bats! The feral, black cloud swooped down from the sky and smeared itself between the three men and Kevin's car. The blackness writhed and surged around the men. I could see flashes of light that might have been gunshots, but the blackness was so pervasive it was impossible to know for sure.

Suddenly, the two suited men broke loose from the coal-colored cloud and ran toward their car. I could see moonlight glistening off the blood that covered their hands and cheeks. Only tiny bits of their exposed flesh remained untouched.

The bats, which seemed to have initially focused on the man in charge, suddenly surged toward the two remaining men whose leader lay prone and immobile on the gravel behind them, his light-colored leisure suit stained crimson and shredded beyond recognition. I chose not to view the body from any closer vantage and was thankful the man had fallen facedown.

Suddenly, lights from the newcomer's car illuminated the private road. Apparently, the thugs had made it to the safety of their car. The vehicle kicked up dirt in a wide circle and sped away toward the rest area. Then, suddenly, it swerved left and struck a large hemlock tree. Like smoke from a garbage fire, hundreds of bats spewed from the shattered windshield, leaving only torn flesh behind.

Uncle Finneus had made it in time.

I backed myself thousands of feet into the sky until I could see only the life-lights. My sister's beacon had returned to a healthy shade of yellow. Kevin's, however, remained a perilous shade of pink. Apparently, Mr. Benarrio's seminar wasn't yet over.

I allowed my view to descend again, just in time to see both Kevin and Vicky emerge from the Mustang. Suddenly, Kevin crouched and pointed his gun outward as his eyes darted from the corpse in the road to the demolished car and back again. With his booted foot, he rolled what remained of the leisure suit man over then started to laugh. He was still laughing as my sister raced away. I was thankful she didn't glance inside the wrecked car as she ran past.

Go, Vicky, go!

The tractor-trailer was still parked in the rest stop ahead of her. I wondered if the truck's presence was a gift of good fortune or part of Uncle Finneus' plan. Either way, Vicky ran to the truck and seconds later was climbing into the passenger side of the cab. The big vehicle lurched in a wide arc then surged back to the highway. I followed above and was relieved when the driver pulled into the nearest restaurant parking lot. My sister stumbled from the cab and, crying, rushed straight to a well-lit phone booth.

I merged with her then and was thankful to hear my Aunt Donna's sweet voice: "Hello."

"Aunt Donna," my sister began, "I'm in trouble."

She didn't say much more, nor did she have to.

"Baby, go inside where you'll be safe," my aunt said. "Your Uncle Bert and I are leaving right now. We love you and we'll be there soon."

It was over. The danger had passed.

23

Lives Collide

Clay, a private detective specializing in missing person cases, stood in the bank line and waited for the older woman with the black faux-mink coat to finish with the bank clerk. He could tell the fur wasn't real because he'd grown up next to one of the largest mink farms in Oklahoma, and at one time he might have recognized which litter a particular coat had come from. Though it had been nearly twenty years since then, he still knew that the fur this woman wore had been spun from a cotton-silk combination, probably overseas. It wasn't that he agreed with wearing fur, but he never understood those people who wore pretend fur. Either you wore fur, or you didn't. Why pretend?

"Thank you, Ma'am," the young redheaded teller said as the elderly woman ambled away.

The woman's rude lack of a response didn't seem to bother the young woman as she turned to Clay with a smile. She had two prominent freckles at the tip of her nose, one a little higher than the other.

"Can I help you, Sir?"

"That'd be great, Miss," he said. He had remembered earlier to take off his cowboy hat, but now it was in the wrong hand. He shuffled it to the left hand so that he could reach into his right breast suit jacket pocket. He stepped forward, his boot heels clicking loudly on the marble floor, and slid the check and his deposit slip over to the teller.

She examined the check, looked up at him, and then repeated the motion, several times.

Used to this, he smiled and, after shuffling the hat again, reached into his pants pocket for his wallet. He propped the hat with his knee against the counter and used both hands to retrieve his Oklahoma driver's license, which he slid it over to her.

Her head bobbed up and down a couple more times while she compared his license photo to his face. She shrugged cutely and smiled.

"I'm sorry, Sir, but the manager has to approve this."

"No problem," Clay responded as the teller moved to a counter a few feet away and picked up a phone. He was used to this part, too. At

one time bankers only worried when you took money out of their banks, but now it seemed they were just as concerned when you put it in. Of course,
it probably wasn't every day that an out-of-state customer wanted to deposit a one hundred and twenty-thousand-dollar check. But that's why he had opened an account at one of the national banks, so he could make his deposits, no matter where he happened to be. Even so, it hadn't changed the song and dance he had to go through each time. Patience wasn't just a virtue, sometimes it was a learned skill. He fingered his hat while he waited.

"Good morning, Mr. Gromkis," said the heavyset man with a suit who approached him from the bank lobby only moments after the attractive teller hung up the phone. He reached out and shook Clay's hand with what felt like a clammy dead fish.

Clay politely resisted the urge to wipe his hand on his slacks as he returned the smile which prominently displayed one upper tooth that seemed to be twice the size of the others. It gave the man a hillbilly look that his off-the-shelf suit couldn't overcome.

"I'm Tom Winthrop, the Branch Manager," the man said. "I apologize for the inconvenience, but it will take us a few minutes to verify your deposit. On a positive note, these security measures are the same ones that allow us to keep your monies safe."

Clay forced a smile and nodded. He'd heard this line, or a variation of it, a dozen times in the last two years.

"I understand." He handed the manager a business card from his home branch in Oklahoma. "It might help if you give that number a call. The manager at my home branch should be able to clarify any of your questions."

"I'm sorry, Mr. Gromkis, but we also have the issue of insurance. You understand that your deposit puts your account past the limits of the FDIC coverage we can provide for you. We, of course, could arrange private insurance coverage for the difference."

"Whatever you think is best would be fine, but I think my portfolio insurance with your company should cover it. I'll wait here while you work out the details."

"Very good, Mr. Gromkis," the manager said. "Again, I'm very sorry for the inconvenience."

Even with Donna's direct number, it took about fifteen minutes for them to finish with the deposit. Clay used the time well and made sure he had the teller's phone number before he left. He hoped to spend a few days in town, and she had a pretty smile. He whistled as he slid into the front seat of his late-model silver Corvette. He'd long-since learned to turn the music off before he got out of the car so heard his cell phone ring just as he settled into the seat.

The display screen said the call was from a restaurant in Boston. He didn't know anybody up there, but these days his name did tend to get around. He did a mental calculation of distance from his location in Daytona Beach to Boston. With a few hours' layover for sleep, he should be able to make it in about twenty hours. So much for the pretty girl with two freckles, he thought as he picked up the phone.

"Clay Gromkis."

"Mr. Gromkis, can you help?" a frantic woman's voice said. "It's my son, Jesse. He's been kidnapped."

≈ ~ ≈

I didn't see Uncle Finneus for nearly four months after he had gone to save Vicky. I had actually begun to worry that one of the other damned characters from my extended family might have bested him down below. It wouldn't have done them any good if they had, however, because I had no intention of opening any new basement doors for anyone other than my Uncle Finneus. No matter how nice any shady grandfather this or dark grandmother that happened to be, they weren't getting into my house. It would be Uncle Finneus or no one at all.

In those months following Vicky's crisis, I found myself thinking more and more about life and about the options that only being back on Earth could offer. I desperately wanted to have another chance at running through forests, at having a dog and at growing up in a place filled with people my own age who wouldn't disappear as quickly as they came. But I didn't know if I could live with the risk of winding up back in Under-Heaven. Of course, I knew everyone had to die at some time, but I wanted a chance at a full life. It didn't seem fair that I had only been given nine years the first time around, and there were no guarantees I'd even get that far the next time.

≈ ~ ≈

Jesse woke in the dark, lying on what felt like a blanket on a hard floor. In all his five years of life, he didn't think he'd ever been anyplace

189

so completely black. His head throbbed and when he moved his jaw it felt like something was shifting in his forehead. Could the horrible bear man have broken his head?

Jesse struggled to get to his feet but felt woozy and sat back down. He knew he had to do something but couldn't think of what. Too dizzy to stand, he crawled on his hands and knees along the edges of what turned out to be a small room. The floor was concrete like his school cafeteria, and three of the four walls felt like bricks. The fourth wall was made of wood and had a door in it. Knowing it was dangerous but needing to try anyway, Jesse reached up and felt for the handle. He used it to pull himself upright. His head felt like it was being kicked from the inside, and he knew if he let go of the knob he'd fall.

The knob wouldn't turn. It was locked.

Jesse slid to the floor and crawled back to the blanket. He knew he should have been terrified, but his head hurt so badly he just wanted the pounding to stop. He settled onto his back and tried moving his mouth again. Each time he did, it felt like the bones above his eyebrows were grinding together. He wondered how many five-year-old's had died like this. As tears rolled down his swollen cheeks, Jesse prayed.

He prayed that his father would be okay.

≈ ~ ≈

"You don't think it was the father?" Clay asked. "How can you be sure?"

"Wagner's a screw up," the weathered woman said, "but he wouldn't do that. He loves Jesse as much as I do."

She was young, maybe late twenties, but the years had not been easy ones. Already there were deep circles under her eyes, and her smile had the beginnings of age-creases. Her hair was a cross between dirty blond and brown, but grays were sprinkled at the temples. She wore a tight white waitress uniform with a pink apron. Though her figure was slim, it seemed to Clay more likely a result of undernourishment than health-consciousness.

Clay set his pencil on the Formica counter and reached into his coat pocket. He rubbed at the pewter key chain his mother had given him many years before. The simple movement helped to slow his mind to a methodical pace. These interviews were the most important part of any investigation, and Clay had learned to take his time and be attentive. Though there were dozens of veteran detectives at the Oklahoma

190

Police Department when he left, nearly every major case had been given to him, especially the ones that reflected on the department's reputation. Not only had Clay learned how to solve the majority of his cases, he somehow managed to do it while still playing by the rules. Unlike some detectives he could name but wouldn't, Clay had never roughed up witnesses or dealt with questionable informants, and he had never even once created evidence to put a man in jail. Clay wasn't always by the book, but he believed in the law, and had always been a good representative of it.

While she waited for him to say something, Clay watched her hands quiver. She didn't seem to be on drugs, an assumption he based largely on her logical, even if uneducated, answers to his questions. No, he guessed the trembling came from a genuine fear for her son. He felt certain she was in no way involved. And, as an extension, Clay felt it was unlikely the husband was either. Fathers could be fooled, but mothers usually had an instinct for that sort of thing. Clay also felt certain she wasn't hiding anything. This was clearly a woman who would have shared any information that might have helped bring her son home safely.

No, there was a responsible third party here, but it was too early to guess at who or why.

"You're sure you don't know how I can reach your husband?"

"I'm sure. I've looked everywhere. I called all of our friends and relatives. I called all of his friends, too. I even tried to locate his drug dealers."

"He's an addict?"

"I kicked him out of the house because I didn't want Jesse around that stuff. Wagner tried, but it was obvious he couldn't kick the habit. I even considered getting back together…for Jesse, but when those men burned his truck—"

She broke down into tears.

Clay had been doing this long enough to know emotions came with the job, and patience was about the only way to work through them. While she recovered, he surreptitiously looked over her arms for needle marks.

Nothing.

There were also no marks between her fingers or under her nails. Had her legs been visible, he would have casually glanced there as well. But he already felt confident there was nothing to find. This woman was not and probably had never been on drugs.

"When's the last time you saw your husband?" he asked when it seemed polite.

Apparently, the tears had dislodged a tightly held guilt, because she suddenly blurted out, "I'm sorry Mr. Gromkis. I desperately need to get my son back, but I don't have any money to pay you! I never should have let you drive all this way—"

Again, the tears came.

He reached across the counter and laid a hand on her forearm.

"Mrs. Largess, it's okay. We'll worry about money later. Right now, what's important is finding your son."

Through the tears came a look of wonderment.

"You're still willing to help?"

"Of course."

"Why? I mean…I'm so thankful, but why would you help me?" Probably thinking he had other payment methods in mind, she suddenly pulled away from him.

"I used to be a police officer, Mrs. Largess. I was a detective with the Oklahoma City Police Department and spent almost fifteen years chasing thieves, mobsters and dirty politicians." He purposefully didn't mention murderers. "I left the department when I realized the crooks always seemed to get back on the streets and the politicians always got reelected."

"I don't understand."

"When I find a child and bring him or her safely back home, I am accomplishing something."

"But you can't work for free, can you?"

"Not normally, no. But the truth is many of the parents I have helped are wealthy. They pay me well. Some of them actually keep paying me long after their children have returned home, just so that I can continue doing what I'm doing."

He didn't want to mention that his latest check had come from a man whose child he had found dead. Mr. Imodo had since committed to helping find other missing children before it was too late, and Clay was apparently at the top of his donor list. Now that he thought about it, Clay made a mental note to apprise Mr. Imodo's secretary about this case when it was resolved.

"Are you sure?" she said.

He smiled. "I'm working for Jesse now, Mrs. Largess. I'm going to do everything possible to find him."

"Can you?"

"Yes, I think I can." Maybe it had just been the luck of the draw, but in the last two years he'd successfully found seventeen missing children.

It was unfortunate that less than half had still been alive.

≈ ~ ≈

Together, Grandma Clara and I watched as a new arrival purposefully strode up to nearly every soul in Under-Heaven. She had no angel relative at her side, which seemed odd, and she seemed intent on talking to everyone. The last few people she talked to pointed toward my house.

"I don't like this," Grandma Clara said as the young woman approached my front porch.

I guessed her to be about twenty. She was stunningly beautiful, but her smile gave me the creeps. My reaction might have been, in part, because of her color. Her shoes were shiny black. Her long stockings had colorful stripes rising to her knees. Her skirt was bright pink, and her sweater was dark blue. To top it all off, she had a pink ribbon in her dark hair. There was literally not a spot of white clothing on her.

"I'm going inside," Grandma Clara told me, "and so should you."

I could see why she felt that way, but I had grown used to making my own decisions in Under-Heaven. Though my instincts toward this newcomer were negative, I didn't see how her colors could make her any more dangerous than my Uncle Finneus.

"Hi," she said as she pranced uninvited up my stairs. She extended a hand, which I politely shook. "My name is Mary-Lou Evans," she continued. "It's a pleasure to meet you."

"I think it's a pleasure to meet you, too," I said, not yet sure.

"Oh," she said sweetly as her eyes flicked down at her colorful attire. "I am a little loud for the neighborhood. Sorry about that."

It wasn't my place to share information with the dead—their angel relatives were supposed to take care of that—but this woman seemed more knowledgeable than most.

"You know what the colors mean?"

"Yes, a number of those fine souls explained the basics." She waved absently toward the fountain where several dozen people had gathered to watch the legendary boy of Under-Heaven and the frighteningly colorful woman converse.

"You were murdered?" she said lightly, as though discussing nothing more serious than the weather.

I nodded and glanced down at her blue sweater. No stains.

"Oh, not me," she said. "I killed myself." There was something perverse in the way she spoke so cheerfully about something so gruesome.

"Why?" I blurted then immediately regretted my rude reaction.

"Oh, to follow him."

"Follow him?"

"My stepfather."

"You followed your stepfather to Under-Heaven?"

She gave me a genuine smile that would have left most boys in silent awe. I, however, sensed she was used to manipulating people with her looks. I remained cautious.

"Actually, I'm pretty sure he went to Hell. I'm going there next. I had a little killing to do before I left, but now it's time I took care of the man who started it all." Again, she smiled.

Disgusted, I didn't want to know any more. Personification of evil is a term I might have used as an older soul, but at that time I only knew she was utterly corrupt and happy about it.

"I'm sorry, Nate…it is Nate, isn't it?"

I nodded.

"I probably shouldn't have been quite so open about all this. You are a little…well, white."

"That's true enough," my grandmother Clara said, reappearing on my porch. I felt her hand on my shoulder and was happy to have it there.

"I'm right that I shouldn't have said it, or that he is white?" the young woman asked mockingly.

"Both," Grandma Clara responded.

The beautiful smile grew wider.

"Isn't it funny," the newcomer said, "that an angel has a problem with my honesty?"

I'd been around long enough to know what sarcasm was. However, even including my Uncle Finneus, I don't think I had ever heard anyone use it so acerbically. This woman could smile sweetly and make you feel as though you'd been spit on at the same time. Other than possibly the men who had killed my family, this woman scared me more than anyone I had ever met.

"Shouldn't you be getting along now, young lady?" Grandma Clara said. "I believe your ride is about to arrive."

"Really? That's great!" The woman winked at my grandmother then focused her brilliant smile back on me. For some reason her cheerful grin now looked deformed to me. I could easily have imagined worms crawling in and around her teeth.

"I'm sorry we didn't have more time to get to know each other," she purred. "I could have taught you so much."

Grandma Clara stepped between the colorful visitor and me.

"I'm surprised you didn't ask how I became so colorful, Nate," she said.

I shook my head, instinctively knowing I'd heard enough. She had already admitted to killing someone.

"I killed five men," she said.

"Only five?" my Grandma Clara said caustically.

The girl shrugged.

"Two were boys. But boys will become men—well, would have become men." She winked at me.

I shuddered and found the thought of spending even one more second with the vile woman revolting.

"It's time you left," Grandma Clara said, "and I don't intend that as a suggestion."

Suddenly, I saw Nathaniel standing on the roof of the house to the right of mine. The golden-haired archangel looked menacing. Movement to my upper left revealed itself to be another archangel, alighting on a roof to my left.

Like a celebrity, the evil woman waved up at both of them.

The elderly woman next door, upon whose roof Nathaniel stood, ducked into her house and peered out the window. I wished I had done the same when my Grandma Clara had suggested it.

The murderess grinned at me then backed down my stairs. As she sauntered toward the fountain, a third and fourth archangel settled onto roofs not far from my own. Something sinister was about to happen. What else could attract so many archangels? In confirmation of my thoughts, not one, not two, but three demons fell from the sky and landed heavily around the colorful woman. She made as though to strike out at one of them. It hissed and backed away. She did the same to a second, causing it to cower.

As hard as it was to believe, the demons were afraid of her.

"Kneel," she commanded one of them. Astonishingly, the gnarled, black-skinned creature did as told.

"Thanks, everyone," she said to the gawking inhabitants of Under-Heaven. She seemed to take particular pleasure in waving toward Grandma Clara, me and then toward each of the four archangels in turn. "I have a bit more revenge to seek on a rapist, but maybe I can come back and visit."

She winked at me then gestured for the two standing demons to take her arms. Suddenly, she was being born away, one demon holding each arm and the third cradling her legs. The frightening smile never left her lips.

Any fears I might have harbored about my Uncle Finneus dissipated that day. I now knew the difference between bad and Evil.

≈ ~ ≈

As a teenager, Clay imagined that one day he would be cutting record deals and singing in front of thousands of people. And like the majority of folks in Oklahoma, he'd grown up on country and western. Johnny Cash, Hank Williams Sr. and George Jones had been his earliest idols, and for almost ten years Clay had practiced and perfected his singing voice. Unfortunately, his practiced voice was soprano, which didn't fare well when applied to the gravelly standards of the country singers of the day. His cousin Nelda had once described his voice as "cat with man on tail." His friends had begged him to join the pop music trend more suited to his high range, but Clay wouldn't hear of it. Country was country, and if he couldn't sing country, what was the sense? Times had changed, and in an ironic twist of fate, it was usually the pop stations he found his radio tuned to as he crisscrossed the country in search of children and clues.

He was singing along with the John Lennon tune Imagine when he spotted the tire warehouse at the corner of Alscott and Beamer streets in Boston. The traffic was thick, but fortunately there was a large parking lot and the roads were dry. In keeping with most of the drivers in Boston, he swerved out of his lane and suicidally crossed three lanes of oncoming traffic. His Corvette soared easily into the large paved expanse, and the stunt earned him only two horn blasts from oncoming traffic and one middle finger from an elderly woman in a speeding, green Volkswagen Bug.

As he came to a stop, Clay let the Corvette's motor purr downward before he shut it off. Two young men, probably just under twenty, sat on two of the many stacks of tires outside the large open bay doors. Though it was less than forty degrees out, they were dressed in only dark T-shirts and sooty blue jeans. A small, hand-rolled cigarette passed between them.

Clay got out of the car and pulled his beige, trench coat tight against the bitter, city wind. The two young men blithely ignored him as the small cigarette passed back and forth again. As Clay approached, the taller of the two held the cigarette out.

"Want a hit?"

Clay recognized the smell from his younger days, but beer—not marijuana—had always been his drug of choice. He could have counted the number of times he'd actually smoked the stuff.

"No thanks. How do you know I'm not a cop?"

They looked at one another and chuckled.

The shorter one said, "We thought you were."

"I'm looking for Wagner Largess. Is he around?"

Another glance passed between them. It would have been a great Hollywood comic routine if it hadn't already been so overdone.

"We ain't seen that sack in a couple of months," the taller one said. "Poor fucker went off the deep end with blow. Boss fired him about the same time his bitch threw him out."

"No," the shorter one said, smacking his friend in the shoulder. "That bitch threw him out long before that."

"Oh, so now you're an expert on bitches."

As they bantered back and forth, Clay wondered if they knew how ignorant they sounded. Since it wasn't his job to enlighten them, he said, "So he doesn't ever come around?"

"Nope," the shorter one said. "He wouldn't dare. Not after he clipped the boss for an advance then dissed everyone and left."

"Boss inside?" Clay asked.

"Unfortunately," the taller one said. That earned him a great burst of laughter from his friend. They high-fived each other.

Clay went inside.

There were bay entrances, each large enough to fit a full-sized semi-tractor, complete with trailer. A wooden set of stairs brought Clay up onto the loading dock, warehouse level. The building was old and dimly lit. He could see bright florescent lighting hanging along the furthest aisle to the left. Thinking it might have been an office, he walked that way, the soles of his cowboy boots echoing through the half-empty building. It appeared business wasn't great; though floor-to-ceiling metal racks cradled thousands of tires, there was room for thousands more. Large swaths of the racks sat empty.

His assumption about the office turned out to be right. The door opened into a brightly lit room with one desk off to the right. A man, probably in his thirties, sat behind the second smaller, scarred wooden desk that might once have been staffed by a secretary. Though the man didn't wear a tie with his casual jacket, he seemed much too well-dressed for the surroundings.

Clay knocked but could tell from the calm glance in his direction that the man had heard him coming. Eyebrows rose in question, but the silence remained.

"Clay Gromkis, I'm a private investigator," Clay said, taking a couple of steps into the office.

The man got to his feet, revealing a matching set of dark slacks to go with the high thread count jacket. Comfortable in his off-the-rack suit and trench coat, Clay reached across the desk to take the impeccably groomed hand. The man's grip was firm and confident, but he didn't try to impress Clay with a death grip.

"Harry Bennerman. I have the unfortunate pleasure of owning this place." He shrugged.

Though his personal style was a little flashy, he seemed like a pretty squared away and friendly guy—at least that seemed to be how Harry wanted him to feel.

"This is about Wagner," Harry Bennerman said. It wasn't a question.

"Well, not exactly. I was hired to find his son."

Harry shook his head.

"I heard about that. 'Hope the boy's alright."

"Do you know anything about Wagner's location right now?"

"No," Harry said with a sympathetic nod, "but I wish I did. He and I grew up together, only a few blocks from here, down on Temple. We were good friends in school. When I got a chance to take this place over, he was the first person I hired. For the first three years it was just me and him."

"But you fired him?"

"Have a seat," Harry said, waving toward a couple of chrome-framed office chairs that, surprisingly, were not covered with tire soot. The room was equally as clean with cream-colored walls and an off-white linoleum floor. Harry had a basic wooden desk in one corner to the left and a few tall file cabinets against the right wall. The office was functional with no luxuries. Harry settled into his own rolling cloth seat behind the desk. Clay pulled up one of the vinyl chairs across the desk from him.

"I didn't fire Wagner, Mr. Gromkis. Never could have. As I told you, we were friends right from the beginning. Without him, I never could have gotten this place off the ground. Hell, we even used to do some autobody work at night, just to keep the doors open. Wagner never made me pay the overtime."

"Your crew says he clipped you for a little money before he left."

"Nah, nothing really, just a couple hundred bucks. He's earned it a dozen times over. If he showed up today, I'd happily give him another couple hundred and his job back. No one knows these racks like Wagner."

"So, you have no idea where I might be able to find him?"

"Not a clue. We haven't seen him around here in probably two months, maybe more."

"If you were going to try and find him, where would you look first?" Clay asked.

"That's an easy one," Harry said. "I'd check with his wife. If Wagner ever had a weakness, it was that girl of his. They fought like hound and fox, but he never could get enough."

"Mrs. Largess is the one who hired me to find her son Jesse. She has no idea where he is or I'm sure she would have told me."

Harry nodded. "Then I'd try the old neighborhood. He might still have some connections down there."

Clay nodded. His hand slipped into his jacket and he rubbed his thumb across his pewter key chain. Something about this conversation wasn't adding up, but he hadn't quite placed the oddity yet.

"Do you have any connections you could check on for me?" he asked Harry. "You are from the same neighborhood, right?"

"Sure," Harry said. He pushed his chair back a foot. "I can make some calls, but to tell you the truth I don't really know anyone down there anymore." He leaned forward in a conspiratorial manner. "I kind of grew out of the street scene, if you know what I mean."

Clay nodded and stood.

"Thank you, Mr. Bennerman, for all of your help."

Clay continued to rub his key chain as Harry followed him back out to the loading bays. Just as he'd been ready to go down the stairs to leave, he spun and caught the briefest expression of relief on Harry's face. The look instantly disappeared.

"How's the tire business these days?" Clay asked.

Harry paused as though weighing various responses.

"I hate to talk about it."

"Oh, I don't mean specifically," Clay said, "just overall. Things pretty good?"

Harry smiled and gestured with his hands out, palms up.

"I'm sorry, Mr. Gromkis, but that's not the sort of information I like to make public. It's a business thing. You understand. Of course, we all know how tough the economy is, so no matter what I said it would either be complaining or bragging."

"No problem at all," Clay said. "I'm sorry if I offended you. I'm from Oklahoma, and down there folks'll tell you anything from their shoe size to who they're dating behind their wife's back. I know it's a little different up here on the East Coast."

"No problem at all, Mr. Gromkis," Harry said. "I'll call around the old neighborhood and see if anyone has heard from Wagner. I'll let you know if I learn anything."

Clay thanked him and left. He hadn't provided Harry with a card or a phone number to reach him. It didn't matter, though, because they both knew he never intended to call.

24

Secrets and Hunches

Uncle Finneus arrived back in my Under-Heaven in a most unusual way: he knocked at the front door. My grandmother Alice had been gone for several hours when I went to see which member of the dead wanted me this time. As I opened the door, my uncle's bruised and bloodied body fell onto the entry floor.

"Oh my god," I said, rolling him face up to see how bad the injuries were. As I turned him over, a wide grin spread across his bloody lips.

"Gotcha!" he said jovially.

He got to his feet and shook like my Whiskey used to do when drying himself off. By the time he stopped, all the blood and bruises were gone, his hair was neatly combed back, and his mustache was curled at the ends. He was as dapper as ever.

I didn't know whether to be mad or thankful he was all right.

"Not fair," I said. "I was really worried."

"You must admit it was a fine trick, Young Nathaniel." He said it with a smile.

Not wasting any more words, I hugged him. Whether he was returning the same affection or just keeping up an act that would allow him to stay out of Hell for another extended stay was hard to say, but it was good to feel his arms around me.

"I really missed you, Uncle Finneus," I told him sincerely. "I was scared something awful had happened."

"What, something happen to Finneus T. Buckland?" He placed his top hat back upon his head. "Don't be ridiculous, child. Now, I must admit there was a bit of unpleasantness, but nothing I couldn't handle in my typical dazzling style. There were a few tight bits. You've a dark streak in your ancestry, you know, one that runs right from your grandfather on your mother's side all the way back to the Slavic nations of the seventeen-nineties. If I ever see another Yugoslavian pike again, it'll be too soon."

"Someone tried to stab you with a pike?" I asked, shocked that he could have survived such an attack.

Uncle Finneus chortled.

"This is the underworld we're talking about, Young Nathaniel. Of course, they tried to stab me with a pike, several dozen of them to be exact. But I made short work of that European rabble. For as long as their pea brains can hold a memory, the name of Finneus T. Buckland will bring tears to their eyes and send chills down their backsides!"

"But how could you beat dozens of them?" I asked, as much from curiosity as from admiration.

"Well, it helps if you know those fancy kar-aat-tay moves." He puffed his chest out and did a kick that fell short of knee height. "But, of course, knowing a few tunnels that let you skip right under the bumbling fools' noses doesn't hurt either."

I smiled at the joke, but somehow suspected my uncle hadn't needed to do much sneaking. In the past, I had glimpsed a cobra-like strength reflected in his eyes. Though I doubted he'd be much for fighting fair, I imagined he could handle himself just fine in most any skirmish. I certainly pitied the first soul who had come at him with a pike.

I was ready to offer space on my couch until he could get himself settled again. But he stepped toward my blank kitchen wall, extended his hand and, starting with the handle, a brand-new door seemed to sprout from his palm, quickly spreading itself up and down the wall. He casually opened it, tipped his hat to me then went downstairs, closing the door quietly behind him.

As simple as that, my Under-Heaven had returned to normal.

≈ ~ ≈

Clay spent the rest of the day shopping. It wasn't that he particularly needed anything, it was just that it gave him a chance to mingle with a few of the small shop owners in one of the Boston shopping districts. As he had suspected, each of the business owners he met was happy to answer his simple question: "How's business?"

One clothing storeowner, a woman in her sixties best summed up what most of them had all been saying, "It's not busy like it was a couple of years ago, but it's been steady." A shoe storeowner said, "It's been the worst damn year since I opened. And I've had some rough years." Even the fellow that ran the coffee shop commented, "You can't win in this business, but it's better than sweeping streets." Besides the fact that the economy was obviously tough, each of them had offered an instant response that he suspected they had used dozens if not hundreds of times. With Harry Bennerman, however, it was as if he had never had to answer the question before.

Clay felt that one of two things was true: either the man he had just met was not Harry Bennerman—and, judging from Laurel and Hardy's comments before Clay walked inside, he was—or Harry Bennerman was not and had never been in the tire business. That's not to say he didn't sell an occasional tire or two, but Clay was willing to bet that was not where he made his money. The inner city offered all kinds of illegal ways to make money, but Clay's bet was on drugs, possibly drugs that could be shipped inside the few tires that Harry did sell.

Though Clay knew he was stretching one thin theory on top of another, he wondered if Harry Bennerman might be some type of a drug kingpin. And if he were, what did that make Wagner Largess? Clay didn't have any answers, but the questions were piling up. And, one way or another, he would get his answers because there was a little boy out there depending on him.

And he intended to bring this one back alive.

≈ ~ ≈

In frustration, I splashed my hand into the fountain pool and ended the viewing. I'd only been watching Vicky for a few minutes, but as usual she had been with a boyfriend. The latest was tall with muscular arms bursting out of his tight-fitting shirt. His face was unshaven but had a cropped appearance that made me think he kept his whiskers that way, never letting them grow out too far but never shaving them off either. When Vicky slid into his metallic purple Jaguar convertible, I had seen enough. Though only two years had passed since her boyfriend Kevin had been shot and killed, my sister seemed to have forgotten completely about the danger that type of man had gotten her into. She seemed intent on self-destruction.

I trudged across the grass, across the cobblestone street and back into my house. It was late, and I was as tired as I'd ever been. Recently, my life in Under-Heaven had begun to feel like a chore. Just getting out of bed some mornings took all the energy I could muster.

I followed the noise coming from down the hall and discovered Uncle Finneus sprawled out, head propped up on one arm of the couch, shiny black shoes supported by the other. He chuckled at some character he was watching. Though I had asked him to remove that confounded television a dozen times, it always seemed to find its way back to the corner of my living room. I had never actually seen a TV during my life, but somehow, I didn't think the ones on earth displayed the same kinds of warped, sadistic and just plain cruel images that Uncle Finneus apparently conjured from the depths of his twisted imagination.

Upon seeing me, my uncle sat bolt upright and smoothed his slacks and jacket. I was surprised he hadn't also slipped his hat back on. He was very image conscious.

"Come in, come in, Young Nathaniel. This is an especially funny bit."

I glanced at the screen to see a brunette girl dangling over a pot of boiling water by her hair. I closed my eyes.

"Uncle Finneus, please shut that diabolical box off!"

There was a click and silence. I opened my eyes to find the television completely gone. My corner was mercifully bare again.

"You, my young nephew, are a sore sport." Uncle Finneus rose to his feet and moved back toward the kitchen.

I plodded after him.

"I don't suppose that if I promised not to do that again, it would cheer you up," he said.

I shook my head. For one thing, I knew my uncle well enough to know that, promise or no promise, he would have been just as likely to be watching TV in my living room tomorrow. I didn't like to think of him as dishonest, but I also knew a little promise like that wouldn't even rate on his personal honor chart. Few things did. That said, however, ever since returning from saving Vicky, his previously charcoal black suits were now more dark shades of gray. I suspected it had to do with the sacrifice and risks he had taken to help her, but I also liked to think it had something to do with his roommate. As for me, my clothing and shoes remained pretty much white all the time.

"You have a problem," Uncle Finneus announced.

"Do I?" I asked.

"There's no life left in you, Boy," he said. "You've been moping around this Under-Heaven for almost a year now.

It seemed hard to believe, but it had been over a year since Uncle Finneus had reappeared. Other than feeling a great sense of relief that he was okay, I couldn't remember much else having happened since then. Time sure did fly when you—well, time sure did fly. I settled onto one of my kitchen stools.

"Look at you, Nathaniel. You're a wreck. You look as though you've just walked a hundred miles up hill. Now what's this all about?"

I shook my head. Though I knew the crux of the problem, I didn't think I could bring myself to admit I was bored. And it wasn't just that. Though I loved all my angel relatives, and though I even loved my flawed Uncle Finneus, I just couldn't find anything to be personally concerned about. Nothing I did or could do here in Under-Heaven made any difference. In all the time I'd been in Under-Heaven, I had only influenced one life, the life of my sister Vicky; and even that had only been with Uncle Finneus' help. It seemed to me that nothing I did mattered. It was as though I didn't exist, and in a very real way that was true. Back on Earth I was less than a ghost; I could see but could not be seen. Here in Under-Heaven I existed, but to what end? Of course, I didn't know much about Heaven, but I feared it would be more of the same. Somewhere deep inside myself, I cringed at the thought of spending an eternity of not mattering. And worse yet, I feared that during that eternity, I might not even matter to myself.

"Apparently, I must tell you a secret," Uncle Finneus stated.

I shrugged and didn't bother to guess at what manipulation my uncle was about to try. In many respects I was beyond that. To be manipulated, you had to care about something, and I was finding that harder and harder to do.

"Whiskey," Uncle Finneus said, "did you know that Whiskey is still alive?"

≈ ~ ≈

Clay spent about an hour with Boston Police Detective Patricia Conroy, the lead investigator on Jesse's disappearance. She had only a few leads and nothing that Clay considered of value. Jesse Largess's teacher hadn't seen anything other than a black car driving off. Not only had she not gotten a plate number, she also hadn't been able to provide a possible make or model of the car. Only one of the children had seen anything, a little boy by the name of Heath Gregoire.

"Could I arrange to meet that boy?" Clay asked.

"Not possible. Two days ago, the boy's father let us do the first interview, but said he wanted to wait at least a week before we talk to his son again. Because the Largess boy was his son's best friend, he's worried talking to us will create too much trauma."

"So how much trauma will it cause when his best friend dies because we couldn't talk to him?"

Detective Conroy opened her mouth to speak but Clay shook his head and waved her to silence. He didn't mean to be flippant. On the one hand, he knew every second mattered in the search for Jesse, but on the other, young minds could be fragile and parents had every right to worry. Would it be right to endanger the Gregoire boy when he might not know anything helpful anyway? That was a question that only a parent could answer.

Clay opened Jesse's Amber Alert police file and glanced down through the notes on the interview with Heath. "He described the kidnapper as very big with a black beard."

"That's right," Detective Conroy said. She was a pretty woman, in her early forties he guessed. She wasn't wearing a ring, but her ring finger had a pale line around it. Either she had recently split from her husband, or she made it a point not to wear the ring to work.

"How big is Heath's father?" Clay asked.

"About five foot ten, maybe two hundred pounds. Why?"

"Your guy is probably over six feet, maybe two-fifty," Clay answered.

"You think he's comparing the kidnapper to his father's size?"

"Kids always do."

"Maybe the guy was wearing a heavy down or other puffy jacket. That could make him look a lot bigger."

"True," Clay said. "Sounds like a good question to have the father ask his son."

"Good angle," Detective Conroy said, "have the father ask a few questions for us. Anything else you want to know?"

One of the best things about working with female officers, Clay thought, was that most didn't have ego issues. Detective Conroy recognized that he was more experienced at this sort of investigation and immediately sought his help rather than trying to dismiss him in the midst of it all.

"See if he'll ask his son what cartoon character the man reminded him of."

Her blue eyes looked up from her legal pad.

"You're serious?"

"Absolutely."

"Can that really help?"

"Put it to you this way, if a kid says a perp looked or acted like Bugs Bunny, that's a much different image than Elmer Fudd. Besides, it will be good for the kid's psyche to think of this more like a cartoon than reality."

"Makes sense to me," Detective Conroy said. "I'll see what the father says. How will I reach you when I find out?"

Clay handed her his card. His cell phone was the only number listed.

"You up for drinks?" she asked him as the meeting wrapped up.

"Sorry, but I can't," he said. He was glad he didn't have to make up an excuse. If she was making a pass, she was a little too old for him. Besides, he definitely didn't want to get mixed up in any marital issues. "I've got to get over to that school. I want to look around before it's too dark, and right now there shouldn't be any kids around."

She nodded and agreed to call the principal and let her know that Clay would be poking around the yard. He thanked her and left the station. He didn't know it at the time, but when they met again, Detective Conroy's wedding band would be back on her finger.

≈ ~ ≈

Even I knew that dogs seldom lived to be more than twelve or fifteen years old. It just wasn't possible that Whiskey could still be alive. Besides, Grandma Clara said he died shortly after the sheriff found Vicky. I'd be the first to admit my grandmother often gave cryptic responses to my questions, but she would never have lied to me. My Uncle Finneus, on the other hand, had made an art of lying. How could I believe him?

"It's not possible," I said. "It's been almost twenty years since I was killed."

"Dogs have souls, Nate. Well, some of them do."

Now my ears were perked. Was it possible that my Whiskey was in Heaven? Though I had never seen pets here in Under-Heaven, that didn't mean they didn't move on to a different one or maybe even directly to Heaven. If any dog had deserved a place above, it was my amazing Whiskey. My insides quivered at the thought of being with him again. With a few words, my Uncle Finneus had given me a reason to care. I had always known that one day my parents and I would be reunited, but I had never allowed myself to dream that Whiskey and I—

Tears were streaming down my cheeks.

I would see my Whisky again!

Already, I could envision romping through the clouds, my dog at my side. Though it had taken nearly twenty years, my decision was made. I would move on to Heaven.

Uncle Finneus had one of those sly grins when I focused on him again.

"Feeling better?" he asked.

"Thank you, Uncle Finneus." I hugged him before he had a chance to back away.

Though he endured it from time to time, he had never been one to display too much affection. His personal comfort zone seemed to be arm's length or better. Whenever I got closer than that, he would make an excuse to move away. It probably had less to do with his status in Hell than with his personality. I guessed he had been much the same way when he was alive. As I would have expected, he allowed the hug to go on for only a moment before prying me loose. He did, however, surprise me when he reached down and tipped my chin up so that he could see my face.

"Don't you want to see him?" he asked.

I wiped at the tears and nodded my head.

"I'm going to tell Grandma Clara tomorrow that I want to move on to Heaven."

I'm not sure I had ever seen Uncle Finneus truly surprised before that moment. His mouth hung open, but no words came forth. He stared at me.

"Heaven?"

I knew what was bothering him. If I left my Under-Heaven, his only connection to this place would be severed. My leaving would effectively force him to return to Hell. His vacation would be over.

His face went slack.

Guilt settled around my heart. I had never considered this implication.

"I don't understand, Nathaniel," he said, looking genuinely perplexed. "Why do you suddenly feel the need to Rise?"

"I could wait a little while," I offered. "Whiskey and I have waited this long."

It was as if I had suddenly poured a combined of sunlight and humor onto my uncle's bewildered expression, because his face nearly exploded with happy mirth.

"My Boy, now I understand! I have inadvertently misled you."

My guilt was rapidly being replaced with anger. How could he lie about something as important as my Whiskey?

Then, suddenly, I knew I would have to discuss this with one of my angel relatives. I had to know what was true and what wasn't. What I couldn't understand was why Uncle Finneus had told me about Whiskey in the first place. He should have known I would want to be with my dog.

"I should have spoken more clearly," my uncle continued, his voice having taken on what seemed to be a sincere tone. "Whiskey is somewhere on Earth. He's likely been reincarnated four or five times by now."

Now, it was my turn to be speechless. Why hadn't I ever heard about this before? And if it wasn't true, why would my uncle have concocted such a hurtful lie? My first inclination was to believe him—again—but that could simply have been an extension of my desperate desire to see my dog. The one thing I knew was that I had never spotted a dog soul when looking down at Earth. It's hard to explain, but I had always known the life-lights that I saw in the fountain pool were human, much the way I could always tell which light was Vicky's.

My thoughts were in such turmoil that I considered calling for my Aunt Alice because she was the most direct of my angel relatives. She would be honest and clear when answering questions about this entire issue, and unlike Grandma Clara, she wouldn't lose me with double-speak or cryptic answers. Though sometimes brutal, My Aunt Alice was always straightforward.

"You don't believe me," Uncle Finneus said.

"I want to," I told him honestly.

"Go out and look in the fountain right now," he said. "You'll see I'm telling the truth."

"Maybe I should talk to Aunt Alice first."

"Suit yourself. But if it were me, I'd want to start looking for my dog right away."

"Why haven't I ever seen any animal life-lights before?"

Uncle Finneus settled onto one of my kitchen stools.

"It's because people show up so much brighter than animals that you wouldn't notice them without looking."

"You mean I can't see them?"

"No, I suspect you can, but it will take a bit of focus and practice."

He had barely finished the last statement before I raced out into the front yard, crossed the cobbled circular street and sat at the edge of the fountain. In my excitement, it took me several tries to smooth the water.

≈ ~ ≈

Whoever had taken Jesse had cut the cyclone fencing with bolt cutters. Yellow crime scene tape surrounded the sidewalk and most of the playground. Though it had apparently rained since the original work was done, Clay could still see faint traces of the yellow outline chalk showing where Jesse's hat had been found just outside the fencing on the sidewalk.

Clay paced the area a dozen times, glancing up and down the street as he did so. His instincts rang loudly that Harry Bennerman was involved, but so far nothing other than his relationship to Wagner connected him. In his twenty or more years of investigation, Clay had learned one thing: hunches and instincts were more often right than wrong. His ill feeling about the owner of the tire warehouse was simply too pervasive to ignore.

"Come on, Harry, talk to me," Clay whispered as he rubbed his key chain and ingested the scene.

≈ ~ ≈

"Why didn't you tell me?" I asked Grandma Clara when she arrived the next day. I had been awake the entire night and hadn't left the pool until the morning sunlight made it impossible to discern the dim life-lights of the animals that outnumbered the people on Earth, hundreds to one. Though I would have thought the ratio of animals would have been higher, I soon realized that only certain animals had life forces bright enough for me to see.

"Your chances of finding him are so slim, Nate, it didn't seem right to give you false hope."

"I don't understand why I can't just think of him and zoom in like I do with Vicky," I said.

"Animals are much simpler than people, Nate. Their souls evolve but only slowly and over hundreds of lives. The ones that you can see have probably been in existence since the dawn of man. Young animal souls have signatures so dim we can't see them at all, even from Heaven."

"You can see better from there?"

210

"Yes." She paused. "But it's not the same. In Heaven, you experience Earth more than see it."

I wished she would clarify what she meant by "experience," but Grandma Clara didn't respond well to multiple questions about the same thing. I figured that if I asked, her answer would only further confuse me.

"Couldn't you find Whiskey for me and then point him out?" I asked.

She gave me an uncomfortable smile. I knew her answer was "no" just by her expression. "I would help, Nate, but it would take hundreds of angels working together for months to find one animal soul like that. It's not that we don't love you, it's just that there are so many other new souls to look after."

Though her response made me want to cry, I knew she was telling the truth. One of the reasons I saw so much of my Grandma Clara and so little of my other relatives was that the older an angel became, the longer their lineage stretched out. Angels as old as Amber, for instance, likely measured their lineage in the hundreds of thousands, maybe even millions of souls. Granted, most of those souls were not newly dead, but it wouldn't have surprised me to find that Amber had thousands upon thousands of new charges residing in the under-heavens at any given time. Grandma Clara, on the other hand, was a much more recent soul so she had fewer of us to look after.

"What are my chances of ever finding him?" I asked.

"You might never do it, Nate," she said.

I then understood why Uncle Finneus' had told me about Whiskey. The longer I stayed in Under-Heaven and looked for my dog, the longer he would also be able to stay.

For a while, his little trick worked.

≈ ~ ≈

Clay was seated at one of the many restaurants that crowded Boston's suburban malls. This one was called Swiss Mountain, where they specialized in steak and lamb combinations. The artificial grassy knolls between every few tables and the furniture formed to look like rocks and fallen logs suggested it was a national chain, but in all his time on the road Clay had never seen another one like it. After the meal arrived, he determined that the pleasant atmosphere was fortuitous because the food wasn't very good. He had ordered a vegetarian omelet and French-fries. What he got back was reconstituted egg powder and some unnamable freeze-dried vegetable bits. Fortunately, the bottled beer was okay. He ordered a second beer from his waitress who, like all the other waitresses, was supposedly dressed like a Swedish sheepherder. He hadn't known that sheepherders wore such tight, low-cut dresses. He was happy they did, however. Watching the exposed cleavage was a good respite from the day he'd been having.

His cell phone vibrated against his hip.

Unlike many people, Clay felt that talking on a cell phone in public was not only in bad taste, it was downright rude. He'd once seen a lawyer reprimanded by a judge for carrying on not one, but two, loud phone conversations in the court hallway during a trial break. As far as Clay was concerned, he should have been arrested for contempt.

He quickly made his way to the cashier's booth.

"Excuse me, Miss," he said to the especially busty, blond sheepherder. "I'm at the table over there near the window." He pointed. "I'm just going out to answer a call. Do you need me to leave a credit card or something?"

She blinked demurely and suddenly had much better posture.

"No problem, Sir. I'll have your waitress keep your place."

"Thank you," Clay said as he slipped outside. On another day he might already have been making plans to take the young woman out, but he knew that every minute he wasted was another minute that Jesse remained in trouble. The first few days of an investigation were the most crucial, especially if you wanted to get a child back alive.

The vibrating had long-since stopped, but Detective Conroy's home number was displayed on the phone's small screen. Clay leaned against the front of the building and, not bothering to listen to her voice mail, pressed redial.

"Hello."

He recognized her voice.

"Detective Conroy, this is Clay Gromkis, returning your call."

"I'm glad you did, Clay. I just got done talking with Mr. Gregoire, the father of Jesse Largess's young friend from school. He told me the man we want looks like Bluto—you know, the big guy from Popeye."

"Yeah, I know who he means. Anything else?"

"Yes, his son told him the man had lots of gold chains around his neck."

"The father didn't mind talking to his son?"

"No, he actually called the station to let me know Heath had remembered something else, something he thought we should know."

"What's that?"

"He had an unusual ID for the car."

"Unusual," Clay said. "Unusual is always good. What is it?"

"The boy told his father the car was collectible. He said it was a Blue Line car."

"Detective?"

"Heath's father collects toy Hot Wheels cars. The ones they call Red Lines are some of the most collectible. Rather than white walls, they have red lines around the tires—"

"And the kid says the black car had blue lines on the tires instead of white or red," Clay finished. "Hello, Harry."

"That means something, Clay? Who's Harry?"

"New tires have blue on the white walls, Patricia. When they're mounted most garages wash the blue off. Must protect the white or something. The black car had new tires on it, and the blue hadn't been washed off yet. I'll bet those tires came from a warehouse owned by Mr. Harry Bennerman. That's where Jesse's father worked for the last few years."

"Sounds pretty slim, Clay."

"Yeah, I know. Think you could run a check on this guy anyway?"

"Sure," she said.

"How long will it take?" Clay asked.

"I can have records run a local within a few minutes. National takes a couple of hours sometimes."

"I'll wait by the phone if you can get me a quick rundown."

Detective Conroy agreed. Clay gave her Harry's name and his warehouse address. It turned out to be less than five minutes before she called back.

"Clean as a baby's cheeks. No criminal record, no business troubles, not even a speeding ticket. You sure he's involved?"

Even though she couldn't have seen it, Clay shook his head. "I'm never sure of anything, but something about that guy and his tire business doesn't add up. Even if he turns out innocent on the missing kid, I promise he's prime for an investigation."

"Once we've tracked the boy down," she said, "why don't you drop me your notes. I haven't done a drug prelim for a while. The captain might let me scout this one before turning things over to U-squad."

"U-squad?"

She chuckled. "Just our little nickname for the drug division. Ugly and undercover."

"I like it," Clay said. "Back in Oklahoma, we used to call them 'Roots.' It started as Under-Oakies but then went further."

"No matter what you call 'em," Detective Conroy said, "they don't get paid enough for the crap they go through."

"For the ones that stay clean, that's for sure," Clay agreed. Unfortunately, a lot of them wound up turned or burned for playing too close to the fire. Clay had often thought that undercover departments should either be more careful with their psych evaluations or should be eliminated altogether. Some of the most dangerous criminals in every city were the undercover cops that played both sides of the fence. Some people believed it was a necessary risk, but Clay wasn't convinced.

"Thanks again for all the help," Clay said. He hung up and went back inside the restaurant. Thoughts swirling, he didn't notice a single bosom as he finished his second beer and left.

25

Decisions

My nightly visits with Vicky were now followed religiously with my search for Whiskey. As time progressed, I found myself getting better at discerning domestic animals from wild animals. And, though my instincts weren't always perfect, more often than not I could tell the dogs from the cats. Of the thousands of individual dogs, I found, I had yet to locate one that felt like Whiskey. I'm not sure how many months passed, but at some point, I came to feel my search was in vain.

My previous malaise returned.

As my mood grew somber, my indifference toward most everything and everyone in Under-Heaven became evident again. I loved my relatives and appreciated all they had done for me but that was no longer enough. In my heart, I knew I would soon be leaving Under-Heaven. I knew I again needed a purpose to exist.

Though Uncle Finneus wouldn't be pleased, I had decided to return to Earth.

≈ ~ ≈

Clay drove past the tire warehouse. There was one small white van in the yard and beside it sat a black Chrysler LeBaron. Though the whitewalls weren't blue, they could have recently been washed. Every instinct in Clay's body said this was his guy, but he still didn't have a stitch of proof. Gut and innuendo just weren't enough to work with. Somehow, he had to link the boy's disappearance to this fellow Harry.

But how?

First things first, Clay had to get a new set of wheels. Corvettes were fun but a bit too conspicuous.

Car rental and then coffee, he thought to himself, in that order.

It was going to be a long night.

≈ ~ ≈

Jesse heard movement outside the door of the damp room he'd been locked in. It was probably the bear-man bringing him another fast food meal, but Jesse hadn't eaten a thing in days. His jaw was so painfully swollen that he couldn't chew, and though he sipped occasionally from the drinks, the bubbles in the soda made his stomach cramp. It didn't matter, though, because Jesse already knew he was going to die. He sensed that sometime soon the bad men were going to kill him, and there wasn't anything he could do about it.

His head ached all over and he felt certain that the bones in his face were broken. His fingers were raw from prying at the door and at the bricks in the walls. Only his legs remained undamaged, but they were of scant use because his head swooned every time he got to his feet.

Surprisingly, Jesse didn't feel scared for himself. He had already accepted his own impending death. But he knew his mother would cry when she found out. Most of all, though, Jesse was scared for his dad. He had heard the bearish man mutter nasty things about his father, the worst being what he said when he brought food the last time.

"I'll be glad when your father gets his ass back here and we can bury the both of you."

Gingerly lifting a corner of the blanket he was lying on, Jesse covered his weak, soon-to-be-dead body. He wished he had his stuffed dog to hold onto as he curled up on the concrete floor and closed his eyes. Jesse made a valiant effort to forget that he had ever been born.

≈ ~ ≈

As it turned out, iced coffee wasn't as bad as it had always sounded to Clay. The cappuccino machine at the Handi-Mart had run out, and the clerk warned him the coffee in the dispensers had been there since early morning. The last option turned out to be the caffeine and ice combination he sat sipping in the white Toyota he'd rented only an hour before. He had parked in the Verizon store parking lot across the street from Harry's warehouse. Both the white van and the black sedan were still in the yard. It was possible that no one was in the building, but Clay's intuition told him that someone was. He could see dim light shining into the alley, probably from Harry's office, on the western side of the building. Otherwise the place was pitch black.

It was ten minutes to midnight when a man strode out the side door of the warehouse and got into the black LeBaron. He was a big man, over six-foot-two Clay guessed from the way his head towered over the white van as he walked in front of it. He was not only tall, but also thick—huge by a child's standard.

"Hello, Bluto," Clay whispered.

He knew he was close on this one, but still he didn't have any actual proof. He needed more than a generic black car and a Bluto comparison to get a search warrant for the warehouse. And even that might not have generated the wanted result. Clay suspected that Harry was involved, but someone who had managed to stay as clean as Harry Bennerman would not be dumb enough to keep a kidnapped kid right on his own premises.

Or would he?

Some damn smart criminals had been caught doing far dumber things. If Clay had any advantage at all, it was that Harry probably didn't suspect anyone was onto him. Certainly, the police hadn't shown any interest, and Clay's single visit wasn't likely to have set off any bells or whistles. No, if someone were going to do something stupid, it would be a person like Harry Bennerman who had no apparent reason to fear.

Soon, Clay intended to give him a reason.

The LeBaron pulled out into traffic. Clay waited for several cars to pass then followed. He stayed four cars back in Bluto's same lane. When the LeBaron stopped at a phone booth only a couple of miles from the warehouse, Clay continued on past. He went two more blocks then turned around in a Fancy Hair parking lot, fully cognizant that that criminals tended to use payphones and disposable phones whenever possible. Bluto was still in the phone booth when Clay pulled to the side of the road a hundred feet back.

Clay had the Boston police number on speed dial, but it would have taken twenty minutes to find the right person at this time of night. He took the chance and called Detective Conroy.

A man answered, his voice thick with sleep, "Yeah?"

"I'm sorry to call this late, but—"

Clay didn't have a chance to finish the statement.

"It's for you," the man croaked. There was a slight click and the ruffle of sheets.

"Conroy," Detective Conroy said, sounding a whole lot more awake than her husband. Clay guessed she had children. Mothers always tended to be light sleepers. He didn't remember seeing any photos of children on her desk at the police station, but that didn't mean anything.

"I'm sorry to call this late, Detective," Clay said, "but I need some help, quickly."

"You have a solid lead already?"

"It's getting more solid by the minute. I think I found Bluto. He's at a phone booth on Vanity, right in front of Hollywood Arcade."

"I know the place," she said. He heard more rustling cloth as he imagined her scrambling to the edge of the bed for a pad and a pencil. "He's on the phone right now?"

"Yeah, has been for the last couple of minutes."

"We can trace it. You just need to know where and who?"

"That would be great."

"You're sure that's him?" she said.

"I'm feeling more sure every moment. Thanks for the help."

"No problem, Clay. Do you think I should punch in?"

"No. It'll be a few hours before I can pin anything solid. I hope not, but it might even be a few days."

"You're not a hero, are you?" she asked.

Clay didn't know if she was worried that he'd put the boy in danger by not asking for help, or if she feared he would steal the credit for her investigation.

"I've never been a hero, Patricia. I've always just been a cop."

"I'll have someone call you the second we get the trace."

"Thanks again. Sorry to wake you."

"No sweat. 'Goes with the territory."

≈ ~ ≈

My relatives had been coming and going steadily for the last couple of days. Apparently, news of a reincarnation travels quickly in Heaven. It seemed that everyone wanted to tell me how much they loved me and to wish me well in my new life. The only relative I hadn't seen anything of was Uncle Finneus, which concerned me for several reasons: I feared that maybe my decision had angered him to the point of ruining our relationship or that maybe that our relationship had been nothing but a farce on his end. But the worst of the three possibilities was that maybe I had hurt him when I decided to leave. Surely, he knew how much I would miss him.

I was anxious to see him.

Suddenly, I had another suspicion: would Uncle Finneus stay away, knowing I wouldn't leave without saying goodbye? After all, every minute he kept me in Under-Heaven was another minute he could avoid his return to Hell.

218

No matter the reason, I knew I had to find him.

Grandma Clara, Aunt Alice and Uncle Albert were the last of the angels to leave. They all had the same sad but supportive expressions. Though they hated to see me go, all three had long before sensed my soul would one-day return to Earth.

"I'll miss you," I said to Grandma Clara as I hugged her tightly.

She ran her fingers through my hair.

"No, you won't, Nate, because you won't remember any of this for as long as you're alive. But don't worry, I'll miss you and keep an eye on you down there. And, most importantly, I'll be here to hug my little boy just as soon he gets back."

I moved on to Aunt Alice. Of all my angel relatives, I think she had helped me to grow the most. She taught me about true honor and the goodness of deeds that go beyond your everyday be-a-good-boy variety. I, of course, had long ago learned my Aunt Alice's husband had been caught plotting against the Czar Nicholas and had been killed. When the Russian soldiers arrived at her estate to take vengeance on anyone else who might have been involved, my Aunt took full responsibility and was shot in full view of her three children and all her serfs. With the execution of the Lady of the estate, something the soldiers had been loath to do, the Czar's representatives considered the estate clean of revolutionaries. Thereby, with her sacrifice, my Aunt Alice had delivered the safety of her three children and the wellbeing of their family estate, an estate that had ultimately safely nurtured five more generations until the rise of communism scattered lords and peasants alike all across Eastern Europe.

I hugged my Aunt Alice for a long time.

"You're not so bad," I whispered to her.

"Shhh," she said. "Let's not start rumors." When she finally got free of my grip, she said, "God speed on your next journey, Nathaniel. I, too, will be watching."

Finally, there was my Uncle Albert. It was odd that though he and I had spent little time together alone, he had been a staple of my life here in Under-Heaven. Every few days, he would trundle in some new relative or another; and without him I couldn't have imagined how uncomfortable those introductions would have been. I remembered the way he had first stepped between my Aunt Alice and me. The memory made me smile.

"It appears your time has come, Nate," Uncle Albert said. "I'm going to miss playing tour guide around here."

"And I'm going to miss you," I said. I hugged him as tightly as I had the others.

In apparent embarrassment, Uncle Albert turned his head and wiped at the corner of one eye. I had long-since given up wiping my own tears. They had been running steadily for hours. My time in Under-Heaven was nearly over.

≈ ~ ≈

Clay followed Bluto back to the tire warehouse. As the dark LeBaron pulled into the parking lot, Clay continued on past. When he returned a few minutes later, he again pulled into the Verizon parking lot across the street. Bluto had already gone inside, and once more Clay was left to watch an empty white van and a black car. It was almost half an hour before Detective Conroy called.

"This is Clay," he said, having long-since fallen out of the habit of answering with his last name as most policemen did. He hadn't thought to look at the screen to see who was calling.

"Clay, it's Conroy." She sounded wide-awake. "I just got a call from the techs. Your boy was on the phone with the police department in Ormand Beach, Florida, just one town up the coast from Daytona."

"Damn," Clay said, "why the police department? Can I get that number from you?"

"I'm one step ahead of you, Clay. I called the chief on night shift down there. Seems the name Wagner Largess came flashing across all their screens a few minutes ago, and right after that someone claiming to be his brother called to see if they had heard anything about him."

"Had they?"

"You could say that."

"What'd they nab him on? Something to do with drugs, I'll bet."

"I'm not sure anyone has a handle on that yet, Clay. Wagner was dead when they found him less than an hour ago. They think he was driving a rented van and got car-jacked, but everyone's still shaky on the details. The only thing they found on him was a slip of paper with your guy's name and phone number."

"Harry Bennerman?"

"Yep, the one and only. There was no wallet or ID on the body, but Wagner had a pretty impressive rap sheet, especially when he was younger. Prints were all over our database. Didn't take them long to identify him."

"They say any of this to the caller?"

"Guy on duty said 'no,' but I'm guessing they said enough that whoever called knows something's up."

Clay's mind was running at top speed. Wagner in Florida; Bennerman in Boston; Bluto makes a phone call to Florida; Bluto tells Bennerman—"

"Jesus Christ, Conroy!"

"You got the puzzle?"

"I think Bennerman sent Wagner on an errand, maybe to pick up a load of blow or something down there in Florida. Something takes longer than planned, or Wagner just up and runs off with the product. Bennerman grabs his kid and tells him to get his ass back here with whatever-it-is or the kid dies."

Detective Conroy finished the progression for him, "You think the big guy just found out Wagner's dead or in custody, so now Bennerman has no more use for the kid."

"We have to get in there!" Clay said. He could imagine Bluto pointing a gun in the boy's face even as they spoke.

"I need cause, Clay. I can't get a goddamned judge to let me in there with what we've got."

Clay knew she was going to say that. He had always been a by-the-book cop himself, but he didn't intend to let Jesse die on a technicality.

"What if I threatened to go in there alone, without you?"

"We might get just far enough in to arrest you or drag your dead body out, Clay. You know better than that."

"What about an anonymous tip?"

"Saying?"

"I'm a homeless guy that won't give his name, but I saw a big guy drag a kid into the tire warehouse."

"Not enough. Too vague, only one testimony."

"How about if you also add that Clay Gromkis has reported multiple suspicions about the same location."

Detective Patricia Conroy grunted.

"Yeah," she said. "Yeah, that might do it."

"You need the homeless guy to call you back from another line?"

"No. They won't check me on this unless Bennerman turns up clean and sues the pants off us. If that's the case, none of this will stand up anyway. How sure are you?"

Clay thought about it. This was exactly the sort of thing he never did when he was a policeman, and now he was asking this detective to make up false evidence in order to get a search warrant. But everything added up. It felt right. He could see Harry Bennerman's expression of relief when they had first parted. He saw the Bluto look-alike, the black car, a call to Florida, Wagner's death, and finally he pictured Bluto pointing the gun at the Jesse's forehead—

"Yeah, I'm sure."

"I'll have someone get a search warrant and we'll meet you at the warehouse. How's twenty-five minutes sound?"

"Maybe too long," Clay said, "but if that's the best you can do…."

"Quicker if we can. You think four units is enough?"

"Detective, I'd swing anyone that's free over here, just to be safe."

"Maybe six, then," she said. "See you in fifteen or twenty."

The phone went dead.

Clay sat staring at the large building. He imagined that even now the brute would be on the phone with Bennerman, telling him that his marionette Wagner was in trouble or worse. Bennerman's first thought would be to dump the evidence, in this case the kid's body. Clay just hoped the boy was still alive, but he couldn't get the vision of a gun being pointed at Jesse Largess out of his head.

He had to do something, even if it meant putting himself at risk with the law. He didn't know what Patricia Conroy would think if she found him already inside when she got there, but given that or a dead child, Clay was willing to take his chances.

He opened the door and got out of the rented Toyota. Watching the building closely, he slid a full clip into his 9mm Beretta pistol then strode across the street.

26

In the Balance

Everyone else was gone and I had already said goodbye to my sister at the pool when I approached the door to Uncle Finneus' basement. I had only been down there once, but that was enough to know if my uncle had decided not to be found it would take hours to search the entire area. Even so, I resigned myself to try.

I opened the door.

There sat my uncle, gray suit and pinstripes, on the top step, his back to me. His head was leaning into his hands. I didn't know if it was my imagination, but the material of his suit looked even lighter than it had a few days ago.

"Uncle Finneus?" I said.

Slowly, as though turning on a rusty bearing, his head came around.

"Young Nathaniel," he said, his voice uncharacteristically weak. If I hadn't known better, I would have sworn he had been wearing mascara. Black streaks extended from his eyes down to his chin. He had been crying.

"I've been looking for you, Uncle Finneus," I said. "I wanted to say goodbye."

"Let me come up out of this dank hole," Uncle Finneus said, "so we can have a proper parting."

"I know by leaving here I'm forcing you to go back…down there," I said. "I'm sorry."

My Uncle smiled, and it looked genuine.

"That's my boy Nathaniel, isn't it? He's making big decisions about what to do with his own future but still concerns himself with how it will affect one dark, old man."

"You're not old," I told him with an impish grin. I remembered how he had made that same declaration the day I met him. He hadn't wanted me to call him "grandfather" because it made him sound too old.

"I'm proud of you, Nathaniel," he told me. "When you died that day, I was horrified for you and your family. We see some terrible things down below, but seeing what it did to your soul, that was the hardest part. Then you got up here and worked through all that. Just like a champ, you came out all right. Those people on Earth are lucky to have you going back with them."

I hugged him and was so thankful that all my ridiculous fears about him and our relationship had proven false. Of all my relatives, he was the one I had spent the most time with. I had grown to love my Uncle Finneus for all the things that he was and wasn't. It seemed to me, of everyone I had met since arriving in Under-Heaven, my uncle was the closest to still being human. Lord knew he had his faults, but he had his good points, too. Even if I didn't remember him in my new life, I knew that on some level my soul would miss him.

"I love you, Uncle."

It seemed he completely forgot about his own comfort zone as he drew me tightly into his embrace. For the longest time, we stayed like that. When we parted, it didn't feel as though either of us wanted it to be over.

"What will happen to you, Uncle Finneus?" I asked him. I half-expected his chest to puff out and his bravado smile to appear, but neither happened.

"It's not pleasant down there, Nathaniel," he said, his face somber, "but with a little wit and some luck you can be reasonably comfortable. I have the wit and usually have the luck, so I should be fine."

"Will I ever see you again?" I asked, even though I feared the answer.

This time I got the bravado smile.

"They couldn't keep me down the first couple of times," he added, "so there's no reason to think they'll be any more successful the next time around. We'll see each other again, and when we do, I intend to pound you to smithereens on the chessboard."

We hugged again. As I stepped away, he disappeared.

≈ ~ ≈

Clay crept along the edge of the building and peered through Harry's office window blinds. The overhead lights in the small room were on, revealing it to be empty and the door to the warehouse beyond to be closed. He hoped the closed door would be enough to smother the noise he was about to make.

As expected, the window was locked. He slipped his jacket off and draped it across the glass. With the butt of his pistol, he tapped the pane gently in the corner through his jacket and heard a satisfying but mercifully quiet crack. He took his jacket down and pulled the loose glass shards out of the window frame. Unfortunately, the resulting hole wasn't large enough to reach his arm through. Knowing how risky it was, he placed the jacket over the glass and tapped again. This time, the entire window exploded inward. Definitely not the quiet result he had hoped for.

Clay used his elbow to break the worst of the glass shards away. Then, placing his jacket over the remaining jagged pieces, he pulled himself up and into the room. He left his glass-littered jacket on one of the chairs as he crept over to the door. So far, there was only silence.

Bluto, where are you?

In one way, Clay hoped he had heard the breaking glass. If the big man were investigating the noise coming from the office, he wouldn't be off someplace else killing the child. Right then, Jesse Largess' safety was the only thing Clay could think about. Already, it seemed possible the boy could be dead. Clay blocked that thought from his mind.

Turning off the office light first, he listened against the warehouse door then gently turned the knob. The door creaked only slightly as he eased it open. The warehouse was dimly lit with a pair of fluorescent lights hanging every twenty-five feet or so. Bluto was nowhere to be seen. Clay slipped out into the main warehouse and closed the office door quietly behind him.

What now?

He could hear the sounds of a furnace from somewhere down below, but something else, too. He got down on his hands and knees and pressed an ear to the floorboards.

"Jesus, Harry," he heard faintly through the floor. "I…fucking responsibility…you…I don't…if you want, but…what if he doesn't…maybe…money…shit…body."

Though fragmented, the one-sided bits of conversation gave Clay a ray of hope. First of all, Harry couldn't have been in the building if he was on the other end of the phone—and one criminal was always easier to deal with than two. But the most optimistic thing Clay picked up was that something serious was still going on. He hoped it meant that the child was still alive. It might also have meant he was already dead, and they were discussing who was going to get rid of the body, but Clay didn't even want to consider that.

Knowing he had to find a way to the room below him, Clay slipped off his cowboy boots, held them in one hand, and went in search of stairs. About a hundred feet down the aisle, toward the back of the building, he was rewarded by a wide set of stairs that went down about four feet, stopped at a platform, then turned and went further down. The stairway was dark, and though Clay had a flashlight, turning it on would have been announcing his presence. His amateur entrance had been bad enough.

It was pitch black at the bottom of the stairs, but he could feel concrete through his stocking feet, so he slipped his boots back on. Though silence was important, mobility would be more important when the action began. Clay placed his free hand against a brick wall and moved slowly along it.

≈ ~ ≈

Jesse had been drifting in and out of consciousness so much that he found it hard to tell dreams from reality. At one point, his father appeared, all dressed in a spiffy, black suit and explaining that he had found a new place to live with lots of nice people. But then that dream had been replaced by one with the big bear-like man switching a light on and nearly blinding Jesse.

"Jesus, you're a mess," the man had said and pointed his gun at Jesse's head. It would almost have been a relief to hear the shot of the gun, but nothing happened. Before Jesse knew it, the man turned into his father and left the room, flipping the light off as he went.

Only a short time later, Jesse heard quiet footsteps passing outside his cell. The big man stomped like an elephant, but whoever this was seemed slower and quieter.

"Dad?" Jesse croaked in a low whisper. He could barely open his mouth. As he spoke, he could feel the skin at corners of his mouth crack where his upper and lower lips met. He thought it might be dried blood.

The footsteps stopped.

"Dad?" he said again. Was this still a dream?

≈ ~ ≈

The boy's raspy voice was more like a plea from the grave than a call for help. Clay's heart went out to Jesse. He listened intently at the wooden door but there was no sound of movement or of another voice.

"Dad?"

Clay debated whether it was safe to say anything, but it seemed best to reassure the boy.

"Jesse," he whispered, "I'm here to help you. Can you hear me?"

"Yeah," the young voice came, stronger this time. That was a good sign.

"You need to talk softly, Jesse, okay?"

"Okay." His voice was barely a whisper.

"My name is Clay Gromkis," he whispered, placing his mouth up near the door. "And I used to be a cop. Now I help missing children, children like you. Do you understand?"

"I think so."

"Besides this door, is there any other way in or out of the room you're in?"

"No."

"Do you know how many people are in the building?"

"No, but I only ever see one."

"A big man who looks like Bluto?"

"Yeah."

"Which way does he go when he walks away from you?"

There was a pause, and it occurred to Clay that a five-year-old might not yet know the difference between right and left. He was debating how he could explain it to him when Jesse said, "To the left, from the way you came."

Clay froze. Had he walked right past the guy? Was there a gun pointed at his back at that very moment?

≈ ~ ≈

Jesse heard sirens. At first, they were distant but then they got closer until it sounded like dozens of police cars were close by. He could hear the man on the other side of the door breathing. It seemed impossible to imagine, but maybe he was going to make it out alive.

As he heard the sounds of wood breaking somewhere on the floor above him, he had only one thought.

I hope my dad's okay.

≈ ~ ≈

Clay was both relieved and terrified when he heard the sirens. A moment of panic could send a criminal into a violent frenzy and he could easily imagine that hulk of a man charging down the hallway with a machine gun on steady fire. All Clay could do was to kneel down and keep his gun at the ready. He had considered shooting off the padlock on Jesse's prison, but the noise would have given him away. Besides, the boy was probably safer inside than outside at the moment. The only way Bluto was getting through that door again would be over Clay's dead body. Until local police arrived, it was the best protection he could offer.

Suddenly, there was a crash up above as the police broke down the door to the warehouse. Clay could hear dozens of pairs of feet charging up and down the warehouse aisles. The academies taught officers to run in patterns: run a few feet, stop in a defensive position, reconnoiter then run another few feet before repeating the process. It sounded almost like a rhythmic dance as the teams of policemen moved further and further through the building, Clay held his breath.

What would Bluto do when he heard them on the stairs?

Clay kept his flashlight and gun hands locked together and ready to aim. At the slightest provocation, he intended to switch the light on and begin firing.

"The police are almost here," he whispered to Jesse. "I'm going to stay right here until they arrive, okay."

"Okay," came the soft response; followed by, "Thank you."

Moments later, boots struck the stairway and flashlights darted back and forth in the distance. At any second, Clay expected Bluto to storm out of some dark hiding place and begin killing people, but it never happened. Several lights were bobbing down the stairs. Then, suddenly, he was flooded with bright light.

Clay dropped his gun and flashlight.

"I'm a cop," he exaggerated, holding his now empty hands up and blinking against the glare. It seemed an unimportant lie, measured against the chance that some hyped up policemen might shoot anyone but another policeman.

"I found Jesse Largess. He's in the room behind me."

There was a large commotion coming from the other end of the hallway. It sounded as though they had found Bluto. No shots had been fired. The boy was safe.

~

Jesse's mother was dressed in an attractive blue blouse with a ruffled white skirt when Clay entered the hospital room. Though she still had that weathered look about her, the happy relief had lifted at least ten years from her face. Her smile was warm and genuine.

"Mr. Gromkis, I know I've already said this, but thank you so much for everything. I really thought I'd lost him."

Clay looked over at Jesse in his hospital bed. Most of his face and hands were wrapped in gauze bandages, and a plastic brace was pressed against his chin. He appeared to be sleeping.

"How is he, Mrs. Largess?"

She motioned for them to step outside the room. Once in the hallway, she said, "Just Karen, please."

Clay nodded.

Though she seemed to fight it, the smile slipped from her face.

"Jesse's jaw was broken in two places, and the doctor says one of the fractures extended up into his forehead. Fortunately, his skull only cracked and didn't actually break into pieces. It looks like it will heal without any plates or screws. He'll be in here a while and then laid up in bed at home for three or four months, but the doctor says he'll ultimately be fine."

"I'm glad," Clay said. "But I'm sorry about your husband. I've never been married, but I imagine it must be difficult."

Tears welled at the corners of her eyes, but she wiped them away.

"Wagner was going to die from his drugs anyway. I loved him once, but that ended a long time ago. Unfortunately, Jesse still loved him, so that's going to be tough." Her lips quivered and the tears she'd been fighting began to flow.

Clay hugged her. "Kids are resilient. He'll get through this. I know he will."

"You know what the worst part is?" she said stepping back. "When he went missing, all I could think about was my Uncle Nate. I never met him. He was killed by lobstermen up in Maine almost sixty years ago. They broke into my mother's house when she was just a baby."

Clay couldn't say why, but suddenly a series of chills shot up his spine. The hair on the back of his neck began to rise.

"My Uncle Nate was just about Jesse's age when it happened." Karen's hand went to her mouth. "I was so scared that I was going to lose Jesse the same way. I was so scared that my little boy was going to die."

Chills had grown to envelop Clay's entire body. It was as though a herd of ghosts had arrived to pinch and poke at him. He found himself strangely compelled to know more about this woman's family.

"And your mother?" he asked.

Karen reached into her purse and pulled out a tissue. It was barely adequate, but she wiped it across her eyes and down her cheeks.

"The fishermen didn't want my grandfather to fish off their coast anymore, so they killed him. My grandmother and my Uncle Nate, who was only nine years old at the time, were also murdered. Believe it or not, a dog saved my mother. His name was Whiskey."

Clay felt as though his nervous system had just been plugged into an outlet. Chills and tingles roared up and down his body, a ringing began in his ears. He dipped his hand into a pocket and rubbed his pewter charm.

"The police believe that Whiskey somehow dragged my mother, who was only two years old, out through a broken window. Even though one of the men shot him in the hind quarters, the dog somehow kept her safe until a sheriff found her the next morning."

The ringing in Clay's ears had grown so loud that hearing became difficult. He felt faint.

"Are you okay, Mr. Gromkis?"

Clay nodded and forced the eerie feeling out of his mind. Still, though, his ears continued to ring. There was something so compelling about this woman's story, but he couldn't put his finger on it.

"And your mother," he asked. "How is she?"

Karen shook her head.

"She died a few years ago in a car crash with one of her drunken boyfriends. She sure did have a way of picking the bad ones. It's a trait I'm afraid I may have picked up. The next guy, though, is going to be a saint. I don't care if he's the most boring man on the planet; I want a good man in Jesse's life."

"That sounds nice," Clay agreed. "He's been through a lot. He deserves it."

Suddenly, Clay felt the need to sit. The chills were back, and his knees felt weak. He excused himself and went up the hall where he could sit in a small waiting area. What was wrong with him? Had he eaten something bad earlier in the day? He waited nearly twenty minutes for the odd feelings to pass.

It would have been a good night to find a couple of beers and spend some quiet time in a hotel room, except he had a meeting scheduled in

Ohio for the next evening. Two nights before, an eleven-year-old girl had been abducted right out of a crowded public mall. There were hundreds of witnesses, but the police were having no luck tracking her down.

He made his way back to Jesse's room. The boy was still asleep.

"Mrs. Largess—I'm sorry, Karen."

"Yes."

Clay took an envelope from his breast pocket and handed it to her. In it was a bank check made out to her for ten thousand dollars.

"One of my clients recently lost a child in an incident similar to what happened to Jesse. He wanted you to have this, and he wanted you to call him if there is anything else he can do."

She opened the envelope and peeked inside.

"Oh my god!"

"He's very wealthy," Clay told her. "He paid my fee to help you, and when I told him what had happened, he insisted on helping more." Clay handed her Mr. Imodo's card. "I know he'd be thrilled if you thought to send him a picture of Jesse when he gets better."

"I will," Karen nodded, "I promise."

Clay smiled. "You also have my number should you ever need it."

She hugged him.

"You are an angel," she said to him. "You really are an angel."

Clay hugged her one last time and left the room.

Before he could close the door, she called out, "Would you thank your friend for me?"

Clay peeked his head back in. "Friend?"

"Yes, the policeman from Florida who called a few weeks ago and gave me your number. He said you worked on the last case together."

Clay shook his head. He couldn't remember working with any particular policeman to find the last girl.

"I'm sorry but I don't know who it might have been. Are you sure it wasn't someone from Oklahoma or maybe Texas?"

"I don't think so." Karen rummaged around in her purse and pulled out a pink napkin. She smiled. "From the restaurant I work at," she said in explanation. She unfolded the napkin and read the name.

"He called himself Officer Finneus. Does that ring a bell?"

Clay's face flushed at the mention of the name. He felt as though he'd just become a player in a supernatural movie. Why did these random names and events strike such a strong chord in him? And who was this Officer Finneus? Clay didn't know.

As he left the hospital and followed the Boston signs to the highway, he tried to understand his strange reaction to Karen's family drama. Did it remind him of a similar case, or was it something else? He had driven halfway through the state of Connecticut and his thumb was sore from rubbing his pewter charm when he pulled into the parking lot at a Will Rogers restaurant adjacent to the highway.

The meal was okay, fried chicken and fries, but might have sat in the warmers for a bit too long. Clay finished up a Diet-Pepsi before finally leaving the diner. He was walking back toward his car when a heavyset woman who looked to be in her fifties approached him. She wore a long, white jacket that nearly covered her bare legs. Her shoes were white with short, white socks. Possibly she was a nurse. She had a kindly smile. In her hand was a leash, and at the end of the leash romped a young golden retriever. His amber eyes sparkled with mischief but also, Clay thought, intelligence.

"It's nice to see my boy all grown up," the woman said to Clay.

If it hadn't been for her smile, he might have found her comment menacing.

"Do I know you?" he asked.

"That's my boy," she said. "Always right to the point. Let's just say I'm a relative of young Jesse. You did an amazing job finding him."

Clay couldn't say why, but he sensed he did know this woman. She didn't exactly look familiar, but there was something about her.

"How did you find me?"

The woman chuckled. "It doesn't matter where your soul flutters off to, Little One, as I told you once before I will always be able to find you."

Clay's mind was afire with half-memories and strong feelings of affection for this woman. But none of it made any sense. He had no memory of her. He was sure they had never met before.

"We found him," the woman said, holding out the dog's leash. "It took three hundred angels and nearly forty years to track him down, but you're worth it. We all feel you're worth it."

Clay found the angel comment odd, but no more so than the other statements she made. He felt an almost overwhelming compulsion to step forward and hug her. But instead, he said, "I don't understand."

"He's yours," the woman said. "Or maybe it's you who are his. Either way, you two belong together."

Clay glanced at the dog who was staring intently at him. Something seemed so familiar about those eyes. Clay glanced toward his Corvette and its impeccable seats.

"Thanks, but I'm not a dog kind of guy. I'm on the road a lot."

"I'd like to see your key chain for just a moment," the woman said.

Knowing that his day had just gone from strange to totally off-the-wall bizarre, Clay removed his keys from his pocket.

"I'm not stealing it. It really is my Corvette." He held up the Corvette key. "See."

She smiled. "No, I was hoping to see the other key chain, your charm."

Clay reached into his jacket pocket and pulled out his pewter good luck charm. He dangled it between them. Though he had been rubbing it for years, it had been a long time since he actually looked at it. It was the perfect, even if somewhat worn, shape of a golden retriever.

"May I," she asked and extended her free hand, palm up.

Though he couldn't understand why, Clay didn't want to disappoint this woman. He gently placed the pewter dog into her hand. She slipped the leash into his.

"You've got a little girl to save," she said, "so you probably should be going, Nate."

Suddenly the gale of chills was back, and the internal sirens were ringing. Nate? Why had she called him Nate? On the one hand, she might have been the strangest person he had ever met, but on the other he had an inexplicable desire to wrap his arms around her and just hold her. Was he going crazy?

"I love you, too," she said.

Clay felt himself go dizzy, and by the time he had refocused his eyes, she was gone. He let his eyes roam the parking lot, but there was no sign of her. Confused but strangely buoyed, he opened the passenger door of his car and the dog eagerly jumped in. Clay slid behind the wheel and reached over to scratch his new friend behind the ears.

"How helpful will you be in finding missing children?" he asked the dog.

They were destined to find out.

EPILOGUE

Uncle Finneus sat at the head of the table, a cheerful broad smile spread across his face. To either side of him were Grandma Clara and my Uncle Albert, who looked especially content. Beside him was my Aunt Bertrice who had recently found her way into Heaven. Earlier, my Uncle Albert explained how he'd finally brought Mr. Thomas Edison down to her purgatory to talk with her. Whether the exchange had been proper was a bit of a gray area, but judging from the gathering here, damned and risen alike, my lineage didn't have too much trouble with the gray areas. Across from Aunt Bertrice was an empty chair. At the other end of the dining room table, across from Uncle Finneus, is where I sat, just a nine-year-old among adults.

Uncle Finneus raised his glass to me, "Welcome home, Young Nathaniel. It's good to have you back."

"We've all been so proud of you, Nate," Grandma Clara said, "the way you've helped so many children."

It seemed odd to have them talking about Clay as though he were me. I knew it was true, but I hadn't yet had time to absorb that second life, and it still seemed as though Clay's memories were more of a movie in my mind, rather than my own experiences. I had to admit, however, that it had been an exciting movie, even if—

I glanced down at my otherwise white T-shirt. There I could see a solid red stain in the center of my chest as well as the old stain I had always worn on my shoulder. The details were still a little hazy to me, but Clay had been buying something at a small store when it had been held up. He had been shot. I also knew that Clay had been married and had fathered four beautiful children, and that his first granddaughter had already started school. Though murdered a few years early, Clay had enjoyed a long and happy life.

"How's Russian cheesecake sound?" Aunt Alice asked as she came into the dining room with a large fresh-from-the-oven dessert. Her gown was buttoned high up around her neck and her white lace hoop skirt was wide and elegant. Though some souls might have found her to be stiff and formal, I knew better.

"There's my favorite Russian flower," Uncle Finneus said, gesturing to my Aunt Alice. Of everyone, it was he who had changed the most.

His suit had gone from a medium gray to a gray so light that it would soon be cream-colored. I wondered what Hell would do if one of their own turned white?

Though no one blushes in Under-Heaven, Aunt Alice's body language said she was gushing under my uncle's compliments. She placed the cake down in the center of the table as Uncle Albert and Uncle Finneus rose and rapidly cleared the potato, squash and cranberry dishes away. The smell of the freshly baked cake was heavenly.

Now you might be asking yourself, "Since when is food served in Under-Heaven?" The truth is it's a trend that had just started with my Welcome Home party. We're all independent souls who can make decisions for ourselves, and though there are rules that everyone knows are too important to break, there are others that aren't so much rules as traditions. Sometimes you just have to stretch out and take a little risk. Who knows what rewards you might find?

I slipped a few bits of food under the table where a friendly tongue removed them from my fingers.

I, for my part, intended to take an extended rest and spend time with my family. Already, Uncle Albert was planning a reunion for Vicky, my parents and me. I also wanted to give myself time to absorb Clay's life into my own experience. It was possible that I might even break my own previous record for residence in Under-Heaven, but ultimately, I knew I would go back again. Like the elderly man I had met so many decades before, I knew my ties to life and the Earth below were too strong. Heaven would have to wait for a while longer.

"I want a big piece," I said to Aunt Alice.

"You're the guest of honor," she said cheerfully. She plopped an especially large slice on my plate.

THE END